T. H. S. (Thomas Hay Sweet) Escott

Radolph Spencer-Churchill, as a Product of His Age

Being a Personal and Political Monograph

T. H. S. (Thomas Hay Sweet) Escott

Radolph Spencer-Churchill, as a Product of His Age
Being a Personal and Political Monograph

ISBN/EAN: 9783337079475

Printed in Europe, USA, Canada, Australia, Japan

Cover: Foto ©Raphael Reischuk / pixelio.de

More available books at **www.hansebooks.com**

Randolph Spencer-Churchill, as a Product of his Age. Being a Personal and Political-Monograph

London, 1895

HUTCHINSON & CO.

34, PATERNOSTER ROW

PREFACE.

DURING the greater part of Lord
Randolph Churchill's public course, the
circumstances of my life as an industrious
article-writer on the daily and weekly press,
established frequent points of contact between
him and myself, which gradually expanded
into a mutual acquaintance of a rather intimate
kind. Throughout all the period now referred
to, especially at the time when a failure in
my physical health, after twenty years of
overwork, temporarily disabled me from my
professional duties, I, and those bearing my
name, received from Lord Randolph, as from
other members of his house, many marks of
courteous regard and sympathetic attention.
It has, therefore, seemed in some sort a duty

from me to his memory to place before
the world the present monograph, in which
the chief aspects of his career, with such
collateral circumstances as were necessary to
render the narrative intelligible and interesting to the general reader, will be found in
the main, I hope, not inaccurately set forth.
The time probably has not yet come when
a complete biography of Randolph Churchill,
including as it must the private papers and
correspondence, which he may, or may not,
have left behind him, could be given to the
world; and the present sketch pretends to
be no more than what its title describes.

So far as practicable, the method pursued
here is to let Lord Randolph Churchill's
own acts, or for the most part already
printed words, tell his life's story, and not
to use more comment than time has rendered necessary for a right understanding
of these.

Among the many who have courteously

enlarged my knowledge, or supplied my ignorance, at certain stages of this record, I
would mention with especial gratitude the
names of the Marquess of Dufferin and Ava,
ex-Viceroy of India, to-day H.B.M. Ambassador in Paris; Lord Reay and Sir James
Fergusson, both former Governors of Bombay ;
Sir John E. Gorst, Q.C., M.P. ; Sir Edward
Clarke, Q.C., M.P. ; the present Bishop of
Peterborough, Lord Randolph's former tutor
at Merton ; as well as the Hon. G. C. Brodrick,
to-day Warden of the College. My constant
indebtedness to Mr. L. J. Jennings' admirable
edition of Lord Randolph's speeches, testified
by frequent footnotes; to the author of the
" Diary of Two Parliaments "; to Mr. J.
Comyns Cole's recollections of Lord Randolph's racing career, as privately supplied to
me and embodied in these pages ; give me the
opportunity of associating with the late Mr.
Jennings' name the distinguished patronymics
of other gentlemen whose colleague, during

many years in the service of a weekly news-paper, before, I think, " Toby, M.P.," had become articulate in the *London Charivari's* columns, I, as well as my old associate and friend, the former Member for Salford, had the honour and pleasure to be; and to each of whom I now offer my obliged compliments and thanks.

To safeguard me against the necessity of recourse to newspaper files or magazine articles, I have to thank Mr. R. S. Foster, lately a student at Eton College, for the industry and skill with which, on the Thames, on the Isis, in Birmingham, and in Paddington, he has collected for me all the more authentic traditions and anecdotes that, whether at the seats of his education or in the constituencies with which his name is linked, have clustered around the central figure of the following pages.

Finally, I am particularly appreciative of the services rendered me by my scientific

and obliging friend, Dr. W. S. Hedley, of
3, Western Terrace, Brighton, for his preparation of the statement as to the general
character and course of the malady to which
Lord Randolph Churchill succumbed.

T. H. S. ESCOTT. .

BRIGHTON, *April* 10*th*, 1895.

CONTENTS.

CHAPTER I.

INTRODUCTORY.

CHAPTER II.

BIRTH: CHEAM AND ETON (1849-66).

CHAPTER III.

OXFORD (1867-71).

b

CHAPTER XXII.

SOUTH AFRICAN VISIT—AND AFTERWARDS (1891-4).

RANDOLPH SPENCER CHURCHILL.

CHAPTER I.

INTRODUCTORY.

Why Randolph Churchill's life is more important than its length.—Its duration embraces the recent fortunes and reconstruction of his party at a critical time; his life also is that of an individual who was a microcosm of social as well as political tendencies of the time, for he was always in some kind of evidence—if not politics, pleasure.—Hereditary influences.

THERE may, perhaps, exist some disposition to question whether, after the fulness of public comment in the daily, weekly, and monthly press, on the premature death of the present monograph's subject, there can as yet be a place for the record, in a more permanent shape, of a life concluded before the limit of two-score years and ten had been reached. The answer, as it is believed a satisfactory one, will be found in the variety of incident, the swiftness of movement, the diversity as well as the fulness of occupations, now about to be narrated; finally, in the coincidence of an individual's too brief career, with the irrecoverable defeat as it had seemed, with the restoration and reconstruction as it proved, of a historic party in the State. The story, therefore, of Lord Randolph Churchill's passage through existence, however succinctly told, not only must comprise the tale of personal vicissitudes, more than ordinarily striking in their contrasts of success and failure, light and shade, tragedy, comedy, exultation, despair; but must be also, within a convenient compass, a concentration and epitome; an amalgam as well as a reflection of the dominant characteristics or movements, social not less than political, of an interesting section in the expiring century.

Randolph Churchill's first entrance upon political and parliamentary life was an episode in the most eventful of general elections known to the last two decades. Mr. Disraeli, in the most famous of his earlier novels, inspires his hero Sidonia with the aphorism that in this country, whatever the immediate depository of political power may be, Parliament ever leads the nation to an attack upon it, and the centre of supreme authority is changed.

There is another proposition, which, if at first seemingly paradoxical, will be found upon examination to contain a truth at least as invariable, and not perhaps less profound, than the pithy epigram of democratic Toryism's true founder, whose aptest pupil Randolph Spencer Churchill proved himself to be. Whenever an individual statesman in England has presented himself before his countrymen as the indispensable hero of the hour, the saviour of society, alone able to avert from the realm the doom of chaos and night, the constituencies have proceeded to record their repudiation of his pretensions, to demonstrate the non-existence of such a being as the necessary man, and whatever his past services may have been, to withdraw their confidence from him at the polling booths, to prove, in effect, after the most convincing manner that, instead of being essential to them, he is, in the expressive French phrase, *de trop*. In 1846, upon the repeal of the Corn Laws by a sustained majority of 229, Sir Robert Peel had some reason for supposing his national as well as parliamentary influence would obtain for him the additional powers which he declared were required to preserve the Queen's peace in Ireland. The memorable sequel, with its picturesque surroundings, is familiar to all readers of Lord George Bentinck's life. The party strength, that only some ten days earlier was less by a unit than 230, sank to 219. By a hostile balance of 73 votes the great minister fell, and the author of the abandoned sliding scale, Lord John Russell, reigned in his stead. Twenty-eight years later, Mr. Gladstone made the most direct and, as it might seem, tempting bid to the electorate for perpetuating the Conservative exile from power, in the promised abolition of the Income Tax. Before the first week of the ensuing elections was ended, the compact phalanx of 330 which in 1868 carried the preliminary resolution against the Irish Church had practically disappeared. The most powerful minister of these latter days returned to St. Stephen's in a minority of 106. For the first time in his life, as in the experience of all his contemporaries, Mr. Disraeli carried the country with him, and was nominated

Prime Minister with a working majority of 350,
as against an opposition of 244. How the last
of these brilliant changes of political fortune
was abused or disappeared, till the shadow like
the substance of success had been lost, how far
the subject of this volume was conscious of the
mistakes committed, the opportunities neglected
by the party to which he had attached himself
during this period, will be considered hereafter.
Meanwhile there yet remains to cite another
illustration of a sequence in public affairs which
operates almost with the certainty of political
law. If any statesman could ever plausibly
claim the attribute of indispensability, that
statesman was assuredly Lord Beaconsfield in
the spring of 1880. The victorious bearer of
peace with honour from the Congress at
Berlin, the recipient of ovations such as are
accorded usually to great conquerors in the
field, the hero of London city, the idol of the
organisation called " society," strong in the
demonstrative endearments of his countrymen
as in the Crown's esteem, basking alike in the
sunshine of popular applause, and in the smiles
of the most sagacious among constitutional
and patriotic monarchs who has ever worn the

Plantagenets' diadem, Lord Beaconsfield may well have seemed practically impregnable in his ministerial entrenchments. The historic letter to Lord Randolph Churchill's father, then Viceroy of Ireland, published as the Tory chief's electoral manifesto in the early spring of 1880, warning his grace against Irish evils more terrible than plague or pestilence—namely, the conspiracy which, stripped of its Home Rule visor, would display the lineaments of repeal, was held by the less reflecting of the public to be a masterstroke of genius and policy; to ensure in advance the magnification, to fabulous dimensions, of a triumph that was already certain. Cooler heads and more far-sighted eyes detected a very different omen in the document. No considerable section, either of the public or of the press, paid the slightest attention to the pessimist prophets. On the first or second day of the great national engagement, Stamford, the eminently representative borough, formerly so long associated with the honoured name of Sir Stafford Northcote, returned a Liberal in the place of a Conservative. That incident was at once seen by Disraeli to portend the doom of his fortunes beyond hope of retrieval. The counties followed the boroughs' lead, and he who but a week ago had been the master of innumerable legions, following Mr. Gladstone's example in 1874, resigned before Parliament met, only when it had assembled to find his followers reduced to 243, confronted by a ministerial force of 349, threescore of whom were Home Rulers. What chances of Liberal defeat and Conservative restoration presented themselves between this day and the following 8th of June, when Sir Michael Hicks-Beach's resolution on the Budget proposals once more placed the Conservatives, reinforced by 39 Home Rulers, on the right hand of the Speaker's chair; whether, had Lord Randolph Churchill's advice been followed, such a consummation might not have been anticipated ; or whether, when it had actually arrived, the brilliant politician, now no more, might not have turned the victory already realised to more conspicuous and permanent account, are points to be considered in their place here.

Nor did the politician or *frondeur* absorb Randolph Churchill's identity, exhaust his energies, or monopolise his powers. The heightened social

prestige of the British metropolis after the Second
Empire's collapse and a great diminution of the
French capital's fashionable repute, in other
words, the eclipse of Paris by London as the
chosen home of splendour, comfort, gaiety, bril-
liancy, pleasure, and in this aspect the favourite
resort, above all others, of the good Americans,
whose spirits in the old days were said to migrate
to the city on the Seine, the adoption of Gallic
modes of life and thought, the transition from an
insular to a continental *régime* on the Thames,
the constancy with which the British character,
amid all these mutations, has adhered to its essential principles, occupations, and sports, the increasing, rather than diminishing, ascendancy of
the turf as an institution, uniting round itself, in
a constantly increasing degree, whatever is most
luxurious and opulent, as well as not a little
that is most squalid and debased in our national
economy,—all these developments were compre-
hended within the limits of Randolph Churchill's
life. With each of them he was associated
more or less prominently and practically ; none
of them, therefore, can be omitted from a
monograph whose scope and character it seems
desirable to indicate with some precision.

The few years following the death of Lord Beaconsfield, in their political agitation and suspense, in the delusiveness alike of many hopes and of more fears, in the spirit of political gambling which they generated among various sections of the party, left on the disappearance of the man of genius so long its president and protector, resembled somewhat the party situation depicted in the opening pages of Lord Beaconsfield's final novel, " Endymion," after the resignation of " Lord Goderich," before the interregnum was terminated by the summons of the great duke to the councils of the young queen. All these fluctuations, rapid alternations between abject despair, jubilant forecast of lost ground to be regained, of defeats converted, by a happy mixture of audacity and luck, into triumphs, were reflected in the career, as they may almost be said to have been foreshadowed in the temperament, of Lord Randolph Churchill. Nor do the interest and instructiveness arising from the study proposed in the ensuing pages end here.

No scion of a great house ever presented in his own personality and course so dramatic a contrast between the inherited traditions or prejudices of his race, and the gradually acquired or suddenly developed sympathies of his own mind. His instincts, his views of social existence, his amusements, his tastes, his very bearing and voice, were those of one not unpossessed by the conviction that his descent from the conqueror of Blenheim, through a long line of ennobled and affluent ancestors, placed him in his most democratic moments several degrees above the common herd, and emancipated him from some of the more trammelling of vulgar responsibilities. Allied by his maternal connections with the stock of Castlereagh, in many of the humours and attributes of that political leadership to which events seemed to summon him, he reminded students of political history and character of the statesman who, during his management of the House of Commons, notwithstanding intervals of personal popularity, was regarded generally as the incarnation of reaction from progress towards absolutism. In his quickly varying moods, his incalculable impulsiveness, his momentary humours of autocratic command, his mingled manner of dictatorship or conciliation, Randolph Churchill recalled the historic figure with whom, through Frances, Duchess of Marlborough, he possessed kinship.

The truth would seem to be that unless circumstances, hereafter to be specified, had, some two or three decades ago, conspired to smooth Randolph Churchill's entrance upon political life and parliamentary service, and in doing so called into activity ambitions hitherto dormant or unsuspected, this descendant of the Churchill and Vane-Tempest progenitors would have turned the nobility of his origin to no better account than is done by thousands of young men in every-day life, who, being cadets of great territorial families, regard their station with complacency, chiefly because it affords them a semi-royal road to the pastime of the hour or caprice of the moment. Lord Randolph Churchill was, in fact, saved from the most besetting of hereditary dangers by the keenly curious intellect, the superiority to conventional ignobility of aim, which were the gift of a benignant Nature to himself. Once he had given hostages to fortune, and was committed to a definite struggle with far-reaching aims clearly marked, the ardour and intrepidity that belonged to him by right of birth were converted into forces permitting him only to lay down the sword and abandon the contest when life itself had almost begun to abandon him.

How, amid these diverse agencies of his environment, and these mutually antagonistic tendencies of his character, Lord Randolph Churchill gradually developed, first into an acute parliamentary tactician, then into a cautious, painstaking official, a competent, vigilant, and conciliatory chief, will be shown by the needful narrative of those parliamentary episodes and national occurrences that were incidental to or instrumental in the accomplishment of these processes of evolution, synchronising, as not a few of them will do, with the most politically eventful and personally interesting sessions at St. Stephen's watched by the present generation. For Lord Randolph Churchill, while being the creation and reflection of his age, to some extent, as years passed by, became not an insignificant moulder of its history.

CHAPTER II.

LORD RANDOLPH HENRY SPENCER CHURCHILL,
the second surviving son of the seventh Duke
of Marlborough, by that Duchess who before
her marriage was Frances Anne Emily Vane,
eldest daughter of the third Marquis of
Londonderry, was born at Blenheim Palace
on February 13th, 1849.   No anecdotes of
infantile genius or of precocious aptitude for
and interest in affairs of State can be told of

him authentically. The family portraits * of himself and of his brother, the eighth duke in descent from the great captain who was the founder of the house, show a strong likeness in facial features, rather than in their expression, to each other ; while, in the case of the younger, they disclose the same sort of countenance that is common to most small boys of spirit and breeding, before they are yet emancipated completely from the petticoated dominion on the borderland between nursery and school-room.

The son of a Churchill, who first opened his eyes upon the great park adjoining the Oxfordshire capital of glove making, who delighted in the prospects from the Blenheim terraces of woodland or water, and who cantered his pony as soon as he could ride on the undulating expanses of turf beyond, drinking in with the fancy's, as with the body's eye, the spectacle and the associations of every variety of English pastime, is pretty sure to be a born sportsman. I have never

* One of these is familiar to the public from long having been hung inside the Salisbury Club-house in St. James' Square, 1884–85.

heard of any deer from the Blenheim Park being carted to become afterwards the quarry of dogs and men; but, with the single exception of that recreation which, in its legitimate form, can be witnessed only in the Exmoor country or in the New Forest, and of which the home counties' chases are not very admirable imitations, there is no form of outdoor amusement not to be had within the limits of the park itself, or that was unfamiliar to Randolph Churchill from the day when he was able to grasp a riding-whip, a gun, or a fishing-rod.

The seventh Duke of Marlborough was noticeably free from the pomposity of demeanour, the affected exclusiveness of taste, to which some inheritors of the strawberry leaf appear to be born. His bearing, like his appearance, was that of a simple country gentleman, who employs any surplusage of his revenues in improving and intensifying the healthy pleasures that are part of his inheritance, in doing what he can to brighten the existence of his immediate dependants as of his people generally, rather than in multiplying gorgeous evidence of his own consummate importance, in exploring continents to gratify a humour, or in exhausting capitals to discover a new sauce of life. Randolph Churchill's father was a fair shot, had doubtless been as skilful a performer in the shires as English gentlemen are expected to be, and, unlike his second son, to whom the sea was as hostile an element as to the Marquis of Salisbury himself, was an enthusiastic yachtsman. Before Randolph went to his first school, preparatory for Eton, the historic Tabor's at Cheam, while he was yet in the hands of domestic tutors, almost governesses, he had won local distinction in those rudimentary occupations of the future flier across country, the indefatigable tramper through the heather in quest of Highland grouse, the whipper of Highland trout or salmon streams. Just outside the gate of the Blenheim flower-garden, occupying a considerable portion of the upper section of the park itself, is a long low building—a riding school, erected, if I mistake not, by that chief of the Marlborough house who, prefiguring the liberality alike of Randolph Churchill and of his elder brother, brought forward, when Marquis of Blandford in the House of Commons, a resolution in favour of parliamentary reform.   This structure has been employed for many purposes.   Here, in the days of the seventh duke, tenants' festivities were held. Here, to his credit be it related, the eighth duke entertained, after a day of boisterous enjoyment in the park, many hundreds of children from the East End of London, whom, during the summer of 1885, under the escort of ministers of various denominations, special trains, at his cost, conveyed between their Shoreditch or Whitechapel homes and the Woodstock railway station.   The sight was one to be remembered.   It was the present writer's privilege to witness it.   When the tables, heaped high with cakes in pyramids, or oranges in mountains, had been relieved of their hospitable burdens by the delightfully appreciative little guests, the whole company moved to another lawn in front of the mansion, where their entertainer gave a very few words of address, marked by such good taste and feeling as to leave not many eyes entirely dry.

By Randolph Churchill this covered enclosure was used in infancy for purposes more closely connected with the title of the spot. It was here, doubtless, that he acquired the

2

firm seat and light hand on horseback which
at Oxford distinguished him in the Heythrop
field, or which later, during his father's
administration, subsequently made him in
western Ireland emphatically "the man for
Galway."

About a mile or so down the Blenheim
park is a piece of boggy soil, haunted by
snipe and moorfowl, fringing a dull-looking
sheet of water, rather stagnant, but famous as
the home of eels, exceeding in dimensions
those it has ever been my lot to witness, the
Godstowe prodigies not excepted. The size,
animation, even ferocity of these miniature
monsters, are apt to alarm other than childish
nerves. Several years ago, seated in the little
study in my Brompton Crescent house, I was
startled by a succession of shrieks, from the
shrill treble of a small page boy to the panic-
stricken bass of a middle-aged cook. In a few
minutes the reason of the alarm was apparent.
One of the Blenheim eels, kindly sent by the
late duke, who had remembered my liking
for this dish when prepared in a particular
manner, had arrived that morning. Life could
scarcely have been extinct, or some muscular

energy must have survived, when the noble reptile had been consigned to the basket nearly filled by its girth. It was, in truth, rather a formidable sight. Scarcely less than a conger in circumference and length, this fresh-water serpent, moribund or even actually defunct, menacingly reared its neck and crest, displaying the while a most forbidding set of piscine dentals. "It gnashes," was the exclamation of a terrified Abigail, "its teeth just like one of them lost fiends!" and the excellent woman was very near giving me notice on the spot. It is, perhaps, a proof of Lord Randolph's constitutional intrepidity that, having captured these animals with rod and line, or with net, he faced boldly their expiring terrors, the timidity of cooks or keepers notwithstanding. His, too, was the gun which brought down unfailingly at least its due share of that bird most difficult to hit, the snipe, on the adjoining mainland.

A fisherman and marksman, as he was thus by his earliest experiences trained to be, the subject of this monograph may, with a pardonable exaggeration, be described as having also been born into the hunting-field. Fifty years ago small packs of private hounds were much commoner than they are to-day, not only in North Devon and West Somerset, but in other parts of England as well. Such a pack as this it was Randolph Churchill's fancy to possess. Such an one, a little later, he actually had, hunting his harriers in a genuinely professional manner, to the infinite delight of the Blenheim tenantry and the whole country side.

Between the ages of thirteen and fourteen the future leader of the " fourth party " went in 1863 to Eton, being placed after his entrance examination in the form known as " Remove," in the house of the Rev. W. A. Carter, who, as also the present head master (then Mr. Warre), was his tutor as well. Continuing only a twelvemonth under this gentleman's supervision, Randolph Churchill was transferred to the house now held by Mr. Frank Tarver, but then occupied by Mr. Frewer. In the famous foundation of Henry VII. Randolph Churchill preserved the same characteristics that he had developed at, and brought with him from, the Cheam seminary. He was, that is to say, much as most other English schoolboys between the ages of thirteen and fifteen usually are. Although even now, seeing it by the light of subsequent experience, none of his masters or his friends could have detected during his school course indications of future eminence in any serious walk, the little lad who defied his disciplinarians, or was somewhat disposed to domineer over his contemporaries, revealed in a rudimentary form most of those attributes that, more conspicuously developed and confirmed, served to distinguish the future champion of the mutiny against the insipid generalship of the Conservative front bench. If he could not often, or always, excel, he generally contrived to be notorious ; the first to be involved in a scrape, the first to extricate his comrades from it. He often shirked a lesson, he never feared the birch ; he never shrank from interposing himself between a playfellow and the official chastisement of their associated delinquencies. The one condition he insisted upon from his equals was loyalty to his lead. Provided that was forthcoming, he was himself staunchness and championship incarnate to his followers. As for the public opinion of the place, the criticism of boys not in his set, he cared as little for these as he did for the censure

of the Orbilius of the hour, or as he regarded,
in the House of Commons, the remonstrances
of the satellites of the accomplished statesman
profanely nicknamed by him " The Goat,"
the long-suffering and blameless Sir Stafford
Northcote himself.   It is in the following
manner that a well-known Eton authority
recalls Lord Randolph : " I can just remember
young Churchill as a striking whimsical personality, with full, large, round, astonished
eyes, and a determined, bulldog type of face.
He was addicted to dressing loudly, and I
vividly recollect his appearance one day in a
daring violet-coloured waistcoat.   Botham's
Hotel was in those days a favourite resort
for Etonians, in the way of succession to
Coningsby's " Christopher," where the friends
entertained each other at sumptuous breakfasts
and luncheons.   A special feature of this
hostelry, as well as a powerful attraction to
the younger boys, was a spacious fruit-garden,
celebrated for the size and flavour of its straw-
berries.   During a certain summer this Elysian
enclosure was so pillaged as to cause the proprietor to complain to the head-master, Mr.
Balston.   As a consequence, Mr. Austen Leigh

was despatched to watch, and, if possible, to catch the offenders *in flagrante delicto*. That representative of the highest Eton authority very soon flushed a large covey of juvenile depredators. All of them, however, got away, except Randolph Churchill, who jumped as far as he could towards the road with his pursuer close upon him. They both fell together into the ditch, Mr. Austen Leigh uppermost. Lord Randolph, seeing that any further attempt at escape would be useless, crawled out, much scratched and bruised, into the middle of the road, where, incensed at his own discomfiture, he deliberately sat down, crossed his legs, glared at Mr. Leigh, and with all the vehemence of enraged fourteen, exclaimed, ' You beast ! ' How he escaped the birch after this adventure tradition does not relate."

The implacable opponent of lawfully con-stituted authority, Randolph Churchill was the friend of all his inferiors. The old ground-man of Eton College, Dick Powell, who, as recently as February, 1895, at the age of seventy-five, was still well and strong, expresses himself after the following fashion. " Did I know Lord Randolph ? I should say so, sir !

Him and his brother, the Marquis, were great friends of mine. Lor', how they did use to pitch into me, to be sure! Lord Randolph would pumble me about for ten minutes. He was a rare strong 'un, and then he'd say, ' I didn't hurt you, Dick, did I ?' and I'd answer him, ' Noa, my lord, noa!' But he did, yer know. He was a sturdy young 'un as ever was. He came to say good-bye to me before he left, and I never saw him again after. I heerd about 'im, and I should like to see 'im again, sir, I would!" Nor in the catalogue of Randolph Churchill's Etoniana should there be omitted his frequent encounters with the proprietor of a certain "sock" (sweet) shop, named Alexander. Entering the premises apparently with *bonâ fide* intent, he would suddenly play some wild practical joke, and then rapidly retire to a safe distance outside, that he might enjoy the result, which was, of course, the appearance of the infuriated victim at the door, shaking his fist at his tormentor, and shouting, " Ah, my lord! it's no use my running after you, I know, but if ever I do get hold of you I shall kill you."

Randolph Churchill's progress under Mr. Carter's roof was more prosperous than the time he spent at Mr. Frewer's, now rector of Hitcham, near Taplow. This gentleman remembers Churchill's Puck-like pranks as a source of constant amusement to his house mates, but of great anxiety to the tutor, who describes him as a boy of uncontrollable outbursts of temper, during whose sway he would vent his rage upon any object, animate or inanimate, within his reach. In one of these bouts of fury he took a silver spoon, twisted it, stamped upon it, bit it, and crushed it out of all recognition. "He once," was Mr. Frewer's remark, "shut my son up in the coal cellar"— an incident that, being related to Lord Randolph's other house master, Mr. Carter, drew from that gentleman the observation, "And I've no doubt Master Frewer deserved it." From the first, as at Cheam so at Eton. He was a lad of eminently diplomatic qualities, with much precocity in the art of human management. He loved to be waited upon, and the former inmates of Mr. Carter's house were much impressed by the way in which he would wheedle and cajole people for hours to obtain his point, while if his persuasive arguments proved unavailing, tears of disappointment and vexation filled his large and prominent eyes. His generosity was on the true juvenile, which is the absolutely limitless scale. Leaving-books as presents were then in vogue. Upon one occasion he bespoke nearly the complete stock-in-trade of the most expensively bound volumes contained in the crack bibliopolist's shop to distribute among his departing friends. Thus, with all his native impulses, commendable or the reverse, developed and intensified rather than mitigated or trained, he left at the age of fifteen, after a stay of less than two years, the public school which, more than any other foundation in the country, receives its *alumni* as boys from the nursery, and turns them out as men of the world. Here is what one who, as a boy, with Lord Randolph, both at the Surrey school and on the Thames, deposes concerning his contemporary at this era : " I cannot say that he was generally popular in the school. His temperament was a little too imperious for that ; but when one got to know him one always liked him. That I can conscientiously aver ; and a more straightforward, generous-minded English schoolboy never lived. I never knew him do a dishonourable action.

He has, to my own knowledge, got himself into trouble through shielding others. Whatever he had he was always prompt to share with his mates. Well may my correspondent add, " How this peculiar trait adhered to him through life the history of the ' fourth party ' proves conclusively,"—the reference, of course, being to the parliamentary influence which secured in 1885 his mission as envoy to Constantinople for Sir Henry Drummond Wolff, and his place as Indian Under-Secretary for Sir John Gorst.

From what has been said, it will correctly be inferred that at none of these places did Lord Randolph Churchill apply himself very energetically to the recognised curriculum. His own natural cleverness, supplemented, if necessary, by the requisitioned help of more industrious youths, always ready, as they were, to help him out with his " longs and shorts," abundantly enabled him to reduce to a minimum the risk of serious collisions with the authorities, while systematically shunning any approach to a maximum of exertion on his own part.

When a well-known figure in latter-day journalism, Mr. Edmund Yates, after an inter-

view with the late Lord Chief Justice, was
relegated to six months' seclusion on the
breezy heights of northern London, Randolph
Churchill not only wrote to him a sympathetic
letter—the more kindly from the fact of the two
having then certainly never met more than once
—assuring the incarcerated editor of Sir Henry
James' personal good will, of a general impression that hard measure had been meted out to
the "Atlas" of the *World* newspaper, as well
as of a scarcely disguised feeling that " Lord
Chief Justice Coleridge had made an ass of
himself."   In addition to this missive, its writer
despatched to Edmund Yates a verbal message
by a common acquaintance, the writer of these
lines, to the effect that his confinement would
be much shortened if he went to bed directly
he reached the place of detention, refusing to
quit it till the day of release had arrived.   " It
is," said Lord Randolph, " what I should do,
and on these terms I would willingly take
Yates' place to-morrow."   This remark, now
first quoted, is closely congruous with an
anecdotal observation already printed in a
London newspaper, *The Westminster Gazette,*
and, as I think, bearing internal evidence of its

authenticity. " The ideal life," Lord Randolph is said to have declared, " would be to lie in bed all day, dozing over a book, to dine in one's dressing-gown, and then with all convenient speed find one's way back to bed again." These half-playful, half-serious words, have now a melancholy biographical sound and significance, for they are painfully suggestive of the disguised consciousness of nervous exhaustion that alone can have inspired their utterer with them.

Notwithstanding Randolph Churchill's experiment on the gamut of excitement from " tip-cat " to tiger-shooting, his keen sportsmanship, whether shown over the Oxfordshire pastures or Scotch moors, in negotiating the stone walls of Connemara or in confronting the despots of the African jungle, he eschewed physical exertion if there was nothing in the shape of acute pleasure or heightened emotion to be got out of it. At Eton he was proficient neither on the river nor at cricket ; his youthful, like his maturer, ideal was one of *dolce far niente*. At the same time, he showed and cultivated at Eton a taste for acting. There is still extant to-day a photographic group of

Mr. Carter's pupils taken in character, after an amateur performance of *The Rivals.* In this company Lord Randolph figures as "Lucy," while the present Earl of Donoughmore is " Mrs. Malaprop." These reminiscences of Randolph Churchill's Etonian era must be supplemented by a personal recollection of him, recorded by a contributor to the *Realm* for February 1st, 1895. " I can," writes " J. S.," " recall him at Eton, but only for one amazing moment. It was a summer evening, just before ' lock-up,' and the whole wall, the little old wall so fitted for the height of small boys, which separates the public road from the boarders of Upper School, was thronged with youths, resting after the labours of the day. Even they felt the charm of the stillness. There was no drumming of heels on the wall, only chatter and occasional laughter. On the other side of the road, gathered at the top of Keats' Lane, where in those days was an iron bar for the ' seat of the scornful,' were the ' Swells.' Between these awe-inspiring *aristoi* and us urchins indiscriminate on the wall lay the empty road. Down the middle of that road alone, ringing discordant music from a volunteer's bugle, marched a boy in jackets. It was Churchill, wending homeward to Frewer's. As I recall the ' Swells ' of that time, this progress of a boy in jackets, on his right a long line of his fellows, on his left, for one awful minute, that sublime group at the corner, I feel once more the breathless wonder at audacity so magnificent."

CHAPTER III.

OXFORD (1867-71).

THE contrast between the Eton which Lord Randolph Churchill left and the Oxford which he entered late in the sixties was tolerably complete. At the public school the influences of the new and plutocratic era, under which to-day modern society lives, were not yet decisively felt. Throughout the first half of the present century the majority of boys at Henry VI.'s institution on the Thames were the sons of country gentlemen or professional men—well-to-do indeed, but depending for their incomes so largely on precarious conditions, like the seasons, the value of agricultural produce or stock, and foreign competition, as to be compelled to practise some economy and self-denial, that they might give their sons the benefit of the education which they and their fore-fathers had received. The obligatory virtue of thrift was inculcated strongly upon the young Etonian when he left home ; nor was it hinted obscurely that if he systematically exceeded his allowance, perpetuated gross extravagance, or any other peccadilloes, the result would be the premature close of his school career.

By the time—probably before—Randolph Churchill exchanged Eton for Oxford a complete revolution, socially and economically, had come over the seminary of Keat. The place's dominant tone was no longer imparted to it by the parents and the purses of the average country squire, with his paternal acres heavily dipped in mortgages or charged for marriage settlements. Eton had ceased to be ex-clusively or chiefly the greatest school of England. It was the most fashionable and expensive as well.

The extraordinary development of the national wealth and prosperity between 1846 and 1860, the epoch of railway kings, of brewing, banking, manufacturing, stockbroking, loan-mongering millionaires, reinforced the youthful Etonians of the period, the sons of parents living on the middle zone of prosperity, whether titled or untitled, with contingents of boys, whose fathers laboured under the burden of excessive and newly acquired opulence, placing their offspring under a Hawtrey or a Balston by way of social investment, to relieve themselves of their surplus treasure, at the same time that they gratified their pride by the cultivation, on their progeny's part, of acquaintance with ducal scions or other territorial magnates, whose ancestors had helped to conquer the land for William the Norman. The new men, of course, introduced at Eton, as they long since had done in Belgravia or Mayfair, a correspondingly new and excessive scale of expenditure. The boys who had considered themselves, or were regarded by their comrades as being, capitalists, if they returned after the holidays from the Manor House, the Rectory, or the Hall, with a couple of sovereigns, or, at the outside, a five-pound note in their pockets, were now jostled and eclipsed by the olive branches of the newly enriched, who, not content with merely giving their sons "nothing under paper," did actually in one or two cases propose to open accounts for them at the local bank.

The prestige which is the growth of centuries is not easily destroyed. The names and associations of Eton are intertwined so closely with whatever is most illustrious in the achievements of peace or war, with whatever is most splendid in the fame of statesmanship, letters, and law, as to survive vicissitudes more trying even than those through which it has passed already. If, as an Eton youngster, the future "fourth party's" leader witnessed the beginning of these changes in the neighbourhood of the "Playing Fields," he did not see their final completion, nor, perhaps, had he done so, would it have affected greatly his boyish mind.

At Oxford the new order had been, if not completely, yet in some respects firmly, established when, in 1867, Randolph Churchill began his undergraduate career at Merton. The Oxford with which the freshman then made his acquaintance was indeed still in many

respects the Oxford of the Middle Ages. As
the result of Government inquiries, and the
enterprising efforts of indigenous reformers,
such as the then Provost of Queen's College,
subsequently Archbishop Thomson, nepotism,
nomination and patronage were almost entirely
superseded by a *régime* of the most un-
reserved competition. Alike to scholarships
and fellowships, the best candidates, irrespective
of birthplace or founders' kin, were generally
elected. Common-room opinion throughout
the University would · have been as much
scandalised by the idea of personal preference
or social favouritism influencing an examination
as a school's "invigilator" during the ordeal
of the Hertford or Ireland papers would be
dumfounded at detecting a candidate furtively
resorting to the "Ainsworth leaves," celebrated
in the admirable Coleridgian parody by, if I
mistake not, the present Rector of Lincoln,
"The Rime of the New Mayde Baccalere."
The natural science schools were not yet
recognised adequately, but were in existence.
The law and history schools had long before
become popular. The married fellow, who,
with one or two exceedingly rare exceptions,

had but a year or two earlier been as much
unknown as the unattached student himself,
was now becoming a feature in the place.
The Eton which Randolph Churchill left, by
reason of its exclusiveness and expenditure,
could not be called representative of the
nineteenth-century English people; but the
Oxford in which his residence began, with
its legion of *scholares non ascripti*, its parks
and gardens, peopled with perambulators,
nursemaids, and infants, its suburbs near
Iffley, Shotover, St. Giles's, or the Woodstock
Road, colonised by very-much-married dons
and their families, did fairly reflect the social
or popular changes outside, which hitherto
the University on the Isis had affected to
disregard, or had contrived to ignore.

As yet, not more at Eton than at Cheam,
had the new-comer to the college, whose
warden was then Dr. Marsham, given any
signs that he was likely, eagerly or appre-
ciatively, to enter into the new life of the place.
The then warden of Merton was, like the
warden to-day, a layman; but in his habits of
life, as well as in his social ideas, rather fulfilled
the idea of a country gentleman of the old

school than the head of an Oxford house. The non-collegiate students had not as yet leavened to a very perceptible extent the University; the system of inter-collegiate lectures was still unknown or but partially established. Though it was no longer quite a cloister, the whole social economy of the place was based upon the old exclusive system, under which the society containing him, rather than the individual student himself, was the recognised unit of the community. If in these days Randolph Churchill had anticipated the broadly tolerant and comprehensive spirit, the contempt of sectional and social distinctions, the indifference to the bigotry of conventional usage which at a later period of his life characterised his selection of acquaintances, whether on the floor of St. Stephen's or elsewhere, he might have looked far beyond Christchurch, Merton, or Balliol, for recruits to his visiting list, and, as the Tory democracy's predestined organiser, might have cultivated assiduously the novel order of undergraduates, as more closely allied than students of his own social set to the depositories of electoral power in the country as re-created by successive measures of parlia-

mentary reform. But at eighteen one does
not easily emancipate oneself from the social
prejudices of a modish seminary like Eton,
or from the binding traditions of fashionable
acquaintanceship. Merton had long enjoyed a
cachet of social ascendancy scarcely second to
Eton itself, from which, as a fact, many of its
undergraduates came. Athleticism, titularly to
be distinguished from the cricket field or the
river, was not yet a flourishing institution.
The muscular intercommunion of colleges and
their members, promoted by mutual competition
in jumping, running, and gymnastics, by way
of preparation for similar struggles on a more
august scale, between champions of the two
Universities, was only in its infancy. The
youths representing the best *ton* in the best
colleges still kept very much to their own
societies, or associated outside their respective
walls only with youths of the same calibre
on other foundations. The Union Debating
Society, which had been the training ground
of a Gladstone, a Peel, a Derby, a Cardwell,
or a Carnarvon, had now become, to undergraduates who prided themselves on being " of
the better sort," a lounge or a club. The really

handsome debating hall, with its vaulted roof, decorated by pre-Raphaelite frescoes, was frequented chiefly, not by striplings eager to engage in the mimicry of senatorial strife, but by gentlemen of all ages, anxious to gather from the *Times* newspaper the latest intelligence of the hour, or, it may be, to ascertain from the betting list the exact state of the odds against the newest Derby favourite. Even as late as this, young gentlemen in *statu pupillari* had not annexed a smoking-room in the erstwhile temple of discussion. One chamber, however, upstairs there was, furnished, if I remember correctly, with red baize divans, set apart for novel readers and coffee drinkers. This apartment might have had attractions for the newcomer to Merton in 1867. As a matter of fact, however, Randolph Churchill does not seem at any time to have belonged to the society, though in 1888, when revisiting his *alma mater*, he looked in at its debating hall, and, to encourage the others, took part in an undergraduates' discussion on the Irish question.

The college to which Randolph Churchill's affections were set before he actually began his undergraduate life was Balliol, whither

many of those nearly his contemporaries at
Eton had preceded him. But since the
mastership of Jenkyns—who, after a lapse
of nearly five centuries, filled the seat once
occupied by the Reformer Wycliffe—had re-
modelled the administration as well as created
the modern prestige of this society, the Balliol
matriculation ordeal, though professedly a
qualifying one, was practically competitive,
often not less severely so than a scholarship
examination at an obscurer college. Randolph
Churchill, therefore, had gone to Merton. The
actual selection of this college rather than
Balliol had, doubtless, some influence subsequently on the career and character of the man
himself. Whether, supposing him to have
become one of the subjects of Dr. Scott, the
joint author of the famous lexicon, Mr. Jowett's
predecessor in the mastership, as well as, after
Jenkyns, the finisher of the foundations of its
renown, Randolph Churchill would have
turned out as good a scholar as the present
Lord Morley, or so immaculately orthodox a
nobleman as the present Marquis of Lansdowne,
may be doubted; but seeing his extreme
susceptibility at all stages to his environing

influences, the probabilities are that he would have caught the Balliol tone just as he practically showed his sympathy with the prevailing genius of Merton. In that case, our political and parliamentary life might have had in Lord Randolph Churchill a figure equal to Sir Ughtred K. Shuttleworth in information, to Mr. Arnold Morley in gravity ; but the House of Commons' society in general, his friends in particular, would never have had the Randolph Churchill whom they knew, and whom, in most instances, to know was also to love with a personal affection. Balliol, in truth, has for some time occupied the same place among colleges once filled, under Arnold and his immediate successors, by Rugby among schools. The tendency, alike of the institution traditionally associated with the clergyman of Laleham and Foxhowe, as that of the college now connected with the name of Jowett, is to run different characters into a common mould, to elaborate them within and without to the highest point of finish, to stamp them, notwithstanding their idiosyncratic diversities, with the hall-mark of an identical excellence.

No more efficient corrective probably to the

besetting weaknesses or the congenital defects
of Randolph Churchill's nature could have been
devised than a Balliol discipline during three
years, two of which should have been occupied
with reading for honours in the final school
of *litteræ humaniores.* This preparation it is
which pre-eminently gives to-day an Oxford
training its practical value as a preparation
for the business of life, whether the career
chosen is law, letters, or diplomacy, commerce
or medicine. Few youths, not being philosophers or Scotchmen by birth, find the ordeal
to their taste. It is this very lack of personal
congeniality in the curriculum, this very re-
pulsiveness in the abstract nature of the subjects
studied, which, together with their direct bearing
upon fundamental questions of morals, politics,
or taste, constitute the unique value of the entire
course. That at Balliol Randolph Churchill
would have received a training more salutary
to the future statesman than he was likely
to secure at Merton, that his studies would
have been early preventives against errors
into which, as a politician, he frequently fell,
and have filled the void of ignorances that,
with native frankness, he was the first to

confess and deplore, is certain. On the other hand, the admirable equipments of the well-informed public man would have been secured to the cost of many charms of the natural man. Excrescences advantageously, from some points of view, to be dispensed with, would have been pruned away. The essential fibre of the man might have sustained some injury during the ordeal. In the improving and educating process of the raw material countless and strikingly characteristic attributes, which during his meteor-like course will for ever have endeared the subject of this memoir to those who knew him even slightly, would have been lost. A better balanced and controlled mind would have been the result of this partly reforming, partly manufacturing process—scarcely a more acute or ingenious mind, certainly not so attractive or interesting an one.

Merton, during at least the last three decades, has ever been famous for the possession of a *comme il faut*, or, as it would have been called by the generation of Randolph Churchill's father, a gentlemanly rowing set. For such a society the freshman's Eton

antecedents admirably fitted him. Hard by,
within an easy stone's throw of Merton, were
Lord Rosebery's rooms at Christ Church, in
Canterbury quadrangle, and those of the
present Lord Tweedmouth, then Mr. Edward
Marjoribanks, his special Oxford intimate, in
Peckwater. The more rapid youths of Merton
and of the historic " House " coalesced upon
all non-studious occasions into a common
corporation. Nor had Mr. Cholmeley—then
fellow of Magdalen and proctor, to-day the
venerated and popular rector of Beaconsfield
—many more anxious moments or strenuous
chases than those of which to him and his
" bull dogs" the *viveurs* of the two locally
contiguous and socially allied institutions were
the objects. To the same college as Randolph Churchill, during the same period,
there belonged Mr. Archibald Stuart Wortley,
Mr. E. M. Kenny, the well-known bowler of
Rugby and Oxford, Mr. Leonard Micklem,
of the Eton eleven, the late Marquis of Ely,
Mr. George Markham, and the son of a
former manager of the *Times* newspaper, with
Delane, the creator of its present greatness,
the Honourable Alberic Bertie, now rector of

Gedling, near Nottingham, and Mr. Mowbray
Morris, now the editor of *Macmillan's Magazine.* At Merton Lord Randolph Churchill
kept his terms regularly, cut his lectures,
especially those of the present bursar, who
instructed the future Chancellor of the Exchequer in the Rule of Three ; not more
frequently than others of his day. Randolph Churchill's college tutor was the present
Bishop of Peterborough, then Mr. Mandell
Creighton. This gentleman's lectures, sup-
plementing the quickness and capacity of
his pupil, enabled the latter to win, without
the slightest difficulty, and with not too
much industry, a second class in the history
schools. Nor can there be much doubt that
the opinion formed during his stay there by
the Merton authorities generally is correct,
and that their calibre would, with very little
more application, have enabled Churchill to
obtain a first class, either in the school selected
by him or in any other. One distinctly intellectual taste Randolph Churchill developed
during his Oxford residence. He read and
re-read, till he could repeat long passages of
it by heart, and had possessed himself through-

out of its spirit of solemn irony or scornful antithèsis, Gibbon's mighty masterpiece. The examiners, the late Mr. E. A. Freeman among them, were struck, not merely by the accuracy of Churchill's papers on this subject, but the degree to which the Gibbonian ethos impregnated the literary style in which the papers set were answered.

Randolph Churchill's Merton tutor, to-day, as already mentioned, Bishop of Peterborough, fortunately lives to correct some popular mis-statements about Randolph Churchill's Oxford career. If his relations with the University authorities were sometimes strained, Dr. Creighton, to whom I am indebted for an interesting and valuable letter on this subject, is able to say that in his attitude towards the College management there was no ground for complaint.

During a time of much local excitement— of popular riots at the high price of bread—he came into collision with the police. The inci-dent was turned into political capital in some of the London papers, and Churchill felt himself unjustly treated. " But," says Dr. Creighton, " he was always amenable to expostulation, when wisely administered, and consulted me with freedom on all matters relating to the daily conduct of his life. At first he did not read much, having a constitutional habit of going to sleep in his chair after dinner, often for hours, which he only gradually overcame. But from the first," continues the Bishop, " I was interested to see his growing appreciation of the value of history, especially on its legal and constitutional side. He would take up a subject, and talk about it till he had reached its bottom. As his interest grew, he read more, and finally obtained a Second Class in Law and Modern History at a time when no one was in the first class.

"My attention," to complete this extract, from the Bishop's instructive testimony, " was called to his marked ability for practical politics early in his career. Soon after he came to Merton he deemed it his duty to write a letter in defence of his father, who had been attacked on some question of Woodstock politics. Before sending the note, he brought it to me. I was greatly impressed by its dignity and its dexterity—the former, as the composition of a son about his father, the latter in the administration of a reproof without leaving a loophole of escape."

The tutor's words, after its perusal, were: " I do not advise you to enter into political controversy at your time of life." The answer was : " I have thought it over, and decided that point for myself. What I came to ask you was if you saw anything in the letter which you thought unbecoming."

The tutor, thus appealed to, saw no alternative save to reply, " It you are going to send a letter at all, you could not send a better one."

" That incident gave me," writes the Bishop, "a real insight into Churchill's character, and showed me his capacity for practical politics. He made up his own mind; having well reflected, he chose his ground of attack, and then took every pains about the form of expression. He sought no advice about what he was going to do, but was anxious to do it ' as well as possible.' "

This episode, with Dr. Creighton's sagacious comments upon the facts, shows the undergraduate to have made an appreciable advance upon the schoolboy, and to be the true parent of the politician.

4

The acquaintance with his Merton teacher was maintained after his college days were over. Writing to this gentleman in 1883, Churchill says : " It has always been pleasant to me to think that the historical studies which I too lightly carried on under your guidance have been of immense value to me in calculating and carrying out actions which to many appear erratic. If they ever lead to any substantial result, it will be owing to those years at Merton, when you alone so kindly and continuously endeavoured to keep me up to the mark. It is indeed a pleasure to me to know you have not forgotten your former rather unsatisfactory pupil, and that you follow, not without interest, and perhaps with some hope, a course of which Fate has not yet determined the form or the end."

Still the record left behind him on the Isis is, of course, one of sport and play rather than of intellectual effort or achievement. As when at the school on the Thames, so, too, at the university on the Isis, Randolph Churchill took little part in the more staid or traditional pastimes of the place. He was " neither," in Etonian language, " a wet bob nor a dry bob." He kept a pack of harriers of his own, whose nucleus had been formed so far back as his boyish days. He took an active part in the annual college " grinds," or two days' steeple chase meeting, then held at Moreton-in-the Marsh, long supported by past and present Mertonians, but prohibited and terminated by the Merton rulers in 1875, shortly after Randolph Churchill had gone down. As a matter of course, he rode regularly and eagerly to hounds, the pack with which he most often hunted being that of Mr. Duffield, a sportsman famous throughout the Oxfordshire district for the brevity ot his temper, the fervour of his anathemas, and the fulness of his vituperative vocabulary. This will be as fitting a place as any to give the correct version of an episode that, frequently narrated though it has been, did not occur under precisely the same circumstances as those with which most narrators have associated it. At a certain meet of the Duffield pack Lord Randolph's hunter became very fractious, and, partly bolting, galloped into the midst of the pack. The traditionally insulting questions, with the objurgations usual under these circumstances, were hurled by the master of the pack at the offending figure.

Randolph Churchill being thus made to look for a moment to the whole field ridiculous ; said nothing, but vowed inwardly to bide his chance and have his revenge. That opportunity, before very long, presented itself. A hunt dinner was given at the Mitre Hotel. On the covers being removed, the M.F.H., as chairman of the evening, delivered the conventional eulogy on the sport of kings, the image of war, with less than one per cent. of its danger. Randolph Churchill, who rose shortly afterwards, expressed in enthusiastic but general terms his devotion to every kind of pastime whose object was "to kill something." Then, reviewing in detail various quarries and their pursuit, he wound up : " But if it should so happen that none of the sports I have just enumerated, not even rat-hunting, were available, I might then, as a last resource, attempt to extract enjoyment by following Mr. Duffield's hounds." The meanest faculty of literary criticism will scarcely fail to detect in these sentiments and periods the ring of that invective which twenty years later was levelled against the titular Tory chiefs by the leader of the " fourth party."

When, in 1888, Lord Randolph Churchill revisited Oxford as a statesman of mark, and, though a Master of Arts, took part in the Union debate above mentioned, he was at the evening's close entertained by the Myrmidon Club of his old college, which he had in earlier years helped to found, and of which he had been a leading spirit. This society was one of those purely collegiate, as opposed to University institutions mentioned above, belonging essentially to a bygone Oxford generation, historically significant, of an era whose beginnings coincided with the Oxford career of Randolph Churchill. The Merton Myrmidons had their counterparts in the Phœnix clubmen of Brasenose, in the Canning clubmen of St. John's, in a nameless society of another foundation, as in other collegiate institutions too numerous to be mentioned. Cognate to these societies, but consisting of the better sort of sporting undergraduates from some half-dozen colleges, were the Bullingdon Club, Loder's, and the Eton and Harrow Club. About the end of Randolph Churchill's career, the club known as Vincent's, consisting of a fusion from University and Brasenose Colleges, came into existence. The Myrmidon society held its dinners during its earlier history at the Mitre, but afterwards at the new Randolph Hotel, just opposite the Taylorian Buildings at the top of Beaumont Street. There is a certain monotony in the chronicle of the doings at these feasts. In all cases there are the same narratives of proctors' invasions, youthful concealments in coal-cellars, varied sometimes by the incarceration of indiscreet waiters in pantries or ice safes ; of encounters with proctors and bull-dogs, tempered by conflicts with the city police. If at Oxford in the case of Randolph Churchill the memory of the practical joker is apt to eclipse that of the student, this is not because his intellectual powers, but his habits of application, were of later development than his career on the Isis ; while as for his practical jokes, they were so far superior over the ordinary antics of the place, as seldom to involve any serious destruction of property or of animal life, and not wantonly to select for their butt the retiring student or the nervously unpopular don. His special objective in this variety of escapade was a particularly offensive, insolent, and churlish steward of the college, named Patey.

The Merton College of Randolph Churchill's time consisted, besides the warden and fellows, only of some fifty undergraduates. The contemporary reminiscences of him during this stage of his career are necessarily few, but I believe none of those extant have, thanks to the invaluable assistance and advice of the present warden, the Hon. G. C. Brodrick, as well as Dr. Creighton, been omitted here. But before quitting the subject of this memoir while he was the wearer of a " Commoner's " gown, it must be pointed out that the moral continuity of the Eton schoolboy experiences no solution in the case of the Oxford undergraduate. Small as Merton was, with all its *alumni* on terms of mutual acquaintance, Randolph Churchill, as he had done in the latitude of the " Playing Fields," preserved a noticeable isolation from his fellows. Even with the few members of his own exclusive set he was no more exuberantly and indiscriminately genial than with the members of his own party, or of the House of Commons generally, twenty years later on. But the

faculty of attaching others to him, and so
showing himself a born leader ot men, increased
with his years.   Like Byron, indeed, and many
other masterful spirits not so illustrious, it was
necessary for him to be allowed the lead.   But
this condition once granted, his popularity was
not less remarkable than were his fearlessness
and independence.   No member of Merton
College before or since, no member, for that
matter, of the University, ot the Carlton
Club, or of Parliament, was ever more uniformly liked, or rather signally beloved, by
the few whom he desired for his society or
invited to his coteries.

CHAPTER IV.

GENERAL RESULTS OF ETON AND OXFORD
(1871-4).

Randolph Churchill's position in 1871, on the eve of public life.—The temptations and difficulties of his station.— Educational influences of his home Blenheim life; the Blenheim visitors' book; hospitalities of Randolph Churchill's father and brother, seventh and eighth Dukes of Marlborough; similarities between Randolph Churchill and his brother, then Lord Blandford.

AFTER he had taken his degree, on the eve of starting for the " grand tour," as it was called, when the journey used to be made under such different conditions as well as to such different places, Randolph Churchill presents himself to the observer as a young man whose idiosyncrasies Eton and Oxford, like the private tuition period, had emphasised and intensified rather than corrected. Thus far he had submitted to an imperfectly educational process —an experience, in some degree, informatory and instructive no doubt, but scarcely,

in the best sense of the word, educational.
At Balliol, under Jowett, the academic father
of many great scholars but ot more good
citizens, all this would probably have been
different. As it was, no one knew better
than Randolph Churchill himself at the time,
or in years after confessed it more humbly,
that the time and money expended on his
school or college career could not strictly be
called a remunerative investment. The indomitable will inherited from his paternal
ancestor, who humbled the pride of France
on the field of Blenheim, the unflinching
tenacity of purpose, the bold originality of
political views, his legacy from his maternal
ancestor, Lord Londonderry — valuable in
themselves as these gifts of birth or temperament must, under any circumstances, have
been, their precious utility would have been
increased tenfold if their possessor had ever
submitted himself unreservedly to that succession of corrective forces which his educational opportunities had offered. When the
great Lord Holland was about to submit his
prodigiously gifted son, the future Whig chief,
to tutors and governors, he cautioned them to

beware, above all things, of breaking the lad's spirit. Randolph Spencer Churchill was a child at least as loving, lovable, and brilliantly endowed as Charles James Fox; nor, the human nature of parents being what we know it to be, need one suppose that the seventh Duke and Duchess of Marlborough were appreciably less reluctant to commit so bright, remarkable, and affectionate a child to the hazards and hardships of educational existence as by usage it is prescribed to be.

Not every person really knows, and fewer still adequately realise, the social, moral, and intellectual perils with which, even in this democratic and plutocratic age, the ordeal ot Eton and Oxford, like that ot Eton and the Guards, or diplomacy, is fraught to the probationer who has had the perilous distinction to be born in the purple. There is, therefore, nothing exceptional in Randolph Churchill's case; but for a just retrospect of his opening years the prominence due to the simple historic fact just stated cannot be exaggerated. At Eton, Randolph Churchill picked up not less Latin and Greek than the majority of boys who stay in that seat of learning only two years, who are never sufficiently senior to be in the sixth form, in " pop," or in the boats. With the exception of what he learned at Oxford when he put on a spurt for the history schools, crammed himself with Gibbon in the manner aforesaid, and narrowly missed a first class, the proficiency in any branch of study carried away by him from the Thames or the Isis was, to say the least of it, inconsiderable. When setting forth on his early circumnavigation of the continent, Randolph Churchill's strictly academic studies had not advanced very far beyond the elementary classics of the " Remove." Until " moderations " are safely over, that portion of the Oxford curriculum which is the special use of the place, and the characteristic aggregate of Oxford culture, does not begin. The reminiscences of Horace, Virgil, two or three Greek plays, read in earlier years with his tutor and not yet quite forgotten, were enough to enable Churchill to scrape through the first public examination in humane letters, as they have sufficed to pull others through the same ordeal before as well as since his day, and as they will do so long as the schools exist. Directly the test of schoolboy knowledge, which " moderations " essentially are, had been left behind, Randolph Churchill, if he was troubled with any thoughts of prospective studies, excluded from his forecast alike the philosophers of the Garden or the Porch, and the prose masters who have made the literature of national narrative what we know it to-day. In his father's dining-room at Blenheim Palace he had, as a boy, met the representatives of all that is most distinguished in letters, science, or, above all, in affairs. No great nobleman was more comprehensive or, within wise limits, indiscriminating in his hospitalities than the seventh Duke of Marlborough. This attractive trait in his father's disposition was reproduced faithfully not more by his second son than by his eldest, the late, or eighth, Duke, better known still to a number of friends endeared to him by personal courtesy and kindness as " Blandford." The Marlborough house never knew a head who, as an Amphi-tryon, was more widely eclectic in the choice of his company or sedulously attentive to their needs than the father of the present possessor of the Churchill coronet. The elder of the two brothers had been at times a far severer student than the younger. Never at either University, he had read high mathematics so thoroughly as to be able to find the same pleasure in a treatise by Professor Cayley as other men of education discover in the Odes of Horace. Classics, I fancy, had not the same attraction for him at Eton as catapults—those instruments of boyish assault which had so alarming a vogue in schools some thirty years since, and which were managed by the heir to the Marlborough strawberry-leaf on scientific principles, as well as with rather too infallible precision. Both brothers were French scholars very far above the average ; each wrote it with accuracy, talked in it with ease ; while the elder's conversational mastery of Parisian idiom and accent was not, I apprehend, inferior to that of the late Lord Granville himself. Lord Blandford and Lord Randolph Churchill were both of them considerable travellers. With the exception of an American trip, the younger, probably, was never out of Europe until, in the spring of 1885, he visited India. That portion of our empire the duke had traversed thoroughly and leisurely more than once, from the Khyber to Comorin. He was, too, no mere smatterer in chemistry. The ground floor of one of the wings at Blenheim was devoted to drugs and chemicals of all kinds. Here he often passed hours daily—varying this employment by drives through his estate in a favourite dogcart with a very high-stepping horse, and preferring such occupations to the covert-side pastimes of an English country gentleman, though in these he was no discreditable performer.

The few speeches made in Parliament by the eighth Duke of Marlborough showed extensive painstaking, original knowledge of foreign affairs, expressed in business-like and perfectly adequate language. He was, in truth, as little of a trifler as the erewhile Clerk of the Council, Mr. Charles Greville, himself, in whom, only to the very superficial observer, could the sportsman's front conceal for one moment the statesman's mind, or cloak beneath the professed man of pleasure the profound and sleepless student of affairs. The society chiefly enjoyed by the late Duke of Marlborough was the exact opposite of that in which those who knew nothing of the man sometimes chose to fancy he liked to move, but which, as a matter of fact, the present writer of these lines, in the course of a tolerably close acquaintance of nearly two decades, never saw him enter. Foreign politicians, experienced officials, whether in the English Civil Service or in that of other States, representatives of *la haut finance*—these were the men whom he alone cultivated, or whom willingly he would be at any trouble to meet. It is now an open secret that Lord Palmerston was indebted for his almost superhumanly early and exact knowledge of continental movements generally, and of French politics especially, to the friendly and authentic information from behind the scenes with which he was from day to day, almost from hour to hour, supplied by Sir Henry Bulwer, then our ambassador in Paris. As surely as any fresh departure was meditated by the " Imperial Sphinx " of the Tuilleries, or indicated in the *Moniteur*, so certainly was the gaily omniscient member for Tiverton prepared for the intimation, and forearmed against its consequences. To his own great misfortune, and to the loss, as I believe, of the public service, the eighth Duke of Marlborough never donned official harness. But at least during those years of his life when he was known to me, he worked at foreign politics almost with a Palmerston's industry, and not altogether without a Palmerston's opportunities. Lord Lyons, in his capacity of British representative at Paris, was unsurpassed probably in the annals of latter-day diplomacy ; and of Lord Lyons, his friend and secretary, Mr. George Sheffield, may be said to have been an integral part. The former of this inseparable couple was the habitual guest of the Duke of Blenheim ; the latter seldom failed to accompany his chief, and for very many years was the closest intimate and invaluable informant on all public matters. A member of the great diplomatic club in. London, the St. James', Piccadilly, Randolph Churchill's elder brother, whether in his ducal or ante-ducal style, had maintained a friendly correspondence with members of nearly all the European chanceries ; and if he had never looked into the politics of Aristotle, or, it may be, opened a Latin or Greek book since his Eton days, never failed to peruse the newest of notable volumes on political as on physical science produced by continental experts. The man who, on the few occasions when he met them, did, in their

5

own line of discussion, hold his own with Grant Duff, John Lubbock, Lord Acton, could not well have been the fribble or the fop which the slanderous malignity of prejudiced ignorance has been pleased to depict him.

Chancing to have, from family associations, some knowledge of Winchester School, I was asked certain questions concerning it by the eighth wearer of the Churchill coronet before he decided to send his son, the duke now regnant, to the Wykehamist foundation.   More than one Winchester master of that day could testify to the thorough practical knowledge of the father, then about to entrust his son to their care, as shown by his inquiries into the Winchester provision for mathematical and scientific teach-ing—the two things that principally interested him.   The family resemblance between the two brothers showed itself, as has been already said, in a certain similarity of tastes as well as of facial features.   The elder was practically expert with the turning-lathe, constantly manu-facturing cigarette tubes in meerschaum or amber, boxes in ebony, or caskets of ivory for his friends.   The younger never advanced to proficiency like this, but showed great dexterity in manipulating the works of clocks or watches, taking them to pieces and reconstructing them, just as an ingenious child does with its toy puzzles or dissecting maps.

In a great family, where questions concerning the interpretation of ancestral documents on the subject of heirlooms and dowers is a constant provocative of controversy, some discussions between the collaterals of the same generation, especially when they happen not to be far removed from the ancestral title, are almost inevitable. But from their schooldays to the end of life the relations between the two men now spoken of were, upon the whole, those of friendly goodwill, and not merely ceremonial fraternity. I have before me a number of letters received from Randolph Churchill during different periods of the years 1881-4. A temporary failure of Randolph Churchill's health in the summer of 1882 caused him to leave London, and for some months inhabit a pretty cottage, with delightful lawn and rose-garden, on Wimbledon Common. Here, during his convalescence, I sometimes visited him, always to find him deriving the solace and delight, more potent to cure sickness than doctors or drugs, ministered by the loving care of an admiring, devoted wife, as well as of a gracious and matchless mother ; while on most days, before my call was concluded, Lord Blandford's cab had driven up. ·Subsequently the two brothers went to the Engadine. Writing from Pontresina, under date August 16th, 1883, Randolph Churchill says : " It is quite impossible to do justice to Blandford's more than womanly tenderness and care." The eighth Duke of Marlborough, though not really a partisan of any side, and at no time more than a fitful and precarious supporter of Liberalism, had been once a Parliamentary candidate for an eastern county seat ; and about the year 1884, when a general election was considered to be within a measurable distance, was supposed to have meditated bringing forward a candidate of his own in opposition to his brother for the family borough of Woodstock. I have good reason to doubt his serious entertainment of such a purpose. The mere idea of it was enough to cause some friction in the ducal house. The Randolph Churchills were considering whether, on the eve of their electioneering campaign in the

Blenheim borough, it might not be as well to prevent the possibility of unpleasantness by sending down their own horses and carriages from Paddington instead of, as usual, counting upon the Palace equipages. The Duke had anticipated such a possibility; and while the Connaught Place party were discussing matters, there came a letter from the Duke asking of how many his brother's company would consist. When the Tory democratic leader and his suite drew up in the train at Woodstock Road the sole novelty in their reception was a superbly horsed victoria, which had been provided for the special accommodation of his grace's sister-in-law.

Essential, however, as it was, with a view of correcting certain vulgar misconceptions, to set forth accurately the relations between the two brothers, mutually so unlike, and yet so like, it is an anticipation of our historical sequel, and a digression from the immediate argument. In his felicitous and familiar description of the Rupert of debate, the great Lord Derby, known to this generation, Lord Lytton has spoken of "all Eton having been left in the boy." Notwithstanding the time spent, after

the "playing fields" had been left behind
him, in the society then ruled by Dr. Bullock-
Marsham, Randolph Churchill, on the threshold
of his parliamentary career in 1874, was, in
some sense, little more than an Eton boy,
not yet, as W. Mackworth Praed sings of our
senators, "grown heavy." It is the boast
of England's premier public school that more
than any other she enables her sons to dis-
pense with the completing university course.
Whatever of Latin or Greek he may or
may not carry away with him, the average
Etonian of seventeen or eighteen is already
a man of the world in miniature. No subsequent laurels won in senate-house or schools
would in this respect carry him further.
If Randolph Churchill at Oxford did not
learn a great deal more than his school had
taught him, at any rate he forgot nothing
which he had acquired there. There would
be no greater mistake than to suppose that
the stripling from the famous Thames-side
school is, from the tenderness of his years
or inexperience, in any danger, as a rule, of
wasting his substance, or of being the dupe
of more astute seniors. His escapades and

extravagances are things of the past. By the time the first indications of manly down are visible on his upper lip he is as shrewd a judge of money's worth, has as keen an eye to the main chance and to a good bargain, as any father of a family could possess.

In all these regards, when he entered at Merton College, the subject of these remarks was a typical Etonian. Such he remained when, in the fulness of time, A.D. 1877, he proceeded to his M.A. degree ; and such, with a gradual accumulation of fresh political and mundane knowledge generally, he continued to the end of his life.

Young Englishmen, or, for that matter, Englishmen of any age, are not given to talking about their inner life or psychical experiences to their acquaintances, or even to their friends. Whether there may have been some profoundly serious side to the character of South Paddington's late representative it would, in my opinion, be an impertinence as well as an absurdity circumstantially to conjecture or judicially to decide here. Two things may, perhaps, be said with certainty. No man had more thoroughly seen

through the hollowness of existence, or felt
so habitually as the *blasé* protagonist in
the play immortalised by the late Charles
Matthews, *Used Up*, that whether he
scrambled up the Pyramids, or looked down
the crater of Vesuvius, there was equally
nothing in it. The remark in this vein
attributed to Randolph Churchill is, " I have
tried all forms of excitement, from tip-cat
to tiger-shooting ; all degrees of gambling,
from ' beggar-my-neighbour' to Monte Carlo ;
but have found no gambling like politics, and
no excitement like a big division." The authenticity of this remark may be doubted,
because it is a little more egotistical than its
reputed author's taste might have approved ;
but, historical or legendary, the words give a
very good idea of their possible speaker.
" No man," I once remember Churchill to
have said, " is so entirely alone and solitary
as I am." If this comment seems to any
dropped for the sake of effect, those outside
the family of its author, yet having a fair
knowledge of the man in his various moods,
will recognise in it the expression of a deeply
pathetic truth. The consciousness of this iso-

lation was probably the secret of the surprising interest which Randolph Churchill seldom failed to excite in all women of any breeding, perception, or intelligence. The same besetting sense of loneliness, it may be remarked, can also be found traversing the letters and conversation of the distinguished man from whom, on his mother's side, he was descended, and whom in many things he resembled so remarkably, Sidmouth's colleague during the first two decades of this century, the famous and unhappy Lord Londonderry.

Randolph Churchill has many friends who loved him as few men ever yet have been loved, and to whose eyes his memory will bring tears. Of all those associated with him most intimately in politics or society, there is, perhaps, only one whose knowledge of human nature, and whose insight into the recesses of Churchill's nature, would qualify him to do justice to this complicated and deeply sad topic,—Sir Henry Drummond-Wolff, longtime his lieutenant in the "fourth party," and to-day Her Majesty's Ambassador at Madrid.

CHAPTER V.

THE CAREER BEGUN (1874-78).

Electioneering incident while Randolph Churchill was an undergraduate at Oxford.—The General Election of 1874 sprung upon the country by Mr. Gladstone.— Lord Randolph Churchill Conservative Candidate for Woodstock; returned; maiden speech in House of Commons.—First beginnings of Irish obstruction.—A kind of reminiscence of Oxford experiences.—Great application to parliamentary duties.—Political and Irish education in connection with the Duchess of Marlborough's Irish Fund during the Irish Viceroyship of seventh Duke of Marlborough.—Mr. Disraeli and the Churchill family.

ALTHOUGH, as may be explained by facts already mentioned in sufficient detail, Randolph Churchill, when at Oxford, took no part in the Union debates, he did not, during his undergraduate career,* abstain entirely from boyish politics. At the general election of 1868, following Mr. Disraeli's defeat in the House of Commons on the Irish Church resolutions,

---

* This incident is that glanced at in the preceding chapter by the light of Bishop Creighton's letter.

the representatives of philosophical Liberalism from Oxford and elsewhere made a determined attempt to assert themselves at the polling booths. Prominent among these was the gentleman who is to-day the warden of Randolph Churchill's old college, then one of its fellows, a distinguished member of the *Times* editorial staff in the old Delane days, the Hon. G. C. Brodrick, who at the time now spoken of contested the Blenheim borough against Mr. Henry Barnett, running that Conservative within twenty votes of defeat. Merton College has been generally conspicuous for the lay element in its " common room," resembling in this respect All Souls' among Oxford colleges, and, as perhaps it may be said, Trinity Hall at Cambridge. The Liberal candidate, therefore, of seven-and-twenty years since was not likely to want canvassers among his academic coevals. One of these gentlemen, during the advocacy of his friend's cause, without, as should be added, the knowledge or consent, not less than to the real regret of. Mr. Brodrick himself, attacked the then head of the Churchill house somewhat violently and unnecessarily. This incident brought Randolph

Churchill into the field with a spirited but perfectly well-bred protest against the sentiments expressed and the language used by the academic electioneerer concerning the Duke of Marlborough. Subsequently, a couple of years later, when in Oxford lodgings with his friend Mr. Stuart Wortley—their term of residence within college walls having expired—Randolph Churchill shared the deep interest generally taken by his countrymen in the progress of the Franco-Prussian War, following the campaign daily in the newspaper letters, and more than once resolving to follow it upon the actual battlefields themselves. But though by this time the political ideas of his brother, Lord Blandford, had matured considerably, and were developing into a sober admiration of Mr. Disraeli's great rival, the younger brother's statesmanship probably could have been summed up in the antipathy to Mr. Gladstone, which then, as now, constituted the conventional creed in public affairs of young Eton and younger Oxford.

On a memorable Sunday morning towards the end of January, exactly one-and-twenty years ago, the rumour went round Pall Mall

first, then gradually spread through Belgravia
or Mayfair to Blackfriars, Fleet Street, as well
as to middle-class suburbs and throughout the
whole country, that Mr. Gladstone was bent
on dissolving. On the following Monday
morning the secret was out. The Bath
election, with other like losses in the previous
autumn, had caused "the Government majority
to sink below the point necessary for the
defence and prosecution of the public interests.
By way of bringing it back to the point at
which it could alone be effective," the Premier
was recurring to the judgment of the constituencies. Most of the journals, side by side
with this announcement, contained not only
Mr. Gladstone's address to the electors of
Greenwich, with its promise of Income Tax
repeal when the constituencies should have
made the expected answer, but also Mr.
Disraeli's manifesto to the freemen of Buckinghamshire—those patriots whom he asserted
to be identical with their predecessors in
Hampden's days, and still to return in himself
a constitutional member to the House of
Commons. The points on which the nation
was, through the Greenwich electorate, invited

to pronounce were—first, the execution of the
commission granted to Liberal ministers in
1868, secondly, the further commission they
might think fit to give to their representatives,
as also the hands to which the fulfilment in
the administration of the Government were
to be entrusted. When, six years previously,
Parliament had met, Mr. Gladstone had a
majority of 116. Before the elections of 1874
were over this disappeared ; and having already
sunk before the elections to between 60 and
70, was, when the contest had ended, replaced
by a Conservative plurality of 51. During
the award of the constituencies, Lord Randolph
Churchill carried the Blenheim borough against
Mr. Brodrick, who had once more come forward, by a total of 569 votes, as against 404.
Within a few days the other gentlemen composing the "fourth party" of the future,
Mr. A. J. Balfour, Sir John Gorst, Sir Henry
Drummond-Wolff, were returned respectively
for Hertford, Chatham, and Christchurch.
The net result of the ex-Premier's appeal had
vindicated abundantly the Household Franchise
measure, for which Mr. Disraeli had educated
his party seven years earlier. The Conser-

vative working man had given the most
practical proof of his existence by ejecting the
ex-minister who had promised the middle
classes relief from direct taxation, and for the
first time since the death of Sir Robert Peel
the Conservatives at Westminster combined
power with place.

No circumstances could be more inspiring
than those under which a young politician,
predisposed by hereditary traditions and
personal preferences to trust the democracy,
then entered the popular chamber. In spite
of the past denunciations on his policy, of
more recent anticipations of accumulating disaster to the Tory cause, the greatest captain
whom the new Conservatism has ever known
had led his followers, not, as Mr. Lowe had
predicted, to new humiliation, but to a decisive
triumph. It was what Disraeli had dared to
indicate as imminent in the near future, when,
in the autumn of the preceding year, he had
animated by his presence and encouraged by
his speech the few adherènts to the Conservative cause in the great commercial capital
of Scotland. Notwithstanding the political
philosophers, the French and English theorists

on democracy, the residuum so often spoken of had at last shown the Tory sympathies on which the joint author with Lord Derby of the franchise measure, a short while before, had relied. It was therefore spoken of not unreasonably as a people's victory, won under the Conservative banner for the constitutional cause, against the most powerful mover of the political masses whom this country has ever seen. The superb patience that is the true characteristic of genius was the dominant feature in Disraeli, the keynote of his temper, the secret of his success. Six years previously it had seemed as if the Conservative working man was no less a figment of the Tory leader's imagination to-day than the true blue peasant had been of the young England mind a couple of decades before.

Lord Randolph Churchill's father, the seventh Duke of Marlborough, was one of those peers who had not broken away from Mr. Disraeli when, following the advice first given him by the late Henry Drummond, he had rested the parliamentary suffrage upon the sole intelligible principle of payment of rates by adult inhabitants. The disaster of 1868 had thus been avenged amply by those who in that year were the instruments destined to falsify, as seemed first, the Disraelian horoscope and estimate of the popular mind. The then head of the Churchill family must have been reminded of that ancestor of his who, like also a former Duke of Richmond, when in the people's house, advocated parliamentary reform. Nor on his mother's side were reasons wanting why the great-grand-nephew of Castlereagh should view with delight the issue of the recent appeal to the citizens of the Empire. Traditionally associated to the exclusion of much else he did and advocated with Sidmouth and the " Six Acts," Castlereagh had, at an earlier period, been a true friend of the minor popular liberties of Ireland, not less than after the Congress of Vienna in 1815 he had stood forward as the champion of small and semi-extinguished nationalities. Randolph Churchill may very properly, if he chose, have liked to dwell on these attributes of his maternal ancestor rather than on those which had, on other occasions, displayed him in antagonism to Canning.

As yet, however, the new member for Woodstock had neither written nor said anything signally creditable or remarkable for his thirty-one years. His address to the electors of the ducal borough was sensible, simple, very unpretentious and unsuggestive. Aristotle in a famous passage emphasises the absurdity of political praise bestowed upon boys, because, in the Ciceronian adaptation of the sentiment, *de pueris nondum laus sed spes est.* Nor should it be forgotten that, apart from a bombastic turgidity of invective, the inspiration as much of his epoch as of the man himself, the early election manifestos and House of Commons addresses of " Coningsby's " author were somewhat flat and almost tame. Neither Sir Robert Peel nor the penultimate Lord Derby, the resemblance between whom and Randolph Churchill is in some respects remarkable, were at all precocious statesmen. As they, and for that matter, Disraeli himself, ripened slowly, so, too, did Randolph Churchill. Peel's final overthrower in Parliament was, for a long time after he had entered the House of Commons, only a Hebrew youth of bizarre appearance, grotesque dress, and not attractive manner. Randolph Churchill, when he first sat for Woodstock, and also for some time after, seemed nothing more to many observers than an ordinary specimen of Eton's and Oxford's social rather than educational growth, who had not turned his opportunities to the best account. Deeper observers— notably Sir William Harcourt—there were, who discovered in Randolph Churchill's occasional speeches qualities warranting the expert opinion that his was the material of which great parliamentarians are eventually made, and that the member for the Blenheim borough would undoubtedly go far. The occasion of his maiden speech in the House of Commons was wisely and characteristically chosen. He was too young to recollect the pessimistic apprehensions of Dr. Pusey and other notable academics of the same standing elicited when the Great Western Railway first decided to extend their system from Didcot to Oxford itself; but it was, I think, before the close of his undergraduateship that a second scare was created by the establishment of the Great Western Railway works almost under the very shadow of Carfax. This step was strongly resisted by the local Conservatives. In the clever pictorial satire with which the occasion inspired

Mr. Sydney P. Hall, then, if I recollect rightly, an undergraduate at Pembroke, the Tory leader, the great logician, Professor Mansel, afterwards Dean of St. Paul's, was portrayed as Jupiter hurling from the academic empyrean the Vulcan in whom the collective artisans of the iron road when at their factory employments were personified. During the spring of 1874 the famous cloister was threatened by yet another still more sacrilegious and inevitably fatal invasion. Unawed by the mighty shade of Gaisford, our army reorganisers had advised that the southern seat of English learning should be made a military centre.

Lord Randolph Churchill, to judge from his Eton and Merton days, was not the most likely person in the world to come forward as the soldier of Universities. That, however, is what he did, performing the duties of his championship in a manner which won for him the compliments of the then borough member, Mr. Vernon Harcourt. On the other hand, Lord Randolph was answered by Mr. Harcourt's Conservative colleague, Mr. A. W. Hall, in a speech that gave promise of debating eminence, but in no way daunted the speaker whom it was intended to demolish. This discussion has incidentally an interest and significance for other reasons than the parliamentary *début* of the Woodstock member. During its progress there were heard the earliest premonitory rumblings of Irish discontent, soon to burst in a storm so serious and so prolonged. Randolph Churchill had reminded the patriots from the Emerald Isle of a new and intolerable national grievance. Dublin had long been, without any protest on the part of its *gens togata*, that into which Oxford was to be converted. The Hibernian champions, therefore, discovered in Randolph Churchill's discourse an implied slight on and insult to " Old Trinity." It now became necessary peremptorily to impress on an alien Parliament that socially, morally, intellectually, by achievement as well as by tradition, the institution for which the sister island is indebted to Queen Elizabeth is, has always been, and ever must be, incomparably superior to the foundation that boasts descent from a probably apocryphal founder in a certain Anglo-Saxon sovereign named Alfred, who, if we possessed sufficient information, could doubtless be identified with the first harrier of the pious Celt. Mr. Brooks, therefore, as chief magistrate of the Irish capital, hurled back at the feet of Lord Randolph Churchill a slander upon the Irish members, which he understood the noble lord to have uttered in the course of his remarks. To the same effect spoke another patriot from the snakeless island, asserting that just as Dublin was far and away a better and a finer city than Oxford, so Dublin University, whose graduate Mr. Meldon had the honour to be, was intellectually and physically a greater institution than Oxford University.

Subsequently to this, when Parliament had reassembled after the Whitsuntide recess, the prognostications of inconvenient self-assertion on the part of the Irish members were continued and confirmed. Mr. O'Donnell, a former member of the Indian Civil Service, now member for Galway, wished to raise a question of privilege, but was prevented by the Speaker, who had received a report from the judge trying the petition against Mr. O'Donnell's return, to the effect that this gentleman was not at the present moment a member of the House of Commons.

It was not, however, till the member for Woodstock had been in the House of Commons for nearly a year, that, during the session of 1875, the Irish Opposition had formally organised itself. The chief features on this occasion, in which Randolph Churchill does not appear to have intervened, but of which some mention for the proper understanding of our sequel is necessary, were Mr. Richard Power's complaint that his country should in the Speech from the Throne have been declared in a state of profound peace, whereas he and his friends would not rest content while there remained a single link of the hateful chain euphuistically called the Peace Preservation Act. These remarks prefaced an appeal to the English and Scotch members to give him and his fellow-countrymen a Home Rule Parliament, as well as a threat that if this request were denied they would hear more often than they liked of Irish affairs at Westminster. Subsequently another Irish representative, Mr. John Martin, demanded point blank, in the name of the Irish people, the annulment of the usurpation of 1800, and the creation of a Hibernian Legislature, to be carried out in as friendly a manner as might be, and, if possible, by federal arrangement. This requisition brought another Celtic orator into the arena, Mr. Herbert, who, taking an exactly opposite point of view, denied the right of his predecessors to represent their countrymen. Mr. Martin's manner and words were noticeable because the tranquillity of the one and the audacity of the other prefigured the attributes with which, at a later, period, Mr. C. S. Parnell was to signalise his part in the long controversy that, at no stage, was beheld by Randolph Churchill as an inactive M.P.

Though Randolph Churchill made in abiding characters his mark in the House of Commons during his first session, that of 1874, the only noteworthy episodes in which he figured have been already mentioned. Nor was it before the summer of 1878 that he again asserted himself prominently in debate. The subject before the House was Irish Secondary Education, with copious reference to the project which not even John Henry Newman's genius sufficed to crown with success, the establishment of a Catholic University on St. Stephen's Green. Then, too, it was that the comfortable presence and, as one might have supposed, the inoffensive manner of the President of the Local Government Board, Mr. Sclater-Booth, provoked Lord Randolph's wrath, soon to relieve itself in the memorable outburst against the mediocrities who rejoice in double-barrelled names. If, upon Mr. Disraeli's elevation to the peerage, some two years earlier, the wishes of an active section of the Conservative party had been fulfilled—if, that is to say, the leadership in the Commons had fallen to Mr. Gathorne Hardy rather than Sir Stafford Northcote— then it is possible, and even probable, that the incidents culminating in the rise of the "fourth party" to a power in the State would never have occurred.

Sir Stafford Northcote was the *beau ideal* of a country gentleman, whom inherited opportunities, great local and national position, a real faculty of, as well as a thoroughly practical training in, statesmanship, have raised worthily to a prominent place among public men of the first rank. A tolerably keen sportsman in the shooting covert or with the hounds, a model county magistrate and chairman of

quarter sessions—not because there was anything parochial in his mind, or because he had
any special affinity to the race of Nimrods,
but because the administration of the law, like
the encouragement of traditional and healthy
pastimes, was a primary duty on the part of
a gentleman whose descent was old and whose
acres were extensive—this scion of Devonshire
baronets was, beyond all things, a conscientious,
a capable, a precise public official, educated in
the straitest traditions of Downing Street and
Sir Robert Peel, as well as, unfortunately for
his party pre-eminence, a financial pupil of
Mr. Gladstone.

Just as Dr. Newman's creditable affection
for the Church of his birth never entirely
forsook him, even after he had come under
the Roman discipline,—just as the earlier
associations of Mr. Gladstone himself with the
Conservative party were, after he had finally
parted with Oxford, long a cause of prejudice
and distrust with the Liberals to whom he-
had become indispensable,—as also not more
remotely than 1880 the same statesman's
Conservative adherents to certain traditional
etiquette in the art of Cabinet making seemed

at one moment likely to perplex and jeopardise his newly formed Administration,—so Sir
Stafford Northcote's remnant of loyal admiration towards the transcendent powers and
services of the great man—formerly his official
master, to-day, in the House of Commons, his
official antagonist—was thought by the more
belligerent spirits of his party to secure for Mr.
Gladstone at the hands of the Conservative
leader a considerateness of treatment that
compromised the independence and minimised
the efficiency of the Tory Opposition. Innumerable anecdotes, many of them doubtless
fabulous, were put into currency with a view
of illustrating and emphasising Sir Stafford's
alleged subservience to his quondam instructor,
and therefore his inadequacy as Mr. Disraeli's
successor. Whether Mr. Gathorne Hardy
would permanently have better satisfied these
gentlemen may be doubted. He could not
have led them with more patient attention to
minute opportunities and microscopic openings
than the cautious but vigilant eye of Northcote
detected. On the other hand, he would have
animated them with more inspiriting show of
fight. Hardy could not have introduced one

of Northcote's Budgets in their author's persuasive exposition of its purpose.   Hardy,
however, had, especially during the Public
Worship debates of 1873, showed himself a
modern master of that inspiring rhetoric in
which the older House of Commons chiefs had
excelled.   His well-remembered, rather than
extensive, reading supplied his ready intellect
with a felicitous abundance of apt illustration.
In the course of the ecclesiastical discussions of
Mr. Disraeli's first Ministry, a mouse, starting
from its hole, ran across the floor close to
the Mace.   The House, always ready to be
amused by the infinitely little, or to divert its
attention from grave affairs to any trivial
occurrence, noted the animal apparition, and
tittered.   Hardy alone, happening just then
to be prominent in the debate, recalled a
similar invasion at the Synod of Dort by
a rather larger quadruped, and delighted all his
hearers by a narrative of the circumstance,
expressing exactly as it did the trivial but
absorbing emotions of the moment.   Irre-
proachably free from every suspicion of Glad-
stonianising, Hardy would have fulfilled what
Bolingbroke described as a prime desideratum

in such a leader ; he would have blooded his hounds, and shown them sport. But if the politician who is to-day Lord Cranbrook, whose picturesque figure, rotund voice, clear dissection of an adversary's arguments, rapier-like thrusts, dauntless intrepidity before, during, and after a desperate division, deserved to be bracketed gratefully with the services of Canning and Disraeli himself, there is no reason to suppose that the disruption which came to a point in 1880 and the immediately succeeding years would permanently have been averted.

The truth is, that at this epoch the dominant humour of the Conservative rank and file was such as to prevent their being contented in perpetuity with any captain whatever, had he been even a renascent Mr. Pitt or the ninth Lord Stanley himself. In the memorable and spirit-stirring passage where the Father of History represents the Persian officer as foreseeing in conversation the calamity about to overtake his countrymen at Platea, occur those words that appealed so profoundly to the heart and intellect of Thomas Arnold : " The bitterest pang of all is this, to perceive that one ought to do much, without the power to control anything." The more sober spirits of Conservatism saw, before the event, the extreme perils of that adventurous foreign policy which, oblivious of his own denunciations, endorsed by John Bright, upon Lord Palmerston's militant intermeddling in continental Europe, Disraeli had pursued in South Africa, as well as on our North-West Indian frontier. This line of action, with the disasters it provoked, was quite enough to explain the mystery of the national verdict at the polling booths in 1880.

CHAPTER VI.

WANTED: "A CONSERVATIVE LEADER"
(1878-80).

Randolph Churchill's training for Irish politics under his father's viceroyship.—Conservative discontent in 1880 Parliament, following from consciousness of Conservative mistakes in office between 1874 and 1880.— This culminates in the Bradlaugh question: gradual development of this, and part played in it by Lord Randolph Churchill.—Mr. Bradlaugh's first appearance; earliest disturbance. — Sir Stafford Northcote first endorses Mr. Gladstone's action, then yields to pressure, and his authority over his followers is gone.— Successive stages in the Bradlaugh episode that brought Lord Randolph Churchill to the front.

AT heart, as may be gathered from the foregoing remarks, intensely self-reproachful for not having laid some check upon the adventurous policy of Disraeli, culminating, as it had done, in the overthrow of 1880, the rural and urban plutocrats, the prosperous country gentlemen, the bank directors, mine-owners, large railway shareholders, money-brokers, and financiers generally, who formed the backbone of the connection that Disraeli had not so much led but created, nursed their disgust, as the line taken by the *Standard* newspaper and other Conservative prints conducted upon sober business principles clearly indicated, because they had not, four years earlier, conveyed to their chiefs in Whitehall their disapproval, as practical men, of the modish Imperialism with which Lord Beaconsfield had amused the loungers at clubs and the *habitués* of music-halls.

The Conservative rank and file were, as a fact, in just the temper in which an army, smarting under defeat due to tactical mistakes, wishes to hang a general. This ferment of dissatisfaction was to find its most apt exponents and interpreters in Randolph Churchill and in those whom he attracted around himself. The Adullamites of 1866 had not been more the creation of sectarian discontent or Parliamentary intrigue than the "fourth party," as it was afterwards to be called, was the development and efflux of the dominantly inarticulate disgust at the blunders of their chiefs and their results, prevailing throughout the Conservative forces.

Therefore, and for no other rational cause,

the very excellencies of Sir Stafford Northcote were imputed to him as faults—as marks of timidity and ineptitude, amounting to constructive high treason. Had the Archangel Gabriel assumed the leadership he would, in this temper of his followers, soon have found himself the victim of a cabal. The charges brought against the Devonshire baronet might not have been those preferred against Mr. Gathorne Hardy if Disraeli's erewhile Secretary for War had also proved Disraeli's successor on the green leather benches ; but morally, and in effect practically, if not in detail identically, the result would have been the same. Upon necks impatient of any discipline the first real exercise of authoritative control would have inflicted an intolerable smart. Supposing that Mr. Hardy had satisfied the more exacting contingent of his troops in the Bradlaugh case, he would only have postponed the inevitable rupture, and the revolt against him as the depositary of the principle of leadership would infallibly have been organised on some other issue, and at a later date.

At this stage of his career Lord Randolph

7

Churchill was one of those politicians to whom a revolutionary or stormy atmosphere is the very breath of life. It was his "sturm and drang" period, to quote the untranslatable phrase, the season of tempestuous and destructive initiate, which was to be followed hereafter by industrious attempts to solve certain problems of creative politics. During the sessions of 1876-7, Randolph Churchill, by unfailing attendance at St. Stephen's, mastered the rules of the House as if they were to be the subject of an examination in the history schools. As he was indebted to his exemplary mother—his obligations to whom were repaid by a filial love that was always touching and a filial gratitude that never failed—for many of his best political instincts, so he owed to her the rudiments of his practical instruction in at least the politics of Ireland.

The seventh Duke of Marlborough had been Disraeli's Irish Viceroy. It was to him that the document warning the Anglo-Saxon race of a peril worse than pestilence or famine, unless the men of light and leading should combine to avert it, had been addressed. Never was the Queen's vicegerent in the Irish capital so loyally and effectively helped as to his official labours, and relieved as to his public responsibilities, as it was this gentleman's good fortune to be by the supplementary labours of his wife. The distress fund, raised and administered by Frances, Duchess of Marlborough, was felt as a material blessing and deliverance from Fair Head to Cork, from Wexford to Kilkee. Never were the gifts of charity at once so widely and so discreetly distributed. To ensure that efficiency, and to guard against abuse, the Viceregal Consort constructed for herself the organisation of a State department. She lived, moved, and laboured amid reports from necessitous districts and inquiries into chiefly pressing wants. In all this vast business the Duchess, day and night, week after week and month after month, was assisted by the son she loved so well. Nor, considering his personal acceptability to the Irish people, the amiability of disposition, combined with the dignity of carriage possessed by Randolph Churchill, is it an exaggeration to say that if, when he was yet a parliamentary novice, the Tory Premier before going out of office had given him the Chief Secretaryship to the Lord-Lieutenant, the Fourth Party *frondeur* would have proved a first-rate official, and, by being accustomed thus early to the harness of responsibility, the whole fate of parties, as well as of individuals, might have been different.   Disraeli, however, had always underrated the gravity of the Irish question.   It did not interest him, because it did not appeal to his imagination in the same way as the world-wide empire of his adopted country.   Probably, also, his early associations of Irishmen had something to do with his indisposition to face the facts of Irish history. He never quite forgot, and therefore, one may be sure, never really forgave O'Connell's coarse abuse in his youthful days.   Further, Disraeli had, during many years, been a constant visitor at the Woodstock Palace.   He must have seen, and perhaps patronised, Randolph Churchill so often in his boyhood, that by force of mere familiarity the statesman's keen vision for properly equipped young men had in this par-ticular case become somewhat dulled.   If this especial scion of Blenheim in whom we are now interested had been associated in the great man's mind with the young Stanhopes and

Hamiltons, Disraeli would very likely have
dealt with him after the same manner. Only
a genius almost superhuman could have identified the adult Etonian, who was returned for
Woodstock in 1874, and who, under the circumstances already named, had been initiated so early
into Irish affairs, a potential administrator of
the Empire. At any rate, Lord Beaconsfield did
not exercise this divination ; nor when, after his
translation from the Commons to the Peers, he
once revisited the old battle scenes, and from the
Peers' Gallery came, in his own words, "to see
the Fourth Party," did it occur to him to give
Lord Randolph Churchill a chance. And yet
it may confidently be said that at no period
would Churchill's youth or inexperience have
been such as to disqualify him for the Chief
Secretaryship, filled about that time as it was
by Mr. James Lowther, because his heartiness
of manner rendered his presence palatable to
those Hibernian patriots who most detested
his political principles, and who would, for
much the same personal reasons, have welcomed a politician like Lord Randolph, capable
of demonstrating, as he had shown himself, that,
if no constitutional pundit, his prowess in riding

to the Connemara hounds made him emphatically, in Lever's words, "the man for Galway."

The great feature in the general election
preceding the session of 1880, during which
Randolph Churchill first asserted himself as a
continuously active member of Parliament, was
the loss of the county seats to the Conservative
cause, thus completing the Tory rout in the
boroughs.   Briefly epitomised, the composition
of the new House of Commons was 354
Liberals, 237 Conservatives, 61 Home Rulers.
Thus Mr. Gladstone commanded a majority of
117 clear as against any possible coalition between the legitimate followers of Mr. Disraeli
and the Home Rule disciples of Mr. Parnell.
The Tory leader, recurring to the precedent
of Mr. Gladstone in 1874, resigned directly
the elections were over. A week later Mr.
Gladstone and his colleagues, seated on the
right hand of the Speaker's chair, met the new
Parliament, with Sir Stafford Northcote confronting them as leader of the Opposition.

The name of Mr. Labouchere's colleague in
the representation of Northampton had long
been known unfavourably to many others than
orthodox supporters of the Altar and the

Throne throughout the country. It was probably that very notoriety which prompted
Mr. Henry Labouchere himself conspicuously to
identify, during his election campaign, his own
name, as well as that of the Prime Minister, with
the ex-trooper, whose patronymic was already
a synonym for an unpopular and offensive
propaganda. " Mr. Gladstone," he assured
the Northampton ratepayers, " took a special
interest in the return of the Republican candidate "; and then, improvising for the occasion
the soubriquet for the veteran leader that has
since become historical, proceeded in characteristic vein : " ' Be sure to bring me back
Charles Bradlaugh to the House of Commons,'
were the words addressed to me by our great
chief, that Grand Old Man, before I left
London to-day." By a curious coincidence the
occasion now about to be related was not the
first on which, to the scandal of some of their
countrymen, the name of Bradlaugh had been
associated with that of Gladstone. During
one of his earlier campaigns the member for
Greenwich, as he then was, had seemed to
express approval of certain industrial rhymes
contained in a selection partly prepared by

Mr. Bradlaugh himself, and termed "The
Secularist Hymn-book." That incident was
not quite forgotten when it became known
that Mr. Bradlaugh, having won the seat of
Northampton, would present himself at the
table of the House to inscribe his name on the
Parliamentary roll. The Address in reply to
the Speech from the Throne had not been
voted when, on May 3rd, Mr. Bradlaugh
himself walked up the floor of the House, and
presented, through Sir Erskine May, the Chief
Clerk, a written claim, in virtue of the Parliamentary Oaths Act in 1866, to affirm his
allegiance instead of swearing it on the Bible.
The Speaker referred the demand to the
House. Lord Frederick Cavendish, on behalf
of the Government, moved the reference of
the whole matter to a select committee, the
motion being seconded by Sir Stafford
Northcote, as leader of the Opposition. Just
a week later the House was to consider the
composition of the committee appointed to ad-
judicate on the business. On this occasion Sir
Stafford Northcote was absent. Before he was
again in the Chamber the storm had burst. On
the ground that the Address not having yet been

voted no controversial business could legiti-
mately be transacted, Sir Henry Drummond
Wolff, when Lord Richard Grosvenor, Patronage Secretary, came to the Bradlaugh committee,
objected to any action whatever in the business.
The parliamentary atmosphere had already
begun to be electrical. Further heat was im-
ported into it by Mr. Stanley Leighton's speech,
seconding Sir Henry Wolff's amendment, and
consisting of a bitter personal attack upon
the Prime Minister, as the author of all
parliamentary and political evils. Opposition
leadership, combining, as it might have done,
a fair show of spirit with a reasonable amount
of discretion, would, had it been forthcoming,
have here terminated the whole incident. But
Sir Stafford, to the disgust of his more
pugnacious followers, tamely pledged, as by
his word a few days earlier he had become,
to the committee, was not on the spot.
The ex-Attorney-General, Sir John Holker,
would not encourage an aggressive policy,
advised the withdrawal of Sir Henry Wolff's
resolution, and was followed by the Irish
member, Mr. O'Donnell, who, endeavoured
to aggravate the bitterness existing not only

between the two front benches, but also
between the Opposition managers and the
bulk of the Opposition themselves. Eventually
the previous question was rejected, and the
committee voted. Some ten days after this
the more spirited of Mr. Bradlaugh's enemies
admitted, through Sir Henry Wolff, once more
their spokesman, that oath or no oath, affirmation or no affirmation, they were bent on
excluding Mr. Labouchere's colleague on the
ground of being not only an atheist, and
therefore irresponsible to moral obligations, but
also in the capacity of a seditious pamphleteer,
who had written "An Impeachment of the
House of Brunswick." From this moment
the Conservative leadership, on a point chosen
with great dexterity, because of the prevailing
hatred to Mr. Bradlaugh's reputed opinions,
passed from the hands of the titular Opposition
chief into those of Randolph Churchill, or,
which was the same thing, Sir Henry Wolff.
The next time the House met Mr. Disraeli's
lieutenant in the Commons recanted his former
declarations, and, yielding to the sectional
pressure, announced his antagonism to the
committee, and his support of the amendment

of Sir Henry Wolff. Now, too, on May 23rd, Lord Randolph Churchill first appeared as a protagonist in the movement. In a speech showing the great advance he had made in debating power, the member for Woodstock lifted the discussion to a higher, more interesting and more intelligible level, by arguing that the broad question was whether a professional sedition-monger and blasphemer could have, even under the ægis of the Prime Minister, a seat in an assembly of loyal and God-fearing gentlemen? The next day again the Bradlaugh battle was still in process of being fought, while this same May 24th, 1880, was marked by the Woodstock member's first interposition in the debate, reinforcing Sir Henry Drummond Wolff's objection to the Ministerial policy of a select committee, sanctioned though that had been by Sir Stafford Northcote himself. The controversial struggle was further envenomed and the whole atmosphere additionally disturbed by the bitterness of the Irish members following Mr. O'Donnell against Mr. Gladstone as Mr. Bradlaugh's champion.

A little while before, it should be mentioned,

an open rupture had taken place between
the small coterie on the Conservative side,
championed for the moment by Sir Henry
Wolff, and the official Opposition leaders, who,
as our to-day's Ambassador at Madrid declared,
had supinely not called Mr. Gladstone and
other ministers to account for the breach of
order involved in their walking out of the
House without taking part in a division.
Lord Randolph Churchill was doubtless acquainted with the dagger scene in Burke's
career, which elicited from Sheridan the
parenthetical remark, " Now that he has produced the knife, will not the right honourable
gentlemen give us the fork ? "   At any rate,
during the climax of his speech, denouncing
the secularist at the Bar, the orator produced
a Bradlaugh pamphlet from his pocket, and
flung it down on the floor with a most dramatic
gesture of disgust, amid peals of Ministerial
laughter and thunders of Opposition applause.
An hour after midnight the fruitless and
unseemly wrangles were ended by the adjournment of the debate, with the simple
practical result that Randolph Churchill had
taken another step towards the position of

Fourth Party leader, which he was soon avowedly to fill.

The next day, May 25th, Sir Henry Wolff's colleague in this business sharply criticised the *personnel* of the proposed committee, showing that it included only two Nonconformists, one Roman Catholic, and no Scotchmen. The sole contribution on the part of Sir Stafford Northcote to this discussion was a faint suggestion that the committee advantageously might perhaps be enlarged. But from this moment the blameless baronet ceased practically, as morally he had ceased already, to be the leader of a compact Conservative minority in the House of Commons. Eventually Sir Henry Wolff's motion was lost by 256 votes against 100, when of course the Ministerial proposal was regularly adopted. The last scenes in the first act of the farcical comedy of errors, which was spun out over five years, were, however, approaching.

On June 21st, just before six o'clock, Mr Bradlaugh standing on the now familiar spot just outside the Bar of the House, Mr. Labouchere rose to move the resolution, of which he had given notice, that

his Northampton colleague should be permitted to affirm.   Before the argument was
fairly begun Mr. Bradlaugh had withdrawn.
The sequel of the discussion was signalised by
a speech from Mr. John Bright, displaying
that rare mixture of simple eloquence and
shrewd sense which have given him a place
absolutely unique in our parliamentary annals.
The sense ·of humour that some years before
had inspired the great tribune with the comparison of the Adullamites to a fluffy terrier,
its head indistinguishable from its tail, was, as
might be expected, aroused by a controversy in
which the apologist for atheism was the erewhile Oxford high churchman, Mr. Gladstone,
and the champion of the theological orthodoxy,
Sir Henry Drummond Wolff.   In his characteristic blend of solemn thought and· homely
phrase, Mr. Bright denied the right of Conservative censors to question the honesty and
sincerity of Mr. Bradlaugh, in which, he
declared, he saw the equal of any member of
the House.   The real gravamen or his charge
was that the member for Northampton was
opposed because he belonged to another
social class than that mainly represented

at St. Stephen's. The sympathies of the
people were, he asserted, with Northampton's
excluded representative; "since the lower
classes do nòt care more for the dogmas of
Christianity than the upper classes care for
the practice of that religion."

As if he had not with emphasis enough separated himself from the Wolff and Churchill group
by his previous utterances and vacillations, Sir
Stafford Northcote, before the evening's discussion was over, formulated, in precise terms, his
discovery of the fact that outside the House there
was a general impression in favour of Mr. Bradlaugh's taking his seat without further ado, and
that the sooner the dispute was settled in this
way the better would it be for the dignity and
efficiency of the first assembly of gentlemen in
the world. That result was, however, even
now some little way off. By a majority of 45
(275 to 230), Mr. Labouchere's motion, allowing
his colleague to affirm, was rejected. Some
six weeks of parliamentary time had been, in
this manner, fooled away.

It was now the morrow of Mr. Labouchere's
defeat, June 23rd. The occasion was a morning
sitting, when, exactly an hour after noon, at the

instant prayers were finished, and business was
about to begin, by way of a personal benediction
before work, the burly presence of the secularist
apostle drew as near to the central table as was
practicable.   In an instant an impotent silence
fell upon the assembly.   At last, the invader
having taken his stand hard by the Mace, after
a hurried conference with the Chief Clerk,
Sir Erskine May, the Speaker summoned up
sufficient resolution for the request that Mr.
Bradlaugh would withdraw.   His disappearance immediately elicited from Mr. Bradlaugh's co-partner in the political affections
of Northampton a proposal that Mr. Bradlaugh should be heard.   The motion having
been seconded by Mr. Lyulph Stanley, the
hero of so many encounters stationed himself just before the Bar, at the entry to the
House in front of the Clock gallery.   There
was nothing of arrogance or bluster in Charles
Bradlaugh's deportment upon this impressive
and historic occasion, but much of quiet and
not undignified determination.   The Prime
Minister, as well as the highest legal authorities, had already, he said, in a voice low and
scarcely musical, but deliberate, clear, and pene-

trating into every nook and cranny of the place, declared their conviction of his right to be seated "there" (pointing to the below gangway benches on the Speaker's right). " As for my opinions, Mr. Speaker," he continued, " I did not choose them for myself; I am not ashamed of them. I would forfeit for ever the honour I cherish so deeply of being returned as a member of the House of Commons, rather than slink into my place disguising or hiding my convictions."

"What are you going to do with me?" was the next question, with an artistically contrived cadence of voice, he asked. " Will you declare the seat vacant? Well, I shall be again returned; and what next? I have no wish to wrestle with you for justice," he went on in deprecating tones, "but if the House seeks for the struggle, I shall tearlessly and hopefully submit the cause to a tribunal higher even than this great Assembly, and will ask public opinion to decide between you and me." With these words, occupying exactly eighteen minutes, delivered evidently after the most careful preparation, but without any manifest aid to memory in the shape of notes, and in tones varying from the clear, passionless, rather

8

metallic note of business statement, to chords
vibrating with intense, if suppressed, emotion
at each successive point, the master alike of
his audience as of himself, sometimes applauded with cheers promptly to be checked,
the appellant at the Bar left the Chamber
which had now begun to realise the possibility
of a nineteenth-century repetition of the struggle
with John Wilkes.

Without a moment's delay Mr. Gladstone
declared it to be his duty as leader to sustain
Mr. Speaker's authority, and to submit himself
to the will of the majority.

After Sir Stafford Northcote's suggestion that
Mr. Bradlaugh should be recalled, that he
might be acquainted with the House's final
decision, had met with a not too cordial reception from the Chair, Mr. Labouchere
moved that a resolution of the Conservative
ex-Attorney-General, Sir Hardinge Giffard,
disqualifying Mr. Bradlaugh for membership,
should be rescinded, but at Mr. Gladstone's
advice immediately withdrew the motion.

Within some ten minutes of breathless and
general suspense, the subject of the discussion was once more seen on the open floor

of the Assembly, silent and respectful, but
dauntlessly resolved as ever. The Speaker
narrated to the new-comer the decision hostile
to his pretensions, at the same time calling
upon Mr. Bradlaugh to withdraw. Then
came, uttered with perfect composure, the
reply, to the effect that while respectfully insisting on his right as duly-elected
member for Northampton, Mr. Bradlaugh
respectfully also refused to withdraw. The
leader of the House giving no sign of any
further action, the titular head of the Opposition so far yielded to the Fourth Party's
pressure as to move that the Speaker should
be invested with the power needed to enforce
his authority; in other words, that if moral
persuasion failed physical force should be employed for the Commons' deliverance from
their present incubus. In the division following there were cast 326 votes for the motion,
38 against it.

Meanwhile, Mr. Bradlaugh retained his
position by the table, the sole occupant of
the House. It was difficult not to admire
the intruder's unruffled persistence; but the
only member who, on returning from the

lobby, noticed that substantial and station-
ary form, shaking hands with him, was the
then Radical representative of Leicester, Mr.
P. A. Taylor. Presently the apparition of the
Speaker's emissary, the Sergeant-at-Arms,
Captain Gossett, in his official Court suit,
sword at side, indicated the decisive moment
to be near. During a few seconds these
two, Mr. Bradlaugh and the Sergeant, faced
about, confronting each other, first advancing
then receding a few paces, very much, as
it seemed to onlookers, like timid performers
in the figures of a quadrille. Morally, and
geographically, the Sergeant at last got Mr.
Bradlaugh into a corner in the immediate
neighbourhood of the Bar. After a few more
of these ball-room manœuvres had been exe-
cuted, and the greatly daring agnostic had
technically undergone arrest by the imposition
of the Sergeant's forefinger on his right
shoulder, the House endorsed, while Mr.
Gladstone did not oppose, Sir Stafford Northcote's resolution, brought forward on the
Speaker's suggestion, that Mr. Bradlaugh,
having disregarded the authority and resisted
the power of the Chair, should be made the

prisoner of the Sergeant-at-Arms. The only comment offered on this transaction came from Mr. Labouchere, who pointed out the drollness of a proceeding by which an English citizen was about to lose his liberty because he had done that which the highest legal and constitutional authorities had declared it to be his right and his duty to do. Only 7 dissentients withstood this motion, 274 affirming it. Mr. Bradlaugh offered no kind of resistance, and at once was consigned to "the dungeon" reserved for parliamentary delinquents on an upper story in the gilded Clock Tower.

When, on the following day, June 24th, the House was once more in session, the Premier made no sign of departing from his deliberately assumed attitude of masterly inactivity. In reply to Sir Stafford Northcote, "he had not," he dryly observed, "felt it his duty to bring the matter before his colleagues. He had, therefore, no advice to give."

Recalling, as it might seem to irreverent listeners, the incident recorded in the nursery lines of a French sovereign, who, with all his troops, marched uphill, only to descend, the official chief of the Conservatives, who, some twelve hours earlier, had caused Mr. Bradlaugh to be locked up, on the assumption of parliamentary honour being satisfied, now moved that the offender should be released. But even before this, the Speaker's warrant for the gaol delivery would appear to have been made out ; for almost before Mr. Gladstone had done speaking the incarcerated heretic was once more within the House, while troops of non-parliamentary friends who had accompanied him applauded in the passages outside,

But it had now become clear to the sense of that House, whose collective wisdom is always greater than the individual sagacity of any of its members, that the only alternative to an interminable series of committals and releases on the part of the irrepressible schismatic must be some special legislation. Mr. Gladstone, therefore, submitted a short proposal to the Assembly for legalising, subject to the Law Courts, an affirmation in all cases where an oath was required. Mr. C. S. Parnell, who was gradually becoming a power in the House, expressed detestation of the Bradlaugh tenets, but approval of thus terminating the Bradlaugh difficulty. Another Irish member, Mr. Sullivan, submitted a hostile amendment in the interests of Roman Catholicism. It was rejected by some 40 votes. And on July 2nd, 1880, the elected of Northampton, whom his adversaries had made first a martyr and then a power, seized his seat after attesting his loyalty by affirmation.

CHAPTER VII.

EARLY PARLIAMENTARY ACTIVITIES AND DEVELOPMENT (1880-81).

Exact condition of affairs and parties in the House of Commons and in the country after the termination of the first Bradlaugh episode in 1880.—Sir Stafford Northcote deposed, but not replaced; the Fourth Party masters of the situation; the vacant Opposition leadership; possible claimants personally sketched; Mr. J. E. Gorst, mathematician and lawyer; the son of Fred Burnaby's predecessor, diplomatist and raconteur; Sir H. Drummond Wolff's little ways and anecdotes.—Mr. Henry Chaplin, the Disraelian squire. —Randolph Churchill already real leader of Conservative "forwards" in the country.—Randolph Churchill in Irish debates 1881-2; Randolph Churchill and the Irish members on a frolic when C. S. Parnell's back is turned.—Erin patriots and evening sables.

DURING the series of incidents described in the foregoing chapter the real leader of the House of Commons was the man whom it was all the while excluding from its technical precincts. Mr. Bradlaugh, as we have seen, came and went, appeared, disappeared, and reappeared exactly when he liked. He betrayed no more impatience of the vexatious delays, that he well knew must prove futile, on his formal admission, than a sensible citizen shows because the train for which he is waiting happens to be a few minutes late.

Mr. Gladstone's contention had been, from the first, consistently that the matter was one concerning exclusively the member for Northampton and the Assembly at whose doors he was knocking, of whose titular leader's duty it was no part to precipitate an adjustment of the difference. Thus far there had been no disorderly scenes or violent scandals such as later stages of the dispute provoked. Now, as in the case of parliamentary reform, the then Prime Minister felt time to be on his (and Mr. Bradlaugh's) side. Sir Stafford Northcote was from the first without any clear or practical line of action. Between the unwelcome, unabashed stranger, and the nascent Fourth Party, he swayed vacillatingly to and fro at the impulse of the moment.

The explanation of this uncertainty and these mistakes on the part of a parliamentary official whose experience, shrewdness, tact, and honour were not surpassed, even

if they were approached, by any man on his
side of the House, is, of course, that, as
his initial step in seconding the proposal for the
select committee showed, he was personally
in favour of admitting the newly elected
member for Northampton, however hateful his
propaganda, with the least possible delay.
The House of Commons being always, and
to-day more than ever, the creature of popular
opinion, Sir Stafford knew it instinctively to be
only a question of time when the representative chamber must receive the member whom
the capital of cobblers had chosen for itself.
Having, however, once suffered his hand to
be forced, and his nominal leadership to be
wrested from him by Sir Henry Wolff, the
Devonshire baronet was obliged to make some
show of continuing a struggle that his common
sense had pronounced hopeless. Except for
the purpose of stultifying first, and ejecting
afterwards the Opposition manager, the
Bradlaugh question was not a good fighting
issue.

If Randolph Churchill had then possessed a
few years' more experience, or had been advised
less belligerently by his two senior lieutenants,

Sir H. Drummond Wolff and Mr. J. E. Gorst, he would himself have avoided a contest foredoomed to practical sterility. If any general proposition could have been demonstrably true of public sentiment on this, as on other cognate topics, it was that in regard to speculative theological or religious questions of any kind, the prevailing temper is Laodicean in its tepidity.

Charles Bradlaugh might have been excluded indefinitely from the House of Commons if, and only if, the popular humour outside was fanatically or definitely religious, and upon however less dramatic a scale akin to those national impulses which once found their satisfaction in the Crusades. Had these conditions been fulfilled in the year now spoken of, decades might have gone by without Mr. Labouchere's enjoyment of his parliamentary colleague's company, and during this time it is conceivable that the member for Woodstock might have ridden on the crest of the wave to the real Tory leadership at Westminster.

As it was, the results of the whole business were negative. Sir Stafford Northcote was discredited and weakened.   No sufficient influence in the authoritative quarters, to which he might have looked, had been interposed to revive his moribund prerogative, or to reconstruct the declining discipline of the ranks.   The condition of the Conservative party after Mr. Bradlaugh's triumph seemed indeed even more desperate than after Sir Robert Peel's conversion to Free Trade.   In the latter case Mr. Disraeli stepped directly into the official position which the old chief vacated.   In the present instance no competent successor to the deposed leader was visible.   The air was full of rumours ; many in the last degree impossible and absurd.   The lobbies of St. Stephen's, the political clubs of St. James and Pall Mall, the fashionable drawing-rooms of Belgravia and Hyde Park, were reputed to be the scene of conspiracies and counter-conspiracies, of intrigues and rival-intrigues.

In this universal ferment of aimless activity and confused plot the most unlikely combinations, the least practicable names, were perpetually being thrown up to the surface. One day the quidnuncs asserted that Sir

Stafford Northcote had formally resigned in
favour of Mr. Gorst. The next day the
gossips knew, as a positive fact, that when
Parliament next met Mr. Gladstone's immediate
vis-à-vis would be Sir Henry Wolff. Presently
a parliamentary *gobemouche*, more highly
inspired, more mischievous or mendacious than
his predecessors, was able to show circumstantially that all these prophets were wrong,
and that to the seat of power formerly occupied
by Mr. Gladstone's arch-foe, there would be
voted, by common acclaim of the Carlton Club,
one of the despised Irish race, whose pretensions were highly favoured by the ex-Premier,
then consoling himself for his electoral defeat
with watching the spring flowers blossom in
the glades and gardens of Hughenden. That
preposterous rumour rested, it is needless to
say, upon no better foundation than the
accident of the member for Cavan, Mr. F. H.
O'Donnell, having joined vigorously in, and
once or twice having even led, the hue-and-
cry after Bradlaugh, as well as having made
himself exceedingly disagreeable to the Ministry
of the day on one or two foreign or quasi-
international issues. This gentleman had not

given proof of possessing any higher qualities for the vacant office than his other countrymen. He had all the volubility indeed, and at least all the effrontery, of his race. As an Indian civilian he was an educated gentleman ; as a writer for the *Morning Post* newspaper, whose office was impregnated with the traditions of Palmerston's foreign policy, he had picked up a great deal of available familiarity with the topics of the time.

Of the other and rather less preposterously impossible candidate for the Tory chiefship, Mr. Gorst had, two or three years earlier, occupied for a short while the place of general election manager in the country, formerly filled by Mr. Markham Spofforth, a solicitor, of the firm of Baxter, Rose, and Norton, an acute, trustworthy, confidential agent of the great electioneering Warwick, Lord Abergavenny, and even of Benjamin Disraeli himself. At Cambridge Mr. Gorst had won the third place in the mathematical tripos, as well as a St. John's fellowship, and had, after taking his degree, engaged creditably in academic or educational pursuits before he went to the Bar. But, indisputable though his intellectual eminence was, the House of Commons does not generally love lawyers too much ; nor in Mr. Gorst's case could this lack of cordiality be lessened by a certain demeanour disagreeably reminding honourable members of Common Room councils in their undergraduate days. If Sir Henry Wolff's views of life had been more serious, and his diplomatic apprenticeship had not so entirely deprived him of that fervour which an English party, however small, likes to witness in its protagonists upon solemn occasions, his pretensions to the office would not have been inconsiderable. His personal popularity was far greater than that of Mr. Gorst. He was quick at reply, ready in attack. His good humour was imperturbable. He was liked equally well on both sides ot the House. Diplomacy had taught him to use words, in the manner prescribed by Bacon for wise men, " as counters." A benign Nature, ripened under his social, and' parliamentary experience had given him the happy art of employing invective and badinage, not with bludgeon-like blows, but with rapier thrusts. If, in short, a nineteenth-century version of the poet Horace, adapted to suit the requirements

of parliamentary life, and, divested of his
poetry, can be imagined, Henry Wolff would
have been very much that man. He had, moreover, by this time occupied a parliamentary seat
during nearly two decades. He had profited
by every moment of his time, was thoroughly
master alike of the written laws of the House
as of the unwritten, but not less safely violable,
code of parliamentary etiquette and tact. Between Lord Beaconsfield, as he had now become,
and the accomplished son of Lord Beaconsfield's
compatriot, the great explorer who preceded
Fred Burnaby to Khiva by half a century,
there was a nearer intimacy than between
the Tory veteran and any of the younger
generation.

A close retrospect of this period, then, justifies
the assertion that Lord Beaconsfield, being still
alive and in the full possession of his intellectual
perceptions, ought, as the head of the party,
after the events of the 1880 session, to have
interposed otherwise than by semi-serious
remonstrances sent through Mr. Spofforth to
rescue Sir Stafford Northcote from a clearly
untenable position, instead of leaving that
statesman to add failure to failure, until at last,

after a series of supersessions by Sir Michael
Hicks-Beach or by Lord Randolph Churchill,
he was placed in the asylum of political
ineffectives, the House of Lords, there to
languish, and finally hunted down, to die
literally of a broken heart. That Lord
Beaconsfield, with his incomparable eye to a
parliamentary situation, did not see and act
on the necessity for some such steps as this
is explicable only on hypotheses for which
the still delayed publication of his posthumous
papers leaves us unsupplied with the necessary
data.

Long before this time, before even he had
entered Parliament, or for that matter fully
grown up to man's estate, the bright promise
of Randolph Churchill ought to have been
known to all the guests at Blenheim, of whom
Disraeli was one. Another of these visitors,
referring to a period when Randolph Churchill
was yet in his teens, Sir E. J. Reed, has related
that during his frequent stays beneath the ducal
roof the second son of the family was fond of
talking with him so late into the night as to
cause the visitor, in his own words, " to wish
the young nobleman elsewhere." It is no

exaggeration to say that, some twelve months before Lord Beaconsfield's death, Randolph Churchill, who, not less early, it must be remembered, than 1875, had shown first-class debating powers in his encounters with Sir Charles Dilke on the unreformed corporations, was destined visibly to the real parliamentary leadership of militant Conservatism.

The undisputed ascendancy with which his great years and incomparable service had invested Disraeli assuredly might have enabled him with great propriety to provide against the perils and perplexities of a disputed succession to the House of Commons captaincy on the Tory side. Had this duty been performed, it is no very violent assumption to conclude that, in all human probability, Lord Iddesleigh, a Devonshire worthy in a green old age, full of honour as of years, might still be among us, and that the subject of this memoir, having profited by the judiciously imparted experience of his elders, mellowed by practice, disciplined by experience, trained to full-orbed completeness of achievement, might to-day be leading a reconstructed, rejuvenated party in Parliament, instead of having fallen the

victim to a cruel as well as in some sense
a preventable disease.

Having now firmly achieved unquestioned
pre-eminence on the Opposition benches, Lord
Randolph Churchill, throughout all the Irish
debates, first on the Peace Preservation Bill,
secondly on the Irish Land Bill—the discussion on whose third reading engaged him
in an encounter with the only formidable foe
who at this time confronted him, in the person
of Mr. G. W. E. Russell, of about his own
parliamentary status—proceeded, without inter-
ruption or failure, to improve and strengthen
his hold upon the Conservative party, alike
in the Commons and in the country.

In all those themes relating to the welfare
of the sister island, the local knowledge he had
gained under his father's and mother's *régime*
proved invaluable. The palliative applied
fifteen years ago to Irish distress, known as
the Compensation for Disturbance Bill, was
the most organically innovating transaction
ever proposed by a constitutional Government
for the relief of social and agrarian trouble.
History contains scarcely a precedent for it,
unless, indeed, it is to be found in that

" seisactheia," that wholesale disburdenment of
debtors, by which the Attic legislator sought
to relieve the financial distresses of his native
city and district. It was looked upon with
mute amazement by the contemporary Parliaments of Europe, none of which would have
dreamt of introducing such a measure. The
tone and temper of Randolph Churchill's
criticisms upon that experiment, as upon Mr.
Gladstone's other Irish reforms, the real if
partial grip of the subject, the maturity of the
argument, reinforced at every turn, not only
by official statistics, but by personal experience,
indicated a perceptible advance upon anything
he had accomplished or attempted.

Nor could any one, after hearing his speech
in the second-reading debate, July 5th, 1880,
doubt that the young man (he was only thirty-
one then) who made it would go near to the
highest place. The public, as well as Parliament itself, recognised the gravity, the moderation as well as force, with which, profiting by
his past lessons, Randolph Churchill showed
the very magnitude of Irish adversity to be
the measure of the fraud and imposture which
accompanied it. The truth, he protested,

was that the Bill "had been introduced in panic, for the futile purpose of expediting Government business by pacifying the Irish members."

Mr. Gladstone had long paid Randolph Churchill the marked compliment of personally answering his strictures. Upon the present occasion the Prime Minister made no attempt to disguise the effort with which he drew upon all his resources of dialectic, rhetoric, sarcasm, parliamentary experience, historical knowledge, to confute charges, the result, as he said, of researches which would be more valuable if marked by greater approaches to accuracy.

It is possible that if parliamentary usage had permitted Randolph Churchill to speak again, he might have contrived to retort not ineffectively Mr. Gladstone's taunt of inconsistency, levelled at the Opposition, and resting, as it did, on the not wholly unanswerable plea that Lord Beaconsfield's Land Act of 1870 contained, at the moment of its second reading, the main principle incorporated in the present Compensation measure.

The subject-matter of the other chief debates

during the session of 1880, especially the
Hares and Rabbits Bill, supplied the little
band of Tory democrats with the material
necessary to cement and consolidate them into
that independent unity known as the Fourth
Party. The gentlemen composing this, unlike
Mr. O'Donnell, in some respects their predecessor, who himself constituted a party of
his own, knew not only when to speak, but
when to be silent; and so soon as the discussion refined itself into a technical controversy
between agricultural and veterinary experts, on
the merits of different roots, the genesis of
diverse forms of cattle disease, or the criterion
of the qualities which butchers deem to constitute excellence, Randolph Churchill set a
wise example of rhetorical reticence.

The dimensions of his following rendered
their management easy; but only one who had
passed his silent sessions in mastering details
of parliamentary procedure, and who, above
all, possessed the natural endowment of leadership, could have controlled the movements of
the "fourth party" with the rigour and precision
displayed throughout each successive session.
The chief might be indebted for his acquaint-

ance with constitutional law to Mr. Gorst, and
to Sir Henry Wolff for the point of many of
his questions put to Ministers ; but the choice
of times and seasons was entirely his own ;
and for the importance with which Mr. Gladstone's personal notice and replies invested
himself and his followers, Randolph Churchill
was under no other obligation than to his own
innate acumen, his daily study of affairs, and
his tact, part of it native to him, but part also
acquired or improved by practice.

The session of 1881 witnessed the intro-
duction of Mr. Gladstone's second Irish Land
Bill ; and in the business of candid criticism on
its provisions there existed a certain amount
of united action between Randolph Churchill
and the Irish members, though more than
once the former's words in the House of
Commons were, " We all wish this Bill to
pass." At this time the personal popularity
of the member for Woodstock among the
representatives from the Emerald Isle was
manifested in many suggestive, if trivial, ways.
An extreme, and even funereal, decorum, in
contrast to the reckless or rollicking joviality
of an earlier generation, was now the dominant

characteristic of the Celt at St. Stephen's; his way of life was austere, often to total abstinence from any liquid stronger than water; his speeches were usually devoid of anything within dangerous distance of wit or humour, epigram or fun.

Mr. Parnell, the most imperious chief whom the parliamentary Irishman has ever known, excelled in clear, passionless statement, but avoided all approach to pleasantry in speech, and all geniality in his social manner. His whole existence outside the Westminster walls was cloaked in mystery from those with whom he acted within them. He seldom, or never, went into society; was not, I believe, a member of any London club; while the only occasion on which he made one of an Anglo-Saxon company was a dinner party given by Mr. Joseph Chamberlain during the summer of 1881 at the Richmond "Star and Garter" Hotel. He cannot, indeed, have been said strictly to "lead" his followers, but rather to overawe them, by his majestic isolation, and to coerce them by his frown into being the passive instruments of his absolute will. If the deportment of the parliamentary

patriot from the other side of St. George's
Channel, during the session of 1881, had
afforded us our sole knowledge of the Irishman of the new school, admirers of Miss
Edgeworth and Charles Lever would have
been constrained to confess that the Hibernian sketches contained in their writings were
gross caricatures, and that the "genius of
Erin" was never more falsely libelled than
when her representatives were associated with
the brandishing of shillelaghs, or the aroma of
potheen. At a later day, indeed, glimpses
were permitted us of certain incidents in progress, during the whole of this time, behind
the scenes, while the occasion of their dis-
closure was marked by such ebullitions of
acrimony and vituperation within the committee rooms of St. Stephen's, as to raise
the question whether fiction might not, after
all, be truer than fact, and the delineations
of Charles O'Malley and Harry Lorrequer
be more accurate reflections of Irish life and
nature than the solemn veneer of Mr.
Parnell's manner, or the laughterless Recha-
bitism of Mr. Sexton.

Fortunately for Lord Randolph Churchill,

the human nature even of Irishmen revolted against this sepulchral solemnity of deportment and existence imposed on the Hibernian patriots by the Anglo-American squire, whom an accident of birth had settled in the "beautiful Vale of Avoca." At the voice of Woodstock's representative, the dismal members from the " distressful country" started up, as boys eager to take the initiative from some professed master of prankfulness, intent on any escapade that would relieve the intolerable dulness of parliamentary life in the English capital. Now the amusement was that of "drawing" Mr. Gladstone in the House; now that of putting Ministers in a tight place in the lobby.

A single and not unpicturesque trifle deserves mention as showing Randolph Churchill's influence over the sons of St. Patrick. As a rule, an Irishman arrayed in Anglo-Saxon evening dress upon the parliamentary benches was a phenomenon practically unknown at Westminster. The scion of the Churchills, however, habitually adopted, after nightfall, that costume. Gradually, first one and then another of the senators from beyond the sea, to whom

Lord Randolph had become, in a degree never yet attained to by a Sassenach, a social cynosure, reproduced the sable suits customary in London drawing-rooms for English gentlemen of the nineteenth century.

CHAPTER VIII.

COMMONS AND COUNTRY FROM 1882.

Lord Randolph on the front bench below the gangway in Mr. Cavendish Bentinck's old seat; his parliamentary manner and authority; the cat and the mouse.—The Irish members; Mr. J. G. Biggar; " I should have thought it was a leprochaun"; the traditions of Cheam, Eton, and Merton at St. Stephen's; an hon. member fagged for brandy and seltzer.—The various stages by which Randolph Churchill had now established his position; the " old gang" will not be warned.

By the session of 1881-2, the veteran Mr. Newdegate was not a more familiar personage in the House of Commons than was Lord Randolph Churchill, established on the seat from which he had dislodged Mr. Cavendish Bentinck, exactly opposite to Mr. Dillwyn. That position was never disputed by any of those with whom he acted while he himself happened to be inside St. Stephen's. Nor did any chief of a parliamentary majority ever receive from his followers more deference than was accorded to

Lord Randolph by his two invariable henchmen
Mr. Gorst and Sir Henry Wolff, even though
his occasional followers, Mr. A. J. Balfour,
Lord Percy, and the casual Celt, may have
presented a more independent front. With his
full, quick eyes, " watching," to use his own
expression, " Mr. Gladstone as a cat may
watch a mouse," the presiding spirit of the
" fourth party," the chief incarnation of that
genius of revolt against traditionally constituted
authority vested in mediocrities, toying with
his long moustache, or nursing one of his knees,
Randolph Churchill sat continuously during the
prolonged meetings, the *séances*, which sometimes lasted for five-and-twenty or even thirty
hours at a stretch, in the course of the memorable summer months of 1881 and 1882. It was
really a continuance of the ascendancy that
had been exercised over his comrades by Mr.
Tabor's daring pupil at Cheam school, by the
Myrmidon Club's founder at Merton over his
convives.

Profoundly gratifying to the vanity of so
young a captain, the obsequious fidelity of
that little triad's other members to their
dashing general was of course the worst

experience conceivable for Randolph Churchill himself. Admiration corrects no faults, and widens no horizon, increases no knowledge, but makes for the idol himself many enemies.

The minute and capricious supremacy offered to their . president by his maturer colleagues was illustrated sometimes in a fashion smacking of comedy or farce. Their leader's precise corner below the gangway was keenly competed for during his moments of absence by his two lieutenants. Sometimes Mr. Gorst would anticipate Sir Henry Wolff in its occupation ; or sometimes, on the contrary, the diplomatist, by a skilful strategic movement, would outwit the lawyer ; but whichever of the two had happened to plant himself first on the coveted spot, the unexpected appearance in the chamber of their *generalissimo* was the signal for the two elder gentlemen hurriedly to disperse in different directions, reminding spectators of nothing more than two playful but senior kittens dispersed by the unwarned apparition of the housewife near the milk-bowl.

Many were the characteristic scenes between Randolph Churchill, his neighbours, and his friends, which relieved the intolerable tedium of these monotonous discussions. On one occasion, after some half-dozen hours of nearly continuous debate on a sultry day, Churchill, parched with thirst, in one of those stage whispers audible throughout the chamber, said, to the then member for Chatham, ": Seltzer water!" When the effervescing fluid made its appearance, the orator, to correct any ill effects from the undiluted beverage, while thanking his friend, remarked in the same tone, " A liqueur glass of old Cognac " ; then, having quaffed a beaker, filled, however, by his thoughtful friend with nothing stronger than the purest lymph, with the extreme courtesy of manner never lost in his most imperious moments, the speaker said, so that the House could not choose but hear, " Thank you, my dear Gorst, so much!"

As at school, this determined but most loyal, loving, and lovable despot of his connection always pitted himself against the biggest boy in the playground, or the most authoritative of division masters in school; so, in the House of Commons, Randolph Churchill was never less dissatisfied than when he was crossing swords with Mr. Gladstone himself; and though in a famous speech during the Irish debates of this period the then Premier claimed to have, in his own words, " smashed and pulverised the noble lord," he had produced no more destructive effect upon him than would have followed if Mr. Gladstone had dealt a murderous blow with his axe-handle against his own feather bed. But Randolph Churchill's attacks were delivered with undiscriminating impartiality, and with an ostentatious disregard of persons. Sometimes it was one of his own group, sometimes a member of that "old gang" whose members chiefly excited his wrath, that provoked the onslaught.

There was thus a touch of pathos not less than humour in Sir Henry Drummond Wolff's discovery of a certain resemblance between the controller of his parliamentary existence and the terrible cornet-of-horse, as, in his earlier days, the great Lord Chatham used to be called.

One familiar member of the House of Commons there was whom Randolph Churchill not only never attacked, but seemed to reckon as unofficially attached to his own small brigade. This gentleman was the Home Rule member

for Cavan, Mr. Joseph G. Biggar. His
personal appearance was not attractive; and
when, shortly after his return for the House
of Commons, Mr. Disraeli first beheld him, he
struck the imagination of the Tory statesman
as a Pixie, or scarcely human personage in
Parliament. "Who," in his deepest tones of
wonderment, inquired the great man of his next-
door neighbour, "may that be?" When told
by Mr. Plunket that Cavan had sent the new-
comer to St. Stephen's to support Home Rule,
"Contarini Fleming's" author, adjusting his
glass to his eye, drawled forth, in his solemnest
tones, "I should have thought it was a lepre-
chaun."

Whatever to others this gentleman may have
appeared, to the Woodstock statesman he
seemed all which the credulous youth in the
"Ode to Pyrrha" found the object of his
infatuation, ever golden and immutably fond.
The chief connecting link between this drolly
assorted pair was doubtless the pertinacity with
which in common they then pursued the Prime
Minister. Lord Randolph's rising on the floor
could always be inferred unerringly from the
tempestuous applause emitted from that exact

angle under a side gallery's shadow, where, half concealed, was the fantastic figure of Mr. Parnell's Cavan delegate.

When, on the other hand, the parliamentarian, formerly a curer of hams, displayed his astounding power of talking against time, or reciting, if needs be, half a blue-book, that there might be no progress before the House rose, he was sure not to lack an always appreciative, sometimes an applausive, listener in the organiser of Tory democracy, whose keen sense of the ridiculous failed on one occasion to prevent his referring, amidst tempestuous laughter, " to my honourable friend, the member for Cavan."

More than once during the 1882 session it seemed as if the " fourth party " must be dissolved into its constituent parts. Mr. Gorst had brought in a Bill inoffensive enough, as might have been supposed, if not important, for the recovery of small debts. Something connected with this proposal of the disciple displeased the master ; even the member for Chatham's patience was exhausted, and for about a week the " fourth party " existed only in a state of suspended animation. At this time Sir Stafford Northcote enjoyed comparative immunity from the attacks of his titular follower, while for the moment Mr. Sclater-Booth was also at peace; and though he had nicknamed the Lancashire member and the great Strand tradesman " Marshall and Snellgrove," it is noticeable that Randolph Churchill usually refrained from vituperating Mr. W. H. Smith.

On a certain afternoon towards the close of November 1882 the sprite of the perverse seemed especially busy in the People's Chamber. Lord Randolph, evidently ruffled, rose to speak on an amendment, moved by the Prime Minister, to one of the Irish Bills. The addition in question was not, of course could by no possibility have been, in print. Sir Richard Cross, as he had then become, having previously made a note of the Premier's proposal, politely handed the small piece of manuscript to the noble speaker. This attention, instead of being received graciously by Lord Randolph, the premonitory symptoms of whose health's failure were even at this early stage not quite invisible, appeared to cause him dissatisfaction. " A pretty pass," was his audible exclamation, " we have come to in the House of Commons, when we have to consider amendments passed about from hand to hand on dirty bits of paper."

The truth is that, strange as it may seem, public opinion in a House of Commons elected under Household Suffrage is not shocked, as strangers to it might suppose, by this system of personal recriminations between individual members of the assemblage. About a decade and a half before his own Reform Bill, Mr. Disraeli had placed on record a signal instance of these tactics at the time of his onslaughts on Sir Robert Peel. Subsequently they were illustrated again in the parliamentary relations which occasionally developed themselves between Mr. Disraeli when he was Prime Minister, and the Marquis of Salisbury when he was Lord Cranborne ; in the gladiatorial combats between Mr. Lowe and his ministerial associates, as at an earlier epoch still between Mr. Horsman and those ironically called his friends, or even between Mr. Disraeli once more and his earliest associates, Mr. Baillie Cochrane and Mr. Beresford Hope.

At this time a story went round the smoking-room to the effect that Mr. Biggar had promised

Mr. Gladstone to desist from future attacks if the Prime Minister would ennoble his family with a peerage. The Premier's reply to a question whether this anecdote had any foundation was characteristic and instructive, though evasive. " So far as I can observe," the Prime Minister answered, " the only person who does not feel the claws of Lord Randolph is the honourable member for Cavan."

Two things in the retrospect of this period may well seem surprising—the first, that Mr. Gladstone, night after night, week after week, month after month, endured the ordeal without absolute failure of physical or mental health ; the second, that Randolph Churchill himself bore the incessant strain of his own tactics so well that their perpetual repetition did not relegate the tactician himself to the category of bores.

About this time Sir Michael Hicks-Beach reasserted himself as an active power in the ranks of the Opposition. This gentleman had already served as Chief Secretary to the Lord-Lieutenant, and as Colonial Minister. Like Randolph Churchill himself, he was the embodiment of the Eton spirit ; but a different

Eton from, and a far more studious Eton than, that of which Lord Randolph Churchill was typical. At the Colonial Office especially, Sir Michael Hicks-Beach had shown an administrative perspicacity not less than an intellectual strength which astonished the permanent officials, and which no one had suspected in this very reserved Gloucestershire baronet. During the discussions of 1882 the "fourth party" chief differed from him somewhat sharply, and in committee debates emphasised his preference for the Prime Minister's over Sir Michael's amendments, but these differences implied no abiding feud; and when, at a later period, Sir Michael took office as Chancellor of the Exchequer, he did so to a great extent in the capacity, not only of Lord Randolph's personal friend, but in some sense his official nomination.

Lord Randolph Churchill could scarcely have had a better adviser than this gentleman. Some time later it was indeed, as the result of a co-operation between the Woodstock member and the Gloucestershire baronet, that in the summer of 1885 Mr. Gladstone's Government was placed in the minority; but during the period of the Liberals' agrarian legislation for

Ireland, Randolph Churchill had not come within the range of this gentleman's influence. His object was simple, and steadily kept in view, amid all the complications, digressions, and minor interludes of these sessions, abounding, as they did, rather in active incident than in events of first-rate importance. The net result of this period in its integrity was the completion of the movement begun by the "fourth party," when the session itself was new, and Mr. Bradlaugh first asserted himself. Randolph Churchill had decided that the battle of secularism should be prolonged to its utmost extent, in opposition to his official leader's desire for a peaceful and speedy settlement. The abhorrence with which the Northampton member's ideas were regarded, not merely on the Conservative side, but among respectable, as well as distinctly religious, persons of every school of political thought, led the subject of this memoir to the conclusion that he had an opportunity, certain, not only to discredit fatally Mr. Gladstone and the whole Liberal connection, but providentially adapted to complete Sir Stafford Northcote's and his colleague's official supersession by Randolph Churchill, and any instruments whom he chose to employ.

All, however, which had yet been accomplished actually was to make Sir Stafford Northcote's position impossible, and clearly to foreshadow as inevitable that retirement to the House of Lords, which, however, was not consummated till after a further interval of some half-dozen years. In the same way, though the way for an offensive and a defensive alliance between the Randolphians and the Irish members was being carefully paved, and all but practically complete, it was not to yield any definite results till that eventful June day in 1885, when the adhesion of the Celtic malcontents gave the Conservatives, after a six years' interval, a fresh term of office.

Two things are chiefly important to notice here at this stage of Randolph Churchill's career—the first, that he had now morally deposed his nominal superior, and had, in effect, made himself the real and, for the future, the only possible leader of his party ; the second, that the logical and moral continuity between his political commencement and the point of development he had now reached was complete.

As his great-grand-uncle had asserted himself in the Tory Ministry which followed the Congress of Vienna by placing pressure upon his colleagues in the interests of national independence for the minor peoples of Europe, so from the first moment that, as a Conservative member, he had a seat in the House of Commons, Castlereagh's great-grand-nephew showed his determination not to be reckoned a passive follower of his chiefs, whoever they might be. His maiden utterance, protesting against the quartering of " a roystering and licentious military upon a peaceful and famous university city," was followed by a remarkable contempt for the disciplinary conditions of Conservatism, when, a little later, the expenditure on the Prince of Wales' Indian visit came before the Commons. Mr. Fawcett had proposed that none of these expenses should be charged on the Indian revenues. Lord Randolph Churchill, while not altogether agreeing with the Cambridge economist, found himself still less in sympathy with the arrangements which his commanding officer, Sir Stafford Northcote, then Chancellor of the Exchequer, had proposed. " The time," he argued, " for taking exception to the trip itself had gone by. As for the plans advocated by the Government, he considered them to combine all the possible errors of niggardliness and profusion. Whereas he desired that the Heir-Apparent's journey should be supported with an unsparing, if not a lavish hand, he considered Sir Stafford Northcote and his provisors to have taken steps likely to insure the waste of money, as well as dissatisfaction all round." The same tone of independence animated each of his contributions to the discussions on the unreformed corporations, and were in exact harmony with the pledges given to his Woodstock constituents in his first address. It cannot, therefore, be said that Randolph Churchill had without very distinct warning notes brought his own personality to the front in his party's ranks.

CHAPTER IX.

THE CHURCHILLIAN IDEAS OF CONSERVATIVE POLICY (1880-83).

Prospective importance of Randolph Churchill's approaching visit to India.—Goes a free lance; returns a statesman.—Literary preparations for Eastern absence.— The "fourth party" manifestos of 1882.—Les idées Churchilliennes.—Conservative troubles due to leader not elected by general meeting of party, as after Lord George Bentinck's death in 1846, but by private arrangements of ex-Cabinet Ministers.—The strength and weakness of Conservatism between 1868-74.—The dangers of lordly patronage.—The calamities of the dual control. — Elijah's mantle rent to pieces.— Who will repair and wear it ?—" I," says Randolph Churchill.

His visit to India during the winter of 1884-5 marks a climax and turning-point of an importance not to be exaggerated in the public course of him with whom we are now dealing. By a convenient figure of speech it might be said that Randolph Churchill went to the cities of our Asiatic Empire a free lance and came back a statesman. The elements of constructive statesmanship had not indeed been wanting in many among his parliamentary utterances. If in the House of Commons he was occupied chiefly with invectives against Mr. Gladstone, assaults upon friends or foes as the whim of the moment and the possibility of producing an effect might suggest, he had outside the walls of St. Stephen's laboured with a praiseworthy and, in the eyes of those who loved him, rather pathetic patience, to increase his slender stock of hard political knowledge, and to redeem, so far as might be, the opportunities at an earlier age turned to too little account. This, then, is a convenient point to review the steps by which Randolph Churchill had reached his present conviction that Conservatism, to be effective, must henceforth be democratic, as well as to explain the circumstances under which the traditions of Lord Randolph Churchill's party had become discredited in the constituencies, and also to state the agencies by which his native ingenuity, conjoined with his acquired experience, told him that the disaster of 1880 could alone be retrieved.

The perfectly sincere representatives of an Evangelicalism, not now very fashionable,

sometimes tell us that what religion really
wants is another Reformation on the same
lines as, if on a milder scale than, Luther's.
Mutatis mutandis, that view is in exact
analogy with Churchill's very sober, eminently
reasonable, ideas upon the Conservative neces-
sities of ten or twelve years ago. The best
tribute to the cogency of his arguments advanced to that end is their subsequent adoption
by the men who decried and denounced them
at the time as verging upon blasphemy to
the Tory cause, if not downright insanity.
The whole course of Conservative reorganisation since his doctrines were first advanced
or elaborated is the best proof of their sagacity
and soundness. John Bright lived to witness
all those tenets which, when first put forward
by him, were condemned as iniquities, embraced, and acted upon as rudimentary truths
of the Constitution, and the commonplaces of
every-day life. A similar truth with respect
to Randolph Churchill can now be illustrated
with some degree of circumstantiality.

In the autumn of 1882 the present Chief
Secretary for Ireland resigned the editorship
of the *Fortnightly Review*, his successor being

the individual who pens these lines. Randolph
Churchill had now so patiently matured and
so thoroughly digested into manageable shape
his thoughts upon the then Conservative and
national discontents, as to be able to express
them in print with a clearness which could
not be mistaken and a fulness which left
nothing to complete.* These compositions
are as much a part of their author's parliamentary and political life as anything he ever
did or said in St. Stephen's or upon any
provincial platform. Apart from them as
being the most mature exposition of his
thoughts left by him on record, his relations
neither to past, to contemporary, nor to coming
events can be understood aright.

The starting-point, as well as the central proposition in these papers, constituting, as they
do, one organic whole, is that if the Tory party
is to continue a power in the State it must
become a popular party. There had, perhaps,
though Randolph Churchill does not mention

* See the *Fortnightly Review,* November 1882: "The
State of the Opposition," by Two Conservatives. Also
the *Fortnightly Review,* May 1883: "Elijah's Mantle,"
by Lord Randolph S Churchill.

the fact, been some ground for supposing Lord Beaconsfield, whose activity in public affairs was not extinguished after the reverse of 1880, but whose interest continued with them to the last, with favouring an *entente cordiale* between the Hartingtonian Liberals and his own progressive followers. Churchill, like those about him, protested that a mere coalition with the Whig aristocracy could not avert the downfall of an exclusive .Conservatism, as .indeed Disraeli, in the days of his earlier and clearer political vision, would himself have been the first to insist. Hence it followed in the Churchillian creed that the liberties and interests of the people at large are the only things which it is now possible to con-serve ; that the rights of property, the Established Church, the House of Lords, and the Crown itself must be defended on the ground of being institutions necessary or useful to the preservation of civil and religious liberty, as well as securities for personal freedom, to be maintained only so far as the people take this view of their subsistence.

A year or so before this, in the House of Commons, Randolph Churchill had repelled with some acrimony Mr. W. H. . Smith's apparent disparagement of the Irish peasantry as the inhabitants of cabins.   He now resumed more elaborately that line of thought by re-marking that, " unfortunately for Conservatism, its leaders belong solely to one class, being a clique drawn from members of the aristocracy, landowners, and adherents, whose chief merit is subserviency.   The party chiefs live in an atmosphere wherein a sense of their own importance, of their class privilege, is exaggerated, to which the opinions of the common people can scarcely penetrate.   These chiefs are surrounded by sycophants, who continually offer up the incense of personal flattery under the pretext of conveying political information. They half fear and half despise the common people, whom they see only through this deceptive medium, whom they regard rather as dangerous allies, to be coaxed and cajoled, than as comrades fighting for a common cause."

" The ' fourth party ' combatants had long denounced the disastrously exclusive character of the Conservative party, prior to the House-hold Suffrage Act of 1867.   Mr. Disraeli had, in ' Coningsby,' enunciated a similar principle in its application to the Conservatism which followed the Reform Act of 1832."

No attempt was made to disguise this exclusiveness. The party's strength lay in the counties, where the tacit understanding by which tenants voted for the landlord's nominee enabled territorial influence to secure the representation ; the efforts of the political managers were concentrated on the boroughs, where they endeavoured by influence, social prestige, and too often by bribery, to win a sufficient number of seats to give the faction of the county members the command of the House of Commons. In this object, though sometimes very near success, they never quite succeeded. The Representation of the People Act swept away for ever the possibility of obtaining a majority by manipulating the borough elections, and the disastrous Conservative discomfiture in the boroughs in 1868 brought the change of circumstances home to the party leaders. After that reverse, the aristocratic chiefs for a time retired. They abandoned the cause in despair ; left the Conservative party and Mr. Disraeli, whom they anathematised in private, to their

own devices. This incubus removed, a new
order of things sprang up.

" In the general disaster of 1868," the exponents of Lord Randolph's views continued,
" one part of the country presented a singular
exception. The great manufacturing towns of
Lancashire, Blackburn, Bolton, Saltford, Preston,
Ashton, Stalybridge, Warrington, Liverpool,
had returned Conservative members of their
own selection by decisive majorities. In these
boroughs the people had for some time possessed political organisations of their own, not
blighted by the patronage of lords or landowners, while the unsuspected vitality of
Toryism thus displayed was a surprise, and
ought to have been a lesson for professional
politicians. Between 1868 and 1874 Conservative associations, on the Lancashire model,
grew up in every part of England. They
universally complained of not being patronised
by the aristocratic chiefs of Toryism, scarcely
realising how fortunate for them this lack of
lordly patronage was. There was no tempta-
tion to waste time and energy in organising
demonstrations to which no local magnate
would come. They were thus driven to

devote themselves to registration, and the machinery necessary for an election contest. The victory of 1874, which was totally unexpected by the aristocratic section of the party, was the result. As soon as success was achieved, the men who had stood aloof since 1868 rushed in to share the spoils. A Ministry was formed, composed almost exclusively of peers and county members. Those by whom the campaign had been planned and fought were forgotten. Mr. Disraeli devoted himself to foreign policy, and the interests of the British Empire abroad. Domestic affairs and the management of the party were left to lieutenants, who attributed their position to their own merits, and entirely ignored the men to whom their unexpected elevation was due. The distinction between county and borough members was revived. The latter were made to feel that they were an inferior class ; they were expected to fight the battles of their superiors with loyalty and devotion, but their own interests and wishes were uniformly neglected ; social influence became predominant, it pervaded the whole organisation of the party with disastrous results. The independence of political thought was visited with the severest punishment. To doubt the stability of the Conservative Government, and to point out the decay of the new Conservative associations under the patronage by which they were stifled, was flat heresy. The members of the Ministry desired their followers to speak unto them smooth things, and to prophesy deceits. In promotion to offices in Church and State, while the members of the late Government never forgot the claims of their personal friends, relations, and adherents, those of their political supporters were uniformly treated with disdain or contempt. Such offices as they did not want for their personal friends were given to their political opponents, to gain for themselves a reputation for impartiality.

"In legislation, the interests of the boroughs were subordinate to those of the counties. The Merchants' Shipping Bill was abandoned to make way for the abortive Agricultural Holdings Act. The requirements of the landowners were ostentatiously preferred to those of the people at large.

" The Conservative associations, as a natural consequence of these things, steadily declined ; their numbers increased, but their vitality was gone. Those by whom the work was silently performed gradually withdrew to make way for noisier partisans, whose main purpose was not to advance the Conservative cause, but to recommend themselves to the leaders of the Conservative party.

" The defeat of 1880 astonished the aristocratic section as much as the victory of 1874. It was no surprise to those acquainted with the temper of that great section of the party whose voice never reached the leaders' ears. With the exception of Lord Beaconsfield, the members of the party learnt nothing by their defeat.

" There is no reason to suppose they have learnt anything since. They cling to their position at the head of the party with more tenacity than in 1868 ; for they expect at the next general election to see the phenomenon of 1874 repeated, though at present there is no sign that the reaction will come. Meanwhile they do not mend their policy, for they are unconscious of error. In the House of

Commons the ring by which the party is governed is as exclusive as heretofore. 'We have had a meeting of the late Cabinet, and have decided thus,' is the answer to every remonstrance and suggestion from outside. The ability and sagacity of Sir Stafford Northcote are smothered by the selfish timidity of his colleagues.

"The defence of the interests of the landlords in general, and of landowners in particular, is the object which the entire Tory party devotes itself to compassing. In opposing the Arrears Bill of 1882, the ground deliberately selected by the members of the late Cabinet for resistance to the measure was not the injustice to the British taxpayer, but the inconvenience to the Irish landlord. They did their best to force an appeal to the country on this issue, unconscious of the swift destruction that would have come among them."

With reference to a then recent remark made by Sir Stafford Northcote, at Glasgow, that the hopes of the Conservative party lay in its organisation, this critic admitted "that in some constituencies there doubtless were associations

still composed of earnest workers with unselfish
leaders who labour for the good of the cause";
but these, he insisted, were few, and his cardinal
contention was, "that the entire organisation
of the Tory party must undergo a radical
revolution before it can afford grounds for any
well-founded satisfaction."

The writers therefore continued: "In its existing shape it is managed by a committee in
London, whose names are unknown to the
people at large, and who act without any
mandate from the constituencies. The council
of the National Union of Constitutional Associations, which is elected annually, has no funds,
and is in a chronic condition of impotence; the
constituencies take but a faint interest in its
composition, and it does not possess the confidence of the party at large. The complaint of
the individual associations, prior to 1874, that
they were not patronised by the privileged
class, can be no longer made. They are rather
corrupted by patronage. The increase of
these societies, so far from being cause for con-
gratulation, is rather symptomatic of a growing
disease. The object for which many of them
exist is to hold periodical demonstrations,

whereat some member of the late Cabinet may exhibit his oratorical talents before the admiring crowd. When this has been accomplished, when the local leaders have had the satisfaction of shaking hands with the great man, their zeal collapses, and the association languishes until there is a fresh opportunity of catching a lion. Real work, like that done in obscurity prior to 1874, is never dreamt of. Action between one demonstration and the next is confined to signing petitions in conformity with orders sent down from the Carlton. Occasionally half-a-dozen members may meet and pass a resolution, assuring Lord Salisbury and Sir Stafford Northcote of the loyalty and devotion of the association. This is sent to the party interested, and usually elicits a complimentary reply, which obtains publication in the local, and sometimes in the London, newspapers. The provision of a candidate to fight the next election does not come within the scope of their activity. No local politician would attempt the hopeless task. A gentleman from the Carlton, furnished with a liberal supply of money, is demanded and expected. Such a candidate is almost certain to be defeated,

but there was the consolation of knowing that
he consolidates and rewards the local party,
though he has failed to add himself to the
Conservative ranks in the House of Commons."

The general conclusion of this, the first
deliberate utterance of his political ideas ever
put forth by Randolph Churchill, whether in
Parliament or in the press, is, therefore, "that
the sole actual result of the spread of the
organisation, in which Sir Stafford Northcote
placed so much confidence, was greatly to
increase the number of occasions on which the
members of the exclusive class exhibit them- (¹)
selves to the multitude. So it came to pass
that for the first time the people were confronted by the men in whom they are asked to
put their trust; compelled to witness an idle
resuscitation of a dead Tory Cabinet, to listen
to a vain defence of its policy and virtues ;(²)
while wearied with minute criticisms of foreign
affairs, and knowing all the while, that had the
speaker been himself in office, he would have
done much the same as his opponents. Nor,"
this manifesto insisted, "could these popular
critics fail to note the Conservative champion's
satisfaction with his own position, and his

readiness to defend the order to which he belongs ; but could catch no word of sympathy for themselves, nothing to show that it is their rights, their privileges, which he is zealous to maintain. He is a being made from different clay, and living in a different atmosphere from theirs. If these are the means on which the official managers rely for bringing themselves back to power, they have a long time to wait. Such speeches, delivered by such men, will never turn the hearts of the people against the minister who is at present their idol (Mr. Gladstone), and who, whatever his faults, always exhibits a passionate sympathy with the masses."

Constructive elements were not wanting to this characteristic composition, which, when it appeared, produced a sensation not less general and deep than the most successful of those effusions that, before monthly magazines had superseded pamphlets, periodically proved the literary or political event of a session and a season. That there was a way out of this demoralising and debilitating *impasse* Randolph Churchill had for two or three years contended, alike in conversation, in addresses from popular platforms, or in letters to the daily press. He now argued " that even as it was, the defeat of 1880 had not been without uses to the party." A long-growing discontent among the rank and file had come to a head. Lord Beaconsfield, who for three or four years had ceased to be Mr. Disraeli, was no longer possessed with the spirit, nor conversant with the feelings of the House of Commons. " His patronage, ecclesiastical and civil, nominations and promotions, whether to place or honours, were apparently administered by some Gil Blas or Figaro behind the scenes, who guarded all the approaches to his chief's confidence with sordid assiduity. Without some such support Ministers were powerless except in their own departments. Social influence over-rode all claims of political or parliamentary service. Lord Beaconsfield, failing from old age and infirmity, did not attempt to struggle with an evil which was sapping his power. He was not, however, ignorant of it. More than once he was known to have told some old friends that the dissolution would entail the entire reconstruction of the party organisation.

"He did not conceal from himself the results of the dissolution. 'To you,' he said to a young man during the election, who was trying to minimise the disaster, ' it is nothing ; to me it is the end of my career.' He accepted the result, as was his wont, impassively, regretting only that Lord Hartington had not accepted the mission offered to him by his sovereign. But he never despaired of the future fortunes of the party, nor did he relax his energy, though hoping for no reward. On the contrary, he set himself conscientiously to repair the evil. His most devoted favourites, having reaped their harvest, and expecting nothing further, left him a little more freedom. This he employed by giving more of his time to encourage the efforts of his partisans outside the ring of the Gil Blas and Figaros."

This appeal, which, at the time of its first publication, had so vivid a political significance, possesses now not only a personal interest, but a historic value. The exact position of the constitutional party in the autumn of 1882 is sketched graphically and faithfully in the following sentences :—

" Never   was   there   a   more   enthusiastic

meeting than that held at Lord Beaconsfield's
new house in Curzon Street in 1881, when he
addressed his House of Commons supporters
with all the wisdom of long and unflagging
service. But Lord Beaconsfield died, and left
no successor. Intrigue was rife in both
Houses of Parliament. A proposal was made
at the National Union, presided over by Lord
Percy, for Lord Salisbury's selection as leader.
This was resisted by Sir Stafford's partisans,
and lost on a division by a single vote.
Ultimately a coalition and a compromise were
effected. The Conservative party, unable to
arrive at a conclusion, decided for a duplex
action, and for the first time in its history has
remained for many months without a leader."

The more personal criticisms of this survey
were necessary to elucidate its author's meaning, and are as entirely free from malice,
jealousy, or rancour as in his most heated
moments Randolph Churchill's strictures are
admitted by his closest rivals, and most
resolute opponents, invariably to have been.

Deploring the generally admitted tendency of
Mr. Disraeli, after he became Lord Beaconsfield, to appoint to important offices either

men of aristocratic antecedents or humbler
individuals, content only to receive and execute
his orders, he shows that at one time six dukes
were serving under the author of " Lothair ";
that among the secondary members of his
Government there were also representatives
of the same blue blood ; while in the list of
his Cabinet officers in the House of Commons
the plutocratic element prevails.

Thus Sir Richard Cross and Mr. W. H.
Smith were the favourite counsellors of Sir
Stafford Northcote, while, great as were many
of their qualities, they did not possess those
necessary to secure the plenary confidence of
a mainly aristocratic party.   At this date both
these gentlemen were of comparatively recent
parliamentary standing, had only been once
in office, and, notwithstanding their administrative success, had still to reach the standard
of statesmanlike excellence by which men of
the first rank are judged.   Nor, undoubtedly,
was the opinion confined to the " fourth party,"
that while the counsel of the gentlemen already
named was most valuable, it was not necessarily
more commanding than that of others whose
parliamentary experience was greater.

The first criticism of Mr. W. H. Smith occurs towards the close of this document, and refers to certain experiments of that gentleman to promote the welfare of the working classes which had recently affronted and alarmed many excellent Tories, giving them a notion that the settlement of the Irish Land question lay between Mr. George and the member for Westminster himself.

Of Sir Michael Hicks-Beach, whose great qualities were recognised by no one more generously than by Churchill himself, it is said, while approaching nearer to the chosen circle, he has not thought fit since 1880 to put forward his best energies, or to assert the position to which his abilities certainly give him no mean title. Nor are Mr. Edward Stanhope or Lord George Hamilton spoken of in less handsome terms. The only criticism on Mr. James Lowther was that his daring did not invariably secure the success it deserved. "These six," summed up the writer, "are the group with whom Sir Stafford Northcote is generally surrounded. Their claim to leadership lies in the offices given to them by the discrimination of Lord Beaconsfield rather than in any general recognition of their merits. There is one figure, however, without which the roll of the front bench is incomplete. Few men have laboured so hard or so efficiently as Mr. Gibson. More Conservative than Mr. Plunket, who sighs for coalitions, more active and less easily amused, he has shot far ahead of his genial and less laborious colleague. But he is a lawyer and an Irishman of the Irish, and it would be difficult to rally the Conservative party of Great Britain to a Teucer so closely identified with the interests of Irish landlords."

In the text of this volume it has been shown above that while (Mr. Gathorne Hardy,) now known as Lord Cranbrook, possessed ideal qualifications for the Tory leadership in Opposition, and would probably have satisfied the more belligerent spirits below the gangway, Sir Stafford Northcote's combination of rank, experience, and ability made him practically inevitable. That view was expressed strongly in the confession of the "fourth party" now under examination. Nor was it denied that with any other antagonist than Mr. Gladstone the Devonshire baronet would have filled the position excellently well. It is indeed possible, as the Randolphian section believed, that Mr. Disraeli might never have relinquished the lead of the popular Chamber in 1876 but for the conviction of Mr. Gladstone's retirement being virtually already accomplished. " With Lord Hartington as leader of the Liberals," as the present manifesto continues, " Sir Stafford might have held his own. He is able and respectable, rich in information, experience, and memory; good tempered, astute, accomplished; a thorough man of business, a man of resource; but he is too amiable for his ambition, which is great, and in trying to play a double part, that of caution and daring, he is at times taxed beyond his strength. With Mr. W. H. Smith on one side, and Mr. James Lowther on the other, he resembles the babe between the two mothers, which Solomon decreed should be divided."

No one will now deny the reasonableness of Lord Randolph's contention that these internal discontents might have been avoided if the Liberal example on Mr. Gladstone's retirement, or the Conservative precedent on

Lord George Bentinck's death, or more recently the peers' example after the departure of Lord Beaconsfield, had been followed; and at a meeting summoned for the purpose at the Carlton Club, a single chief for the whole Conservative army, peers and commoners alike, had been elected on the vote of the assembled legions. As events in 1882 abundantly proved, the dual leadership, or rather a leadership, placed indefinitely in commission, was a fatal cause of weakness and disorganisation. Lord Salisbury could not consult the feelings of the House of Commons save through Sir Stafford Northcote, while the same reserve must prevail over the communications between Sir Stafford Northcote and the peers.

It is important to remember that the views now put forth by Lord Randolph through his lieutenants were not entirely novel. They were the reflection of convictions and complaints openly expressed in private, but by no means confidential conversation; they even found occasional expression in the regular Conservative press during its conductors' more independent intervals. Special point was given to their statement in the *Fortnightly* pages of November of 1882 by the fact that " in the recent session the two leaders, in their respective Houses, had, on the amendments of the Arrears Bill, been deserted by a large portion of their following. That, of course, meant simply a state of chaos, to which no one could foresee a satisfactory end. Lord Salisbury and Sir Stafford might travel together, advertising their loyalty to each other, but how as to their followers ? "

The official reply to all charges like these was, " that the choice of a Tory leader could not be made till the Conservatives returned to office, when the conflicting pretensions of individuals would be decided by the Sovereign's summons. Meanwhile the sheep were to be satisfied with wandering leaderless in the desert, secretly sceptical as to whether their Aaron and Moses were destined to enjoy the promised land."

The most specific allegation now advanced against the titular managers of Conservatism was that " the Tory cause had of late been sacrificed repeatedly to an Irish coterie inaccessible to any political motive outside

Ireland. But for the determination of the rank and file of the party, as the Arrears Bill progress had showed, to resist this Irish invasion, the country might in the autumn of 1882 have been convulsed by a dissolution which would almost have exterminated Conservatism as a political power. But with the adjournment of the House the Irish circle seemed once more to prevail. Lord Salisbury and Sir Stafford had consented to give a joint entertainment at Belfast, the consequence of which will probably be mischievous, and must be futile. 'What English element,' it was asked, 'can be stimulated by the meditated duet of the two Conservative potentates in the Ulster capital?' The Conservative element in Ireland is Protestantism of the hottest type, fanaticism of the deepest orange, and at this time it did indeed seem as if there were danger of a war of creeds. Were the Conservative leaders, with the Catholic Peers and Commons of England in their favour, meditating an appeal to the Orangemen of Ireland, and raising a crusade against the Pope?"

To examine, somewhat more in detail, "the Opposition attitude during the recent Irish legislation, ' what,' it was asked, ' had been the meaning of the first amendment proposed by Lord Salisbury to the Arrears Bill, and pressed upon him by those who had deserted him?' The object of that measure had been first to find some compensation for the Irish landlord, even at the cost of the British taxpayer, and to tranquillise Ireland by the suppression of evictions for arrears. Yet the amendment forced on Lord Salisbury by the band of Irish barons who surround him would have made the success of the Arrears Bill dependent on the pressure of those very gentlemen, who, at their own option, were to be compensated by the British taxpayer, or would have kept Ireland in a state of ferment, equally expensive, by a continuation of the evictions. The taxpayer was entirely overlooked. What a cry for the country! And this was a course in which Lord Salisbury was encouraged by the front bench in the Commons. Had he been able to call a meeting of members of Parliament, or to learn from any other gentleman than Mr. Gibson the feelings of Conservative non-official members, he would have been spared the unpopularity of making the motion and the annoyance of withdrawing it.   Mr. Gibson, with all his ability, labours under one great disadvantage.   He is member for the University of Dublin, and consequently is in no greater communication with the English, or even Irish, popular constituencies than if he were a member of the House of Keys or the States of Jersey.   Possibly Egypt may emancipate us from Ireland.   Possibly by some united action on the part of the Conservative party as a whole a leader may be chosen by a common suffrage of both Peers and Commons, able to guide the policy, command the confidence, and enlist the loyalty of politicians both inside and outside the Houses of Parliament. The Lords follow a lord of their own choice, the Commons do not implicitly follow a commoner who is chosen for them, though there is not as yet any disaffection towards him.   But whom does the party follow?   Joint action does not attract joint loyalty.   Elijah's mantle has been torn in two, and until the pieces are joined there can be no cohesion in the Conservative ranks."

CHAPTER X.

LORD RANDOLPH'S REVOLT: ITS CONDUCT AND CONSEQUENCES (1883-4).

The state of things in the Conservative party on Lord Beaconsfield's death, 1881.—The Tory Leadership in commission.—The history of Conservative management from 1867.—Mr. Disraeli and Mr. Spofforth.—" Are you trying to upset my Reform Bill?"—" I don't believe a word of it."—Official efforts to nobble the Tory press. —Dead set of Tory prints in London against Randolph Churchill.—The bad boy who will not obey Mrs. Harris and Sarah Gamp.—Immense popularity of Randolph Churchill in the provinces and provincial Tory press.— Comparison between Lord John Russell's and Randolph Churchill's style.—Randolph Churchill strictly according to precedent.

LORD BEACONSFIELD's death in 1881 had removed the last semblance of a check upon the Churchillian insurrection against Lord Beaconsfield's successor in the Commons. Had the Tory chief, still plain Mr. Disraeli, survived, the "fourth party" would not have reached even the embryonic stage of its existence. Had the moral authority, which his mere

life carried with it, been a fact subsequently to
1881, Lord Randolph Churchill's rising would
not have gone much further than the abortive
movement of hostility to Mr. Disraeli during
the Reform Bill period of 1867, when, under
the conduct of two or three Conservative
M.P.'s, now no more, and others, a coalition
between the Adullamites of Liberalism and
the malcontents of Toryism perished at the
moment of its inception.   Even as it was,
Lord Beaconsfield, though he took no personal
trouble with the " fourth party " leader, dis-
paraging his influence considerably long before
his own death, speaking of him, on more than
one occasion, half contemptuously as " Dilke
and water," did do something to reduce the
enfant terrible of the party to subordination to
his own nominee.

The verdict of the consummately gifted,
unmatchably astute statesman who educated his
connection up to Household Suffrage, was that
Randolph had talent, but wanted ballast and
discretion, and that the first lesson he had
to master was the platitude that those who
aspired to lead must first learn to follow.   This
message was actually conveyed and delivered

to Randolph Churchill by a gentleman, happily
alive to-day, who, with good reason, enjoyed
Mr. Disraeli's undivided confidence in all
matters of party organisation.

The fortunes of the Conservative party
between 1868 and 1874, during the Disraelian
era, had been largely retrieved, and the whole
organisation reconstructed by the indefatigable
industry and electioneering skill of Mr. Markham
Spofforth, of the historic firm of Messrs. Baxter,
Rose, Norton, and Company, working under,
and in confidential collaboration with, the then
Lord Nevill, now Marquis of Abergavenny.

The circumstances under which this parliamentary solicitor first received the implicit
trust of Mr. Disraeli, and was installed by him
in a position where his Liberal analogue was
the late Mr. Drake, are so characteristic alike
of the prevailing suspicions of the time and of
the self-reliant perspicacity of the great Conservative genius as to deserve some permanent
record here. In those agitated hours of now
nearly three decades since the political atmosphere was full of intrigue and rumours of
intrigues, of cabals and conjectures of cabals.
Markham Spofforth's success had of course

made him enemies. "I am told," were Mr.
Disraeli's words on seeing him one day, "that
you are trying to upset my Reform Bill."
"Do you believe it, sir?" asked the lawyer.
"No," said Disraeli, pausing for a moment,
and looking at him very straight in the face,
"I do not."

The statesman had good reason to con-
gratulate himself on his sagacious incredulity.
Never was party better served by business
personage than the Conservatives by this hard-
headed but urbane son of the law. When
Markham Spofforth, having organised victory,
resigned his post, that he might restore to his
business the energies he had devoted to the
party, the office of Conservative manager was
practically without any incumbent until 1870.
In that year Mr. John Eldon Gorst, subsequently of the "fourth party" and of the
Salisbury Cabinet, was appointed to the post,
remaining at it till after the election of 1874.
Mr. Gorst never formally resigned, but a paid
official, Mr. Skene, was nominated for the
special business of the 1880 election, and
Mr. Spofforth's successor, who never received
any salary, withdrew gradually.

After the events of 1880 the present Sir J. E. Gorst was asked to reorganise the whole Conservative machinery under Mr. W. H. Smith. The plan did not prove practicable ; was, after a year or two, abandoned ; and Captain Middleton, the present business manager, was installed in the office.

Nothing, of course, could have been more unfortunate or ill-advised than these constant changes just enumerated. In many respects Mr. Gorst was admirably qualified to fill Mr. Spofforth's place. His intellectual powers and position are attested sufficiently by the fact that, being two years junior to Mr. Leonard Courtney, he was third Wrangler in a year or two following that in which Liskeard's representative won the blue ribbon of mathematical science, and that, about the same time as Mr. Courtney, he was elected a fellow of St. John's. The scientific mind, habituated as it is to deal with certainties, does not, perhaps, in all cases best accommodate itself to those concerns where probability, always the essential guide of this life, and compromise, belong to the material essence of affairs.

Impolitic Randolph Churchill's open and

audacious strictures upon the post-Disraelian
Conservative managership undoubtedly were.
Disloyalty to titular chiefs is a charge to which
they were constructively open. They compromised, however, no one but Randolph
Churchill himself; they belonged to the same
category of partisan expedients as from the
days of Canning to those of Disraeli and Peel
had received the sanction of traditional wont.
If Mr. Disraeli had lived again under a similar
condition of things, he might not perhaps have
employed Randolph Churchill's precise tactics.
Instead of newspaper letters and magazine
articles he would probably have written another
novel. The accusations brought by Churchill
against the social arrangements of his own
political interior, the satire upon the " Daimios,"
" Gil Blas," " Figaros," and so forth, recall,
with nearly a verbal fidelity, the taunts placed
in the lips of Coningsby and Buckhurst at the
" Venetian oligarchy," when the general election
of 1841 had given Peel his great majority.
Nor can any one possessing the smallest sense
of literary effect, or of fiction's potentialities,
read the expressions wherein the situation was
summed up by the " fourth party " leader,

without recognising in them the materials and the inspiration of a novel of the period, likely to have been more instructive and not less interesting than the majority of those provided for the circulating libraries by the society chroniclers of their epoch.

That the split continued, that the schism deepened and widened, during each successive year, was unfortunate alike for Conservatism as for the subject of this monograph ; but with the exercise of such conciliatory tact as fairly may be looked for in the ranks of a historic connection was assuredly not inevitable. If Randolph Churchill was not (and thus much may be readily admitted) a very docile or easily controlled spirit, the persons whose business it should have been to approach, discipline, and, if possible, tame him, left in their dealings with him no conceivable error uncommitted. Repeatedly during the quarter of a century anterior to these events the official agents of Conservatism had endeavoured to undermine the independence of the Conservative press. Mr. Ralph Earle, whom Mr. Disraeli had attracted from the Paris Embassy to his own secretarial service, had great literary gifts, a quickly constructive mind, and was adapted signally to the office of censor of Conservative journalism. With that view an understrapper from Downing Street did, as a matter of fact, approach the then editor of the leading Tory print. The journalist plainly told the Whitehall emissary that he would tolerate no idea of such interference, and asserted his independence by an exposure of the whole transaction the next day in a scathing article. Nor, to say that which is true, in distinction to that which is so often asserted as perhaps to be some times believed, is there an atom of foundation for the fallacy that to-day the most powerful of Tory ministers conceivable could dictate its policy to the humblest of Conservative broadsheets.

The party managers, however, at the time now spoken of, studiously circulated the rumour, taking especial care that, invested with all possible appearance of plausibility, it should reach Randolph Churchill's ears, that the animadversions on the "fourth party," published daily by the Tory prints, were the faithful echoes of Downing Street *communiques*. The

only result of this device was to embitter
the imperious mutineer against the Conservative press of London, and to harden him
in his defiance alike of written reprimands √
and oral protests. He denounced the manu-
factured opinion of the capital with a vehemence,
or lauded the sincerity and independence of
provincial declarations with a fervour recalling
Mr. Chamberlain himself. In effect, Randolph
Churchill had, by the years 1883-4, become the
idol of the Conservative democracy whom Mr.
Disraeli had called into existence, and whom
he himself was summoning into full activity.

The Conservative press of the provinces,
to an extent far greater than the London
Conservative press, depends for its commercial
prosperity upon being the exact reflection of
popular Conservative opinion. The leader of
the " fourth party " had now become the
leader of militant Toryism throughout the
United Kingdom. When personally rebuked,
lectured, and remonstrated with by Metropolitan journalists in paragraphs which were
an amplification of the sententious message as
to the necessity of future leaders being followers
first, Churchill, with not unnatural triumph,

pointed to the more animating appreciations
of his conduct published daily by provincial
broadsheets.   He was, as he thought, chal-
lenged ; he took up the gauntlet in much
the same fashion that Mr. Gladstone did
repeatedly, and that assuredly Disraeli would
have done on the supposition of a reversal
of his actual experiences, and if, instead of
being, as he was, the idol of the upper circles,
the middle classes, and the clubs of London,
he had enjoyed the popularity and confidence
of the provinces, while looked at askance by
the critics of Westminster and the *quidnuncs*
of Pall Mall.   Lord Randolph's words were
habitually identical on this subject with the
spirit, and almost with the letter, of those
utterances on the same subject from Mr.
Gladstone, Mr. Bright, Mr. Joseph Chamberlain
himself, and other popular leaders : " London
opinion is always wrong ; the masses in the
country are never wrong."   Paradox or truism,
platitude or fallacy, the proposition thus put
has long since become the electioneering com-
monplace of politicians who, for the moment,
do not find themselves at one with their official
colleagues in the Downing Street councils.

The obligations under which Toryism of all grades, during the years now spoken of, was to the member for Woodstock, entitled Churchill to treatment much more appreciative by the Tory prints of the capital, much more considerate, to say the least, by the official managers of the connection. Such bye-elections as Conservatism did not lose were won upon his platform. Such diffusive or propagating power as the constitutional cause possessed was derived from his energising activity, or was inspired by his indefatigably aggressive example. It was the part of publicists, animated by a wise love for the cause, whose representatives began in the year 1880 to be in Opposition, frankly to have acknowledged facts so patent as these, and not, in their loyalty to Carlton edicts, or in their zealous anticipation of hints from auguster quarters still, to have lectured this rising or risen champion of provincial Con-servatism, with at least a compact phalanx of the Tory democracy behind him, as if he had been a rebellious schoolboy or a crude academic doctrinaire.

If the object of these rather indiscreet

homilies had not possessed deep loyalty to the connection which flouted him, as well as a strong democratic fibre of his own, he would have taken his monitors at their word, would have withdrawn his name from the true blue caravanserai next door to the Reform Club, and would have boldly bid for the succession to Mr. Gladstone. In that hypothetical ambition he might, or might not, have succeeded. One thing is certain. In the event of such a secession, the Conservative defeat at the winter elections of 1885, instead of decisive, would have been overwhelming; dissentient Liberalism would to-day be an unknown product, Mr. Gladstone's Home Rule Bill of 1886 would have become law, and before now, from the Giant's Causeway to Cape Clear, from John O'Groat's to Beachy Head, Conservatism would not have had an inch of ground for its foothold. There were other special inducements that are known to those behind the political scenes which might have conceivably moved Randolph Churchill to separate himself from the politicians, by whose rank and file, as well as by whose captains, upon one plea or another, without, or possibly even with,

good grounds, he was taunted with words
and conduct injurious to his party, or with
courses subversive of its internal discipline,
or its external efficiency.

An acute, and by this time thoroughly trained
observer of men, of events, of individual character, as well as of political under-currents,
Churchill must for years after the Liberal victory
in 1880, and especially after John Bright's partial
but frequent withdrawals from affairs, have
noticed multiplying signs of incompatibility as
to personal and political temper between Mr.
Gladstone and Mr. Chamberlain, which rendered an eventual disruption morally certain,
even though that consummation should, as was
the case, actually be delayed until the sole
link, connecting the two men in the person of
the great tribune, representing the midland
capital with the then President of the Board of
Trade as his colleague, should be severed, not
at once by Mr. Bright's death, but by his
adoption of the Unionist cause.

There was at this moment only one man
in the country who could at all be matched,
on any platform outside the midlands, against
Mr. Gladstone. That distinction belonged to

Churchill.   He knew it; he was aware also
that the thread of relationship then associating
the Hughenden and Highbury statesmen was
of the most precarious kind.   Nor can he have
failed to be conscious of the strong probability
that Imperial affairs would issue in an early
severance of the heir to the Dukedom of
Devonshire from the member for Midlothian.
If, therefore, as is historically the case, Woodstock's representative not only took no step
towards the place whither circumstances seemed
to beckon him; if, to state a further fact, whatever the casual observations of his social
moments in the privacy of club or domestic
life, he discovered an identity of view between
Lord Salisbury's opponents and himself; if he
made no overtures to the groups whom his
presence would have amalgamated under the
dark blue and yellow flag, nor invited from
them any serious advances to himself, the
explanation assuredly must be found in a more
deep and unselfish devotion to the political
colours, less of his choice than of his birth, than
that with which Randolph Churchill is credited
by half-informed and superficial, if not malignant,
appraisers of his conduct and motives.

Churchill's speeches were, no doubt, sometimes violent ; his epithets were often intemperate ; his personal invective was not infrequently of the sort called "unmeasured"; but for every phrase he coined, every gibe he directed at the statesmen who were constrained, certainly through no motive of love, from purging their deliberations of his presence, he could have found parallel and justification in precedents accounted more unimpeachable than that of Disraeli against Peel, in the decorous fold of Whig orthodoxy itself, especially in Lord John Russell's rhetoric during the tension of that statesman's relations with his colleague Palmerston.

Political memories in these days are short ; but a man need only be on the sunny side of middle age to recall the bitter diatribes with which, at the zenith of his power, the " My dear John Russell " of the Greville Memoirs delighted audiences of staid merchants in London city, and by means of which he did not a little towards confirming the ascendancy over his countrymen that his ancestral prestige, united with his own genius, had won for him.

" Johnny's at his dirty tricks again ! "   These were the words that went the round of counting-houses and emporia east of Temple Bar, which, with various rhetorical embellishments, were whispered in more fashionable resorts nearer Charing Cross, and which, as being far more eloquent comments on the occasion than any words of Delane's best writers, summed up the habitual practices of the mighty little Whig orator, the John Russell, to whom Palmerston so often boasted of having given " tit for tat."

CHAPTER XI.

WESTMINSTER AND PROVINCIAL CONSERVATISM (1882-4).

The Conservative Associations' Union Meeting at Sheffield, 1884.—Consequences following from the assumption of Elijah's mantle, and the committal of Randolph Churchill to the principle of decentralisation in modern Conservatism.—Differences in the camp healed by compromise; Randolph Churchill resigns chairmanship.

As regards the comparison drawn in the previous chapter between the Conservatism of the capital and the provinces, there may be some who would demand further proof of the propositions advanced in commenting on this contrast. The simple historical facts, conclusively demonstrating as they do the correctness of the picture already given, are these :—

When, during the summer of 1884, the National Union of Conservative Associations met at Sheffield, the differences between the two sections of the parliamentary party were at their height. On one side all those Tory M.P.'s who were of Cabinet rank, or had held any high office, together with the majority of the rank and file in the House of Commons, were upon the whole in favour of Sir Stafford Northcote's Fabian tactics ; holding that, as the London *Standard* had recently put it, it was no part of rational Conservatism to lead forlorn hopes in electoral contests, and that Randolph Churchill had perpetrated a fallaciously antithetic jingle when he talked of the chief object of an Opposition being to oppose.

The acceptability of the Churchillian policy to a preponderance of Conservative delegates was placed on record beyond the possibility of mistake in the capital of cutlery, at the date we have now reached. A plebiscite in favour of the "fourth party's" leader was all but unanimously given. The struggle between the two Tory factions was severe, and, for the time, decisive. The Conservative moderates mustered all their forces in the Yorkshire town, whipped up to the last man their supporters throughout the country, with the view of excluding Randolph Churchill from the Council of the Association.

Lord Percy himself, like Mr. Balfour, an occasional adherent of the "fourth party," represented the antagonism of the aristocracy to the man whom formerly he had fitfully followed ; Mr. Northcote, Sir Stafford's son, vicariously placed his sire's personal authority and official weight in the same scale as the great Northumbrian house. Sir Edward Clarke, a future law officer and a favourable specimen of middle - class constitutionalism, threw in his lot with the dukes and squires. Mr. Henry Chaplin, himself more than once reputedly in the running for the reversion to Sir Stafford's leadership, one of Mr. Disraeli's favourite country gentlemen, who had modelled his oratory on the pattern of his late chief, but who seldom inspired the Disraelian form of words with the Disraelian fire, and trusted to a certain pomp of delivery to cover an unkind suspicion that sentences pretending to be epigrams might in reality be only platitudes, had left his broad Lincolnshire acres for the battle-ground in the more northern shire. Mr. Ashmead-Bartlett, content for the moment to merge his pretensions to supremacy in an absorbing loyalty to official discipline, and to appear as the passive follower of a statesman whose Toryism resembled his own as little as the Conservatism of Peel was like the reaction-ism of Sidmouth, united his own efforts with those of the parliamentarians already named, and many others, to suppress the man whom the Tory democracy too plainly delighted to honour, and if not to shut him out from the Associations' Council, then to render it impossible for him to accept the chair-manship.

Two supporters, and two only, upon this occasion Randolph Churchill had. Sir Henry Drummond Wolff, a personal friend of Lord Salisbury, as of the whole Cecil family, a frequent guest at Hatfield and in Arlington Street, was not afraid to jeopardise these exalted associations, or to compromise his own diplomatic future, by refusing to dissemble his regard for the man who, politically, had made him. Nor did the lawyer's caution which accompanied the intellectual power of Mr. Gorst permit him either to desert the politician in whom his admirer discovered the latter-day equivalent of that terrible cornet of horse—in other words, the younger Pitt's father.

In the sequel, the decision reached reflected beyond a doubt the general feeling of the country. By a majority at least half as large again as his most sanguine adherents had anticipated, Churchill was elected to the presidency of the Tory delegates assembled from the boroughs and counties of the United Kingdom. Had the new chairman no other thought, as he has been credited with possessing, than of his own advancement, he would have been content with his victory. Events had shown clearly that, unless they were prepared to drive him into a hostile camp, the chiefs of Downing Street, as the understrappers of Whitehall, would have to accept Churchill practically on his own terms. It was, in other words, plain that if the general election, then prospectively imminent, were to give the Conservatives a majority, no Administration of which he was not a part could survive a session.

Churchill, therefore, could not have been animated by any purely selfish motive in favour of compromise.

That, however, was the practical issue of

the greatest victory which the "fourth party" had yet won. To Churchill himself, a so-called split in the Conservative connection could have been only a source of profit. The more troubled the waters, the less he had to fear from fishing in them. But he was still anxious to play the game according to the rules. He knew that among the more orthodox of those whom he had already rallied to his side, there was a prejudice not less great against precipitating a party disruption than is excited in a fox-hunting country by the farmer who sets a trap for the Reynard which has robbed his poultry yard.

The newly chosen Chairman of the Tory democracy of England, summoned to that office by the direct voice of the masses them-selves, when he reflected that his new fol-lowing throughout the constituencies must at best be a divided one, and that the impaired efficiency of an inharmonious organisation must either emphasise a Tory defeat at the ballot boxes, or minimise the fruits of a Conserva-tive victory, at once let it be known he was in favour of compromise. In his own eyes, as well as in those of others, he had come to

Sheffield as representative of a great, and, from his point of view, a sound principle, which had already been formulated definitely and explained at length in the pages of the *Fortnightly Review.*

According to this theory, the Conservative reverses sustained at the last appeal to the country were due to the aristocratic and official patronage of local Conservative associations. The Westminster wire-pullers, the Downing Street magnates, the St. Stephen's whips, were the defenders of a highly centralised electoral management—a parliamentary bureaucracy, with its headquarters within speaking distance of the Treasury bench, devoted to execute the behests of traditional authority, and to foster provincial allegiance only on condition that Conservative workers out of London and throughout the country took the same view of Conservative requirements as was held by the Carlton Club's committee and the panjandrums of Whitehall.

The politician, who a year previously had nailed his colours to the mast in the manifesto entitled " Elijah's Mantle," * who,

* See *Fortnightly Review*, April 1883.

since then, had repeatedly pledged himself to employ his popular authority for the adoption of a decentralised form of party management, who was either the head of a Tory democracy or nothing, could not be expected to efface himself, to cancel all his former achievements by converting provincial agencies into offices for the registration of metropolitan decrees.

On one side was the head Conservative committee, nominated by Lord Salisbury and Sir Stafford Northcote, consisting of Lord Henniker, Mr. Whitley, Mr. Thomas Salt, Mr. E. Stanhope, and the party whips.

By the specific promises of his written programme Churchill was pledged to bring back his party's organisation to the point at and the conditions under which it had achieved so great a triumph two decades earlier. That this pledge might be redeemed, it was necessary for him to still oppose that weak but widespreading arrangement "which enervated the vigour of the provincial organisation by focussing all initiative in London." "Unless," he had maintained, "this ceased to be the case, unless, in other words, the secret of

Lord Beaconsfield's theory of government is appropriated, understood, believed in, sown broadcast among the people, unless Elijah's mantle should fall upon some one capable enough and fortunate enough, while carrying with him a united party, to bring to perfection those schemes of social reform and local autonomy which Lord Beaconsfield had only time to dream of, to hint at, and to sketch," Randolph Churchill had maintained consistently that Lord Beaconsfield's great work would be wasted or undone. Churchill was taunted with wishing to raise the committee of the Conservative associations in their National Union to the height of overawing and dictating its action to the London chiefs.

That he had been, with his great and facile receptivity of mind, much impressed by the power which, through the Birmingham organisation, Mr. Chamberlain exercised upon his colleagues in the capital, is likely enough. He was young, ambitious, energetic. He had been treading thus far the uphill path of an opposed career, had been successful precisely in proportion as he had acted independently of his titular superiors, or with the avowed

purpose of forcing their hands. For this, as
for his entire course of indifference to his
superiors' protests, he had the sanction of
historic precedents. It was, as in his latest
written declaration Churchill had reminded his
readers, by allying himself with Lord Palmerston that, "in 1852, Mr. Disraeli had upset
Lord John Russell's Government. It was by
consenting to act with Mr. Gladstone and with
the Radical party in 1857 that Mr. Disraeli
ousted Lord Palmerston. The next year
Disraeli was a second time able to upset
Palmerston because he once more followed
the Radical lead under Mr. Milner-Gibson."

When, in 1874, Mr. Gladstone's great rival
was, for the first time in his life, placed in
power as well as in office, he did not conceal
his conviction that Liberalism was done with
for the rest of the present century.

Six years later the Conservatives were as
hopelessly depressed as in 1874 they had been
exalted. The famous apothegm of the dead
Tory leader, humorously describing, as not very
long before his death, in conversation with
Sir Charles Dilke, he had done, the normal
course of ministries, is, perhaps, less widely

known than it deserves to be. "Your reverses," he said, on the occasion now referred
to, to the gentleman named, "are beginning
a little too early. For governments in general
this should be the order. The first year things
should go pretty well; the second year there
should be mistakes; the third year Ministers
should see, and the country should feel, that
they are mistakes; and in the fourth year
should come the smash."

In the case of the Gladstone Cabinet of
1880 the Beaconsfield programme did not seem
in any fair way of fulfilment. The Administration was now about to enter upon its fifth
twelvemonth. The return of the Tories to
office was in danger of being deferred to the
Greek calends. The old Greek legislator
boasted of having taken the people into
partnership. This is exactly what Churchill—
who, by-the-bye, knew more Greek than most of
his enemies or friends gave him credit for—was
bent upon doing. Consistently he maintained
first that it was necessary for their efficiency that
the Conservatives should not lose the traditions
of office; secondly, that to renew those experiences and avert that evil, it was essential

14

for them to place Mr. Gladstone in a minority
on the first occasion which fortune might offer
or ingenuity create.

As he reminded the world in the document
just quoted from, so recently as 1880, at the
great Bridgewater House meeting of the
party, Lord Beaconsfield had impressed upon
his followers the immense benefit which the
Conservative party had derived from having
been able in 1857 and 1858 to place themselves
in touch with Downing Street once more for
a short period, while the political victory of
1866, following from the coalition between Tory
ultras with malcontent Whigs, whose principles
were even more divergent from modern Conservatism than were the views of Radicalism
itself, had enabled the Tories, reinforced by
Radicals, to hold office for two years, and
during that time to pass a Reform Act, which
laid the foundation of the modern Tory party.

Nor upon this occasion did the writer, with
intelligible complaisance, fail to point out that
seventeen years earlier the erewhile Lord
Cranborne, to-day Marquis of Salisbury, joined
hands with Mr. Bright in the overthrow of
the Conservative Government he had just left,

or that in 1873 Lord Salisbury's master, Mr. Disraeli himself, by a temporary alliance with the Radicals and with the Irish, had defeated Mr. Gladstone on the third branch of the " Irish Upas Tree." The opportunities, it was urged, were daily presenting themselves, but because Lord Beaconsfield's lieutenants were not imbued with his sagacity the chances were not improved.

" Nor," he explained, " would it have been in any way incumbent upon the Conservatives to have taken advantage of any defeat of Mr. Gladstone by grasping at office themselves. To have weakened and discredited the Liberal majority by hostile and repeated attacks would not only have been fair, but in my opinion was imperative in dealing with a Government who had obtained office by methods more un-scrupulous than English politicians had ever yet resorted to."

Now, in words not unlike those which Disraeli himself might have enunciated, come the sum and substance, the essence, epitome, and amalgam of the political philosophy held, or strategical policy pursued, by Disraeli's aptest pupil. "The real moral of Mr.

Disraeli's long parliamentary tactics, which Lord Salisbury probably appreciates, but thinks it inexpedient to explain, is as follows : 'Take office only when it suits you, but put the Government in a minority whenever you decently can. To the first half of this maxim there are no exceptions. To the second half the exceptions are extremely rare, and in dealing with them this rule may be laid down. Whenever, by an unfortunate concurrence of circumstances, an Opposition is compelled to support the Government, the support should be given with a kick, and not with a caress, and should be withdrawn at the first available moment.'"

It was not the enthusiasm of comparative youth, or the optimism of ignorance, which caused Randolph Churchill, in 1884, to paint the possibilities of the immediate future in roseate tints, nor did he fail to base his calculation upon hard facts. Although disorganised, to some extent demoralised, by defeat, the Conservatives throughout the English provinces, in the year now spoken of, were strong, numerous, and confident. At a general election they might then have been expected, as indeed, six months later, they actually did, to carry a considerable number of counties and boroughs. The evil feature of the situation was the irreconcilable hostility to the Tory party of Scotland and Wales. While despairing of any conversion to Toryism in the Principality or in the sister island for the present, Randolph Churchill was satisfied to hint, in words curiously resonant with the Disraelian ring, that, "if Lord Beaconsfield's spirit could for a moment animate his statue, just unveiled by Sir Stafford Northcote at Westminster, an Irish policy might be suggested which would captivate the Celtic race. This, however," he added, "is so dangerous a subject, that I pass from it with haste."

For the rest, the politician who now boldly claimed the succession to Disraeli was content with adopting as his motto the *sanitas, sanitatum, omnia sanitas* jingle, turned to such good account at Manchester, in 1871, by Mr. Disraeli himself. This policy, properly understood and rightly practised, would, he explained, "embrace a social revolution, which, directing attention from wild longings for organic change, and beginning with the little peddling boards of health, would rise to Lord Salisbury's plans for ameliorating the dwellings of the poor, to Lord Carnarvon's ideal of national insurance, would include Sir Wilfrid Lawson's temperance propaganda, would reclaim, or preserve, commons and open spaces as desired by Mr. Bryce, would construct people's parks, while opening to the masses museums, libraries, art-galleries, would not disdain the public wash-houses of Mr. Jesse Collings. Public and private thrift must animate the whole, for it is from public thrift that the funds for these largesses must be drawn, and it is by private thrift alone that their results can be utilised and appreciated."

Next came the vindication of the nomenclature adopted by Churchill for the connection with which he was identified. " The expression, Tory democracy, has excited the wonder of some, the alarm of others, the great and bitter ridicule of the Radical party. It has unfortunately been subjected to some discredit in the lips of Mr. Forwood, the Conservative candidate at the last Liverpool election, who used it without knowing what he was talking

about. But the Tory democracy may yet
exist; the elements of its composition only
require to be collected ; and the labour possibly
may some day be performed by the man, whoever he shall prove, upon whom the mantle of
Elijah has descended."

The programme to which the "fourth
party's" chief stood committed before the
Tory democracy at Sheffield was therefore
perfectly clear and unambiguous. To promote
its practical execution he now agreed that
the whole question of the Conservative associations' presidency should be referred to
the dual controllers of Toryism in either
House of Parliament. This offer, politic or
not, was at least magnanimous. Churchill
was aware he was thus accepting an arrangement by whose terms there would be a practical identity between the advocate and the
judge. That the decision, whatever its exact
nature, must be practically hostile to the
appellant chiefly interested was a foregone
conclusion. His previous experiences, however, not having been entirely lost upon him,
had warned him there was more to hope
from leisurely progress and judiciously timed

self-assertion, than to fear from delay. The award of his two superior officers was what he had expected, and even hoped it would be. The moderates, if they had succeeded in making his own position untenable, thought it prudent to avail themselves of their victory to a very limited degree.

Sir Michael Hicks-Beach by this time scarcely disguised his sympathies with Churchill's belligerency in preference to the tactics of "front bench" inaction, although the traditional restraints of official etiquette compelled him to acquiesce in the prescribed abstinence from more spirited courses.

It was in favour of this clear-visioned, hard-headed, intellectually vigorous politician, that Randolph Churchill, almost within a few days of his original election, resigned the chairmanship. The sequel is now matter of history, and will hereafter be traced more minutely in these pages. The politician, by whom Churchill's opponents had superseded him, gradually became a convert to the Randolphian type of Conservatism, and in this capacity ultimately joined in the revolt against Sir Stafford Northcote, to find himself, on

Sir Stafford Northcote's elevation to the Upper House as Lord Iddesleigh, Chancellor of the Exchequer, and Leader of the House of Commons. Thus, though not in the way he might have imagined or preferred, the Sheffield Congress of 1884, together with the events following from it, signalised incomparably the greatest triumph as a popular and party leader gained by the man whose career we are now following.

The old Athenian law punished with death those who in times of sedition refused to take part with one side or the other ; the assumption, of course, being that the majority would rally round the legally established authority, and that the revolutionary movement not crowned with a certain measure of initial success must hopelessly collapse. In Randolph Churchill's case, the failure which alone makes treason punishable had not, as experience had twice proved, followed upon his audacious independence.

First, in 1880, he had taken his own line with regard to Mr. Bradlaugh, and had compelled his titular chief, already committed to the Gladstonian policy of the select committee, to confess his tactical error, and retrace his steps. Secondly, within a *lustrum*, in the year with which we are now occupied, he had won ✓ the most critical victory possible in these days of political organisation ; and when the attempt was made to oust him from his position, had, with a certain air of condescension, declined to prolong the contest, on the condition, however, as it proved practically to be, that he should, through his superior officers, nominate, in Sir Michael Hicks-Beach, a substitute of his own way of thinking.

The politician who had thus stamped indelibly the characters of his own individuality upon the development of Conservative policy had some reason to think that, as the sole representative of democratic Conservatism in a Cabinet based, like all Cabinets, on the popular vote, his resignation at a date yet to come, of the highest office, next to the Premiership, which a politician could hold, was not likely to be accepted tranquilly by the then head of the Queen's Government.

CHAPTER XII.

THE POLITICIAN'S PASTIMES (1883-4).

*Early signs of exhaustion and fatigue; a life of incessant
excitement with no real rest or pause; Randolph
Churchill's day. — The Carlton Club. — Connaught
Place; Lord and Lady Randolph as entertainers;
constant succession of guests.—The Earl of Lytton,
the Marquess of Dufferin, Fred Burnaby, Condie
Stephen, the Editor of the "Times," etc.—Sunday
luncheon parties in London; the "Fourth Party"
at Lady Dorothy Nevill's, Lady Jeune, etc., etc.—
Saturday to Monday visits to Brighton; the Orleans
Club.—Sir H. D. Wolff, Sir George Wombwell, Sir
Robert Peel.—Saturday to Monday at Baron Ferdinand
de Rothschild's, Waddesdon Manor; description of the
place; the creative power of wealth.—Notable guests;
Sir William Harcourt, Mr. Joseph Chamberlain,
Lord Ribblesdale, Lord Charles Beresford; the late
Sir William Gregory, Baron Huddlestone, Sir Henry
Hawkins; educational value of Gregory's society and
conversation.—Churchill as a classical critic.—The
visit to India; guest of the Viceroy, Lord Dufferin,
of Sir James Fergusson or Lord Reay at Bombay.—
Enlightened views of Anglo-Indian politics, great
popularity with higher-class natives, and not attacked
even in the Anglo-Indian press. — Anglo-Indian
journalists characterised.*

EVEN at this comparatively early period in
his course the natural effects of weeks, months,

even years, passed amidst the excitement of parliamentary manœuvres and the whirl of popular campaigns were beginning to be too visible upon a constitution, capable, indeed, of great exertion, because informed by an indomitable spirit, but never too robust.

His elder brother had already travelled through the greater part of our Indian Empire. Lord Blandford's narratives of Asiatic scenery, sport, and incident appealed strongly to the tastes and imagination of Randolph Churchill. The affairs of Hindostan are never long absent from the scene of parliamentary discussion. Blue-books and volumes of travel illustrative of this subject had been read by him eagerly since his return for Woodstock. His intellectual tastes, resembling in this respect those of the late Duke of Marlborough, were scientific first, and literary afterwards; above all, he possessed the geographical instinct and the topographical organ.

His friend, Mr. Gorst, in his capacity of adviser to the Gaekwar of Baroda, had brought back with him accounts of India profoundly interesting to his chief below the gangway.

Some change from the exhaustions and excitements of Westminster and Pall Mall Randolph Churchill manifestly required. The idea of recreation that should take the form of repose was repugnant to his fervid, restless temperament. The only sort of a holiday he would willingly allow himself was a change of scene, a variation, but not a suspension of excitement. He could never be brought to see that his whole being, physical, mental, and moral, required something more to recruit its habitually spent energies than a week or two at Monte Carlo, with nights passed at the Casino, and with days relieved by racing in pony carriages up and down the Cornice Road; or, in his most sedentary humours, by a rare fortnight's angling in Highland trout-streams; or, perhaps, in the rooms at Newmarket, freshened though these might be by breezes from the contiguous Heath.

In this, as in so many other aspects of his character, Randolph Churchill was the faithful exponent or reflection, the veritable product of his social age.

Polite society has at last come nearer to solving the problem of perpetual motion than it ever yet has done at the most frivolous epochs of its history. The daily chronicle of the *Court Circular* reads like the record of revolutions which never cease, of gyrations through social space that know no pause.

The only perfectly tranquil hours enjoyed by Randolph Churchill since his embarkation on the tempestuous sea of political action and party intrigue were those spent with his wife and children, together with his mother, inside the walls where he had first seen the light ; for the most part, after his brother had become the possessor of Blenheim. Here he led the life of a country gentleman, interested in the personal welfare of cottagers on the family estate who had known him since infancy, sometimes riding, more frequently driving, and occasionally, perhaps, at the due season of the year, bringing down a snipe, or fishing up an eel in that quarter of the park favourable, as has been already described, for such sports. But in a general way his acquaintance with rural scenes, sights, and sounds was made under circumstances which afforded little real change of his London environment.

In that overgrown social organisation for the interchange of modish hospitalities known as the London season, Randolph Churchill crowded into each successive period of twenty-four hours at least as much of diversified sparkling and exacting existence as ordinary mortals succeeded in concentrating into an entire week. At Westminster he was a professional politician, toiling in the lobbies, the smoking-room, or within the Chamber itself, just as if he had been dependent upon the heart-straining, nerve-destroying routine for his daily livelihood.

Like most men of ability, as well as of any social or political mark, he only dined out for a purpose; and infinitely preferred taking his meals at his own well-appointed house in Connaught Place, whose library and drawing-room windows commanded an unbroken view across Hyde Park from the Marble Arch to the Knightsbridge Corner. His luncheon was often consumed at the Carlton Club; the interval was then one not of recreation, but the protraction of the most highly wrought tension, occupied less in the refreshment of physical being than in a series of socio-political reconnaissances or electoral interviews. He took, moreover, scarcely less domestic interest in the Carlton *ménage* than in his own Tyburnian establishment. He never lost his boyish taste for clubs, and displayed something like a neophyte's eagerness in ensuring that no caterer's anachronisms were perpetrated in the joint-stock palace in Pall Mall, that the earliest plovers' eggs from East Anglia were upon the sideboard in spring, and that the larder was replenished by Brobdignagian hams of prime excellence, the production of which was a secret confined to Sir George Wombwell's tenants in the Easingwold district.

Even when he reached his home for lunch or for dinner he kept open house for his friends. At the later of these meals there were celebrities from the four winds of heaven to be entertained during the London season—ambassadors like Lord Dufferin, first from Constantinople, next from Paris, to be received by Lord Randolph with semi-royal state suited to a potentate who unclosed his doors to plenipotentiaries from the Empire's uttermost ends; or, during his period of Parisian service, the late Lord Lytton, son of the man in whom, rightly enough, Randolph Churchill recognised one of the century's forces, had come over on a few days' leave of absence, furnished with despatch loads of Continental and cosmopolitan news such as the French capital alone can yield. There, too, would often be Fred Burnaby, fresh from another expedition like the ride to Khiva; or Mr. Condie Stephen, bringing a budget of unpublished intelligence from the remotest East. Valentine Baker, on furlough from Egypt, where, in the Khedive's service, he had long since renewed his European reputation and retrieved his tarnished laurels, was not unlikely to present himself about the same period beneath this cosmopolitan roof. Lord Wolseley habitually gave *éclat* to these entertainments; and his instructive conversations on the military resources of the British and Oriental Empire of the Queen were eagerly listened to and carefully treasured up by the man who, even before his appointment to it, had sometimes looked longingly upon the Indian Secretaryship of State.

London possessed no more accomplished or

15

charming hostess than the brilliant lady whom, shortly before he entered Parliament, Randolph Churchill had made his wife.   But it was impossible for her or for any other ladies of his family materially to relieve him of the strain constituted by these functions, combining, as they did, for the guests the charm of homely comfort with the splendour of State ceremonial.   For Churchill, in his capacity of host, was never happy till, with the self-sacrificing consideration that is the note of the highest breeding, he had seen all about him at their ease.   Informal and friendly as the host and hostess aimed at making their entertainments, the effort which they entailed on the master and mistress of the house was not the less on that account.

Nothing increases the strain of social functions more than the consciousness of their subserviency to a political end.   There can be no real ease in those private reunions which, for all persons assisting at them, are accompanied by a haunting conviction of time lost, if no visible contribution to the practical end in view seems at any given moment forthcoming.

Digestion and temper, spirit and flesh, soul and body alike, suffer from the wearing intensity of the ordeal; nor are matters much improved and the jaded host more likely to repair the waste of tissue when, on his own guests' dispersion, he seeks relaxation in pursuits that may prolong the vigil to the small hours.

"E'en Sunday dawns no Sabbath day to me." The master of 2, Connaught Place, like many others of his set and of his time, could not have found a more appropriate motto for his weekly existence than the piteous plaint in the prologue to the satires of the Twickenham bard. From the time of Waterloo the first day of the week has been habitually that on which momentous incidents in secular life are pleased specially to enact themselves. If there be a possibility of a Cabinet crisis, the affair is sure to come to a head while the church bells are ringing; if those resorts popularly supposed to be *emporia* of State gossip, "the clubs" as they are vaguely called, but in reality very much less instructive as to their atmosphere than a moderately informed drawing-room, can ever repay the trouble of a visit, it is during the hours which should be consecrated to Sabbath repose.

There were two houses to one or other of which, when he was in London, Randolph Churchill seldom failed to pay a Sunday visit about the luncheon hour. The first of these was the little establishment of the accomplished and experienced Lady Dorothy Nevill, the traditional hostess of the " fourth party " in Charles Street, Berkeley Square, under whose roof amicable meetings, and even cordial reconciliations, of Sir Stafford Northcote and Lord Randolph had more than once taken place. The other was the dwelling of to-day Lady (then Mrs.) Jeune, in Wimpole Street.

Of late years, however, Randolph Churchill cultivated increasingly the habit of inhaling some supply of country air during the interval between one working week's end and another's beginning. In the pretty rooms of the Orleans Club, Brighton, whose windows were full in view of the unbroken sea prospects, the " fourth party " chieftain found as much repose, perhaps, as he was likely to tolerate anywhere. During some years his boy was at a Rottingdean preliminary school; nor was the bright

and joyous father ever more happy than when
he had obtained for his little son an *exeat*
during the mid-day meal in the club dining-
room, at a table whose other occupants were
perhaps the to-day Ambassador at Madrid, Sir
George Wombwell, or Sir Robert Peel.

But the most general haunt of Randolph
Churchill on the summer Sabbaths was the
palace built for himself, on a point of naturally
sterile and almost treeless soil in Buckinghamshire, by Baron Ferdinand de Rothschild. The
south of England probably does not possess a
more conspicuous triumph of art over nature,
a more splendid instance of wealth's creative
power than the Gallic *château*, surmounting a
gentle upland in the home county, known as
Waddesdon Manor. The frontage, with its
glittering spires and golden pinnacles, recalls
the royal state of Fontainebleau or Versailles.
The trees, beneath whose shadow a Churchill
discusses last week's debates with a Harcourt,
the spectacle of the two incomparably beautiful
daughters of Lord and Lady Feversham, the
Ladies Hermione and Helen Duncombe, often
added picturesqueness to the scene, almost
personifying, as in their matchless endowments

of countenance and complexion they seemed to do, the respective loveliness of the morning and evening tints. Nor were directly educational influences wanting to these hospitable occasions. The master of Waddesdon has himself made his priceless collection of *vertu* the object lessons, as it were, of modern history, and can so explain their significance and associations to his visitors as to turn them into real instruments for the increase of their knowledge.

The man who, as I now write, leads the House of Commons, is even among literary persons a noticeable figure. The late Anthony Trollope himself yielded to him in accurate knowledge of Samuel Johnson's epoch, and of the intellectual constellations in the Johnsonian firmament. Especially is Sir William Harcourt familiar with the political and literary history of the period embraced in Sir Lascelles Wraxall's Memoirs. Another habitual, and, for all who were privileged to meet him, most instructive companion at these gatherings was the late Sir William Gregory, formerly member for Galway, who had not only been acquainted intimately with all the leading personages, political, literary, artistic, or scientific of the century, but who had also maintained amid his active career his scholarly attainments, and was never happier than when giving in social intercourse unobtrusive proof of his Greek and Latin scholarship's well-preserved accuracy and elegance.

Sometimes, too, Churchill showed himself not quite to have forgotten the classical reading he had done at Oxford or at Eton, or perhaps before he went to either.

I remember, as it were but yesterday, a discussion started by Gregory on the exact meaning and true translation of the Virgilian words, descriptive of a horse's motion : *Sinuantque alterna volumina crurum.* Randolph Churchill astonished more than one present by a really ingenious and fresh version of these most difficult words, which, while satisfying the literal demands of the scholar in Gregory, fulfilled also the technical requirements of the sportsman as represented by Lord Ribblesdale and Charles Beresford. " I had no idea," good-humouredly exclaimed Sir William Harcourt, " Randolph, you carried so much Latin away from school!"

The fact is, that Churchill had somewhere secreted about him an amount of diversified materials of culture which, if utilised or improved by moderately studious habits, would have surpassed the acquirements in not a few cases of the superior critics who lamented an ignorance that was on their part a pure assumption.

Severer, and, to Randolph Churchill, not less valuable visitors were frequently met with in this Buckinghamshire country house. There, hour after hour, the late Mr. Justice Huddlestone, or the present Sir Henry Hawkins, would unfold for him those stories of social and popular, which, not less than legal knowledge, our judges acquire, and which, to a professional politician, are invaluable. There, too, General Keith-Fraser, than whom the whole question of military organisation possessed no more travelled critic or practical authority, instructed his civilian hearer in the main principles of military defence or expenditure so far as they affected England's political or commercial development.

All this time, we may suppose, Charles Beresford, fresh from his Nile adventures, in

the intervals of lawn tennis or picquet, in the
shade, discusses the mysteries of handicapping
with a Kinsky or Calthorpe ; or, as the representative of their common host, conducts some
of his fellow-visitors to stables, whose four-
legged inmates are only housed less splendidly
than the lord of the manor himself. The
living components of the miniature garden
of acclimation on the central lawn are inhabitants of a pavilion modelled after one at St.
Germains.

If there was ever an Englishman to whom
might be applied the Tacitean phrase, summing up one of the notabilities of a decadent
Empire, *Illi placuerunt magnifici aparatus*, that
man was the politician to whom the preten-
tiousness of British villadom was an abomi-
nation. His eye for the picturesque was less
keen than for the gorgeous ; bright colours,
ample dimensions, large effects—these were
the things that appealed most forcibly to his
imagination. Born in a palace, accustomed
from earliest infancy to broad acres stretching
in endless perspective beyond stately terraces,
his earliest playground a labyrinth of lofty
galleries, a single one of which would almost

have held a regiment, Randolph Churchill had little experience of, and not probably more sympathy with, the modest dimensions of existence in the middle zone of our English polity.

In addition to this, at Waddesdon, as perhaps at other country houses of the same kind, which his own experience does not allow the present writer to describe, Churchill really seemed to re-create his energies.   The favourite pastime of young ladies and æsthetic undergraduates, which consists of hitting a ball over a net, was left by him to such indefatigable athletes as the commander of H.M.S. *Undaunted*, and the present master of the Queen's buckhounds.   For Randolph Churchill there were the vicissitudes of keen observation, with passive repose, from a hammock erected under a cedar that might have come from Lebanon, varied by discussions with Mr. Chamberlain on party organisation, with Sir William Harcourt, now on parliamentary rhetoric as an art, now on the Augustan age in English letters, or, perhaps, the delighted listener to those reminiscences of statesmanship, statesmen, art, literature, diplomacy, which

Sir William Gregory had not then enshrined in a published autobiography.

One thing may be safely said of these occasions, that never was he with whom we have now to do seen to more advantage than at such times and in such company.

Rest, however, was needed ; and to be candid, every one saw that the repose must be sought at some spot more remote from London than the Wimbledon villa to which he repaired a few years earlier, and amid surroundings more restful to the nervous system than the Riviera.

In the November, therefore, of 1884, when there seemed a pause in the party warfare, some time after the temporary settlement of the vexed problems of Conservative organisation and discipline—[the Conservative Associations' presidency being transferred from Sir M. Hicks-Beach, then successively to Lord Claud Hamilton and Mr. Ashmead-Bartlett,]—and of the Franchise Measure, whose negotiations extended from the session into the recess. Randolph Churchill cancelled all his existing engagements on the plea of a condition of health making foreign travel and rest a necessity, proceeded to arrange for the

fulfilment of an ambition he had first conceived when his elder brother returned from
his travels in Hindostan's remotest parts, prepared his outfit, bade his Birmingham friends
a temporary farewell, and, at the end of
November 1884, started for Bombay.

Here he was, on his arrival, as subsequently
on his departure, the guest of Sir James
Fergusson, then Governor of that Presidency,
shortly to be succeeded by Lord Reay. The
itinerary included, of course, all the Presidency capitals. His experiences embraced all
the most famous monuments of the old Mogul
power, all the proudest sights of Anglo-Indian
imperial pomp.

The chief interest of the visit for English
readers lies in the enthusiastic reception given
him by those native advocates of Home Rule
for India to be found among the better-edu-
cated classes of the native populations.

To a degree which he had not himself probably anticipated, these quick-witted subjects
of the English Crown recognised in him the
champion of local autonomy, official decentralisation; the principles of which, in their
application to the organisation of English

parties, he had espoused so earnestly, and, up to a point, so successfully, at the Sheffield Congress.

The truth is, he had now reached a point, alike in his mental development and political career, at which the transition from the irresponsible sharp-shooter of politics, was about to be transformed in the responsible holder of office. Change he certainly had at this epoch, but not rest. As he travelled he mastered from official documents the history and associations of the places he saw, the exact significance of the functions at which he assisted. Macaulay himself never worked harder during his stay beneath the tropical sun than did the " fourth party's " leader.

There are no tribunals of popular opinion more critical than the broad-sheets of our Asiatic dominions. There are no publicists less easy to satisfy, more irreconcilable, to the verge of wrong-headedness, than the gentlemen who comment on the diurnal incidents of British power in the editorial sanctums of Bombay, Calcutta, Madras, or Allahabad. These critics, very often wielders of a finished and effective pen, sometimes endowed with a correct insight into affairs, are, so far as an individual experience may be trusted, journalists with a grievance to a man. No general officer in the Senior United ever protested more vehemently that the Empire, civil, as well as military, was going to the dogs, than the oracles of the Anglo-Indian press.

Either, as they insinuate, the representatives of power on the spot are the servile creatures, the mechanical instruments of the faction which happens to possess power for the moment at Westminster, or else, should they happen to use their own discretion and act on their own initiative, they are arrogant, incompetent, treasonable, jacks-in-office, beggars-on-horseback, who will assuredly, unless speedily removed, light up the flames of another and more destructive Sepoy mutiny, or not rest content till a Cossack captain is acting-Governor at Candahar.

Above all things, these directors of Anglo-Indian opinion profess to hate and despise the English Member of Parliament. It is perhaps little exaggeration to say that no sooner does the representative of a British constituency receive the hospitalities of Government House,

than these publicists would live to deal out to
them the same sort of treatment as that to
which the human fiends of Cawnpore were
subjected in the dire events of four decades
since. Then it is that the editors of these
organs show themselves, during many years
past, to have been keeping their eye upon the
newly arrived political visitor. The unprepared
victim of these attacks in print reads in the
broadsheet of the Presidency whose guest he
happens to be, an account of his past career,
drawn by a fancy whose pen is dipped in gall,
a disquisition on his private and social life, by
a word-painter, whose colours are supplied
alternately from the palette of ignorance and
the brush of rancorous invention.

The experience of journalistic criticism
acquired by Churchill in England might possibly have prepared him for some of these
onslaughts in India. As a matter of fact, not
a pen was raised against him. No arrogance
was discovered in his manner, no ridiculous
assumption was detected in his talk. The fact
is, that when Randolph Churchill pleased to
be so, there could exist no more delightful
companion, more perfectly equipped with that

courtesy which has happily been defined as
"generosity in small things," no politeness
more deferential, no urbanity more unruffled.
If in England he often showed in his demeanour attributes the reverse of these, the first
explanation is the uncongeniality of the environment wherein he found himself; the second, as
is now generally known, was the unsatisfactory
condition of his health, threatened, as it had
been long before its actual failure, by a subtle
as well as a morally, physically, and intellectually disorganising disease. Nor were his
Indian successes only those of the social or
popular kind. The most capable and critical
body of public servants known throughout the
civilised world, as the Anglo-Indian bureaucracy
unquestionably is, was impressed profoundly by
the justice, the liberality, and the originality of
his views.

CHAPTER XIII.

POPULAR PROGRESS, 1884; *CO-EQUAL LEADER-
SHIP WITH OFFICIAL CHIEFS.*

*Randolph Churchill's career helped, not hindered, by
official opposition; carries all his points; leads Opposition to Liberal Reform procedure in session and
recess of* 1884.—*Manchester and Carlisle demonstrations.—Reform Bill passed Autumn session* 1884.

BEFORE Lord Randolph Churchill started
for India Mr. Gladstone had fulfilled his
promise of completing the electoral reforms,
introduced by Mr. Disraeli in 1867, by em-
bodying in a Bill the proposal so often laid
before Parliament in private motions by Mr.
G. O. Trevelyan, for the extension of Household Suffrage from boroughs to counties. The
objections taken by the House of Lords to the
Ministerial measure had been avowedly based
not on principle but procedure. The hereditary
legislature's contention was that the Prime

Minister should bring forward his whole scheme
at once, accompanying the enfranchisement
proposals with a scheme for redistribution of
seats. That demand was supported by Randolph Churchill. The Conservative party,
therefore, during the year 1884, found its
attention divided between two momentous
topics—the first, that of party organisation,
about which enough for our present purpose
has already been said ; the second, the policy
to be adopted by the Tory leaders in the
representative chamber towards the Government on the one hand and the Conservative
peers on the other.

In the course of the first fortnight in
May, it will be remembered, the Sheffield
differences had been composed by the resignation of Randolph Churchill as chairman,
by his persistent refusal to accept the honour
of re-election upon any terms ; in fact, by his
practical abdication in favour of Sir Michael
Hicks-Beach. This arrangement, however,
had no sooner been arrived at than the champions of the Constitution began once more to be
at feud amongst themselves as to the course to
be adopted with regard to the Franchise Bill.

Unqualified resistance to a measure that was the logical corollary to the admission by Mr. Disraeli of the urban householder within the pale of the Constitution was of course out of the question.

Early in the month of May 1884, the Conservative party met in conference at the Carlton Club, under the presidency of their titular leaders, among whom Randolph Churchill, in virtue of his acceptance of the Northcote-Salisbury award respecting the Associations' presidency, had a prominent place. It was, however, premature to assume that he had renounced the right of private judgment, or merged the privilege of independent action in his general toleration of Toryism's dual control. In the House of Commons, Mr. St. John Brodrick proposed an amendment which would have involved the rejection of the measure.

Previously, following upon a series of votes of censure for their Egyptian policy, brought forward against Ministers by Conservatives, a number of attacks upon Mr. Gladstone's new Reform Bill had been made. Randolph Churchill now refused to be accessory to one of these efforts at overthrowing the measure, or to regulate his vote in the House of Commons by Mr. Brodrick's amendment. It would have been indeed a plain violation of his pledges to the democracy whom he hoped to Conservatise had he met with any unqualified negative Mr. Gladstone's scheme for crowning that edifice of parliamentary liberties which Churchill's master, Mr. Disraeli himself, had in all but its actual entirety raised. The precise terms of Lord Cairns' amendment, which, July 6th, 1884, carried in the Upper House, would have indefinitely postponed reform, pledged the peers to concurrence in a well-considered scheme for the extension of the franchise, and only to reject a measure which, while providing for the wholesale creation of new constituencies, was not accompanied by provisions for ensuring that the new machinery should not come into operation except upon an entire scheme. This amendment had been carried by 205 votes to 146 in the Hereditary Chamber within a month of the date traditionally fixed for the session's close. Mr. Gladstone's reply to the hostile demonstration of the hereditary legislators was a brusque statement that the Franchise Bill would reappear in an autumn session. The whole recess, therefore, of the year now being dealt with, was given up to political agitation throughout the country.

Randolph Churchill's antagonism to the Liberal statesman, that had begun with the Bradlaugh question nearly five years earlier, now entered upon its acutest phase. The charge against the Prime Minister, first formulated in the House of Commons, then reiterated with all those additions and embellishments of popular invective suitable for provincial platforms, was that by needlessly withholding the chief details of the enfranchisement clauses, the Liberal leader was guilty of "a criminal and dissolute waste of public time," not for the purpose of widening the pale of popular privileges, but with a view, disingenuously concealed by him, of fomenting an agitation during the summer months against the House of Lords.

"If," Lord Randolph Churchill contended, "the Peers had been dealt with in a decently civil manner by the Premier, they were generally prepared to approach the whole question with open, unprejudiced, and impartial

minds.   If," he said, on the third reading, " the
Premier had addressed the House of Commons
in the tone and manner in which afterwards
he declared the Ministerial purposes with reference to redistribution, no conflict between
the two Houses would have been provoked,
and long before July the measure would have
advanced well on its way towards receiving
the Royal assent."

" The constitutional crisis was provoked,"
according to Lord Randolph, " entirely by the
President of the Local Government Board,
and by a silly person of the name of Schnadhorst.   The Liberal party in Parliament wished
for nothing less.   They were not prepared for
it ; they could not turn it to any good account."
But the person named " Schnadhorst," in
whom, just then, Randolph Churchill affected
to recognise the incarnation of all political evil,
" was meeting somewhere with his myrmidons
in the back slums of Westminster in order to
concert measures for supporting their great
master and their great friend."

Randolph Churchill taunted Mr. John
Morley, and Mr. Gladstone himself, with a
timid reluctance directly to challenge the Upper

House to a formal contest, by impeaching them in the Commons.

" I know," he said, " that there are honourable gentlemen, particularly the member for Newcastle" (Mr. John Morley), "and the member for Ipswich " (Mr. Jesse Collings), " who are very fond of getting up in this House, and then careering about the country and calling themselves the people of England."

This burst of rhetoric led on the speaker to compare these gentlemen with the animal to whose asinine mind it occurred that great power, dignity, and profit would accrue to him by his investment of himself in the lion's skin ; " but surely," he warned the First Lord of the Treasury, " no one ought to know better than himself that it is the easiest thing in the world to detect the difference between the demagogue's bray and the people's roar."

These, and many other like declarations at Westminster, after the prorogation, before the Indian visit, had been followed up by speeches emphasising the same argument, pitched in much the same key, with such variations as time and place appeared to prescribe, throughout the great industrial centres of England.

On these occasions Randolph Churchill was accompanied generally by Sir Michael Hicks-Beach, who, as his nominee, had occupied the place in the Associations' committee vacated by Churchill, as also by Sir Stafford Northcote and Lord Salisbury; for both these states-men had in effect surrendered to Randolph Churchill at discretion, and had conceded those conditions of local autonomy and freedom of provincial initiative in the work of Con-servative organisation for which Churchill had contended.

Thus, notwithstanding his nominal discom-fiture in the metropolis of the West Riding, Lord Randolph was now confessed by his titular chiefs to be not less indispensable than themselves to the leadership of the party. Instead of being, as it was under the North-cote-Salisbury arrangement, a dual control, it had become a triumvirate, the lead in which was taken practically by the creator of the "fourth party."

Churchill, even where he had seemed to suffer eclipse, was now practically triumphant along the whole line throughout the entire Kingdom. Ostensibly, indeed, he appeared

as the follower of, and spoke in deference to
the Devonshire baronet and the Hertfordshire
marquis, but the multitudes who cheered him
knew instinctively, and recognised applausively,
the fact that a Salisbury and a Northcote
appeared by permission, and spoke under the
patronage of the erewhile mutineer.

Throughout the first half of the recess deep
answered to deep ; the challenge thrown down
the first week on one platform was taken up
and answered the second week on another.
Thus it was that on August 8th a Liberal
attack on the Lords at Manchester a few
days earlier elicited a counter demonstration of their constitutional supporters almost
immediately afterwards.

The whole summer of 1884 bore testimony
to the established and sustained influence of
Randolph Churchill, alike in the councils of his
party and in the country.

Now, for the first time, he achieved in the
great manufacturing capitals of Lancashire the
same kind of popularity and influence which
he had won in the Oxfordshire market town
that had witnessed his birth and that contained
his constituency. The last fortnight of July

beheld, as has been said, a mass meeting of Liberals on the Irwell to strengthen Mr. Gladstone's hands in his reform struggles against the House of Lords. The first week in August there was held in the same city, and in the same place, the Pomona Gardens, a responsive meeting to protest against Caucus dictation, and to support the House of Lords' demand for a complete Reform Bill.

The same enthusiasm now welcomed alike Lord Salisbury, Randolph Churchill, Mr. Chaplin, and Sir Michael Hicks-Beach as they took their places at the rostrum. Churchill's speech had, as its refrain, the assertion of the Tory party, so often previously made by Mr. Disraeli, as by all the members of the Young England clique successively, to the real championship of the popular cause, and the indefeasible claim of "those beautiful spirits and swift," who, from the days of Falkland to Bolingbroke, or to those of "Canterbury Smythe" himself, had been Conservatism's leading lights, to rescue the multitude from misrepresentation by Radical ochlocrats.

His opening words struck, as usual, the keynote of Churchill's speech. "The Radical

party, with Mr. Gladstone at its head, is out-
raged and indignant with the Tories because
we have adopted as our party cry, ' Appeal to
the people ! ' "

By this time Randolph Churchill's platform
style was fully formed ; it was unlike his House
of Commons manner in many respects. His
opening sentences enunciated the burden,
refrain, and outline of his address ; his vivacity
enabled him to hold his audience's attention
without flagging till the last sentence of the
address was reached. The very appeal for
which the Conservatives contended was,
according to Churchill, then actually in process ; "the only difference between the operation, as advocated by the Tories and carried out
by the Liberals, being the former's insistence
that the popular judgment should be ratified by
the popular vote, and the latter's shrinking
from the ordeal of a dissolution. The great
feature of the nation's political history since
1832 was the growth of popular Toryism,
because, as at the commencement of the
eighteenth century, so at the end of the
nineteenth, that party was showing it to be
the one which protects popular freedom, which

defends and enlarges popular rights, which neither grinds, nor drives, nor tyrannises over the people, but which seeks ever a fair and free and full expression of the nation's will ; and," he continued, " it is because we have truth upon our lips, honesty in our hearts, and patriotism and love of our great Empire and the Queen overruling and guiding all our acts, that we are able to meet, without shame, the men of Lancashire assembled in their thousands to-day."

One quality was possessed by Randolph Churchill in a degree not inferior to that in which it had been forthcoming with Mr. Disraeli throughout his early electioneering campaigns—the cool audacity of dealing with an opponent's taunt, founded upon notorious facts, as if it were only a malignant and baseless fiction.

The domestic condition of Conservatism at this epoch was known to be one not merely of disorganisation, but of positive dissolution. The party was, in fact, reduced to its elements ; the presence that day in the cotton capital of a Churchill, as a Salisbury's co-equal, proved this to be the case. If, that is to say, the

Conservative discipline had been what it was during Disraeli's life, Randolph Churchill would not have been suffered to have a place on the same platform as Disraeli's titular successor until he had worn the white sheet of penitence in Downing Street, or had burned the candle of contrition before Arlington House. He had done none of these things. He had openly gloried in his obduracy, had defied the mandate, violated the traditions of the Westminster chief; had converted his resignation of the Sheffield chairmanship into a practical triumph, not less than a moral victory, by successfully exacting from the two arch-controllers of the party those adaptations to local requirements which he considered to be necessary for the effective discipline of the Conservative forces, and which had been so long unconditionally denied.

To-day, at Manchester, nothing made this despot of his party more indignant than the manner in which Radical orators " perambulated the country, declaiming about Tory disunion. Well," he added, "let them! We know," he continued, in the veritably Disraelian vein, "that Tory disunion is a phantom and a fiction, the ridiculous figment of a disordered and dissipated Liberal imagination."

Next, the Manchester orator proceeded to turn the tables upon his opponents. " So far from there being any such thing as Tory disunion, it was the Radicals who were at loggerheads with each other. On the one hand, were the two great Liberal leaders, the Premier and Lord Hartington, declaring that they will be no party to abolishing the House of Lords ; on the other hand, were the Radical swarms crying out that the abolition of the Peers is the only thing they care for, that the Franchise Bill is a stalking-horse which they cannot be troubled with any longer when the demolition of the Peers seemed to be within their grasp."

As for the hereditary legislators lacking confidence in the people, and therefore withholding from them suffrage, Churchill solemnly assured his hearers this was an impudent lie. By insisting on redistribution, the Peers only showed their desire to make improved representation immediate and certain, rather than distant and doubtful. " There was, however," he admitted, " one set of persons in whom the House of Lords had no confidence. But these were not the people of England, but the Ministers of the Crown. Herein the hereditary legislators were truly reflecting the national spirit, and therefore, at this moment, were in more entire harmony with their fellow-countrymen than they have ever been."

It is to be noticed that these are the arguments, almost the exact words, in which, just ten years later, Lord Salisbury described and justified the action of the aristocratic chamber towards Mr. Gladstone's Home Rule legislation. Randolph Churchill committed mistakes of judgment, temper, and taste ; but to condemn the general results of his career is to denounce the fundamental and most vivifying articles of the Conservative creed, as these have been held and acted upon by the most orthodox pillars of the Constitution, from the time of Bolingbroke to that of Chatham, from Chatham to Canning, from Canning to Disraeli. For at least two decades all the national victories won by Conservatives have been secured on the "popular ticket," to use the American phrase. The tactics with which Randolph Churchill's name will always be identified, whatever their merits in themselves, have, and alone have, stood the test of experience, and received the prestige of success. From the time of his maiden speech at Westminster in 1874 he had been consistently what he now was.

From the first of his great platform efforts at Hull, on the last day of 1881, when perhaps he first won the ear of the country by his invectives against the Parnell agitation, by his identification of Liberalism with high treason, and by the comparison, spirited enough, and at least original, between Mr. Disraeli and Mr. Gladstone as party leaders, Randolph Churchill had shown entire consistency with himself.

Without most of Mr. Bernal Osborne's humour or wit, he at least possessed that Irishman's entire lack of guile. He never dissimulated antipathies by fair words, never cloaked ignorance by specious pretence of knowledge, and from the day when he first scandalised the political prudes of Westminster by defining the business of an Opposition as to oppose, never disguised the tactics of party in the cant of patriotism.

Two things Churchill knew better than any

political Telemachus could teach him : first, the political temper of the masses he addressed ; secondly, the language in which he could most effectively convey his ideas to them. So it was at Manchester in the August of 1884.

Having ascertained by experience the innate capacity of the Liberal party for the falsification of political truth, Churchill confessed himself to have been anxious for a moment as to the issue of the conflict provoked by the courage of the Lords. Manchester, however, had reassured him. His confidence now would never waver. " That the British nation having to decide between the House of Lords and its long centuries of tradition on the one hand, and the faults and the follies and the failures of Mr. Gladstone's four years' government on the other, they will, by their wisdom, by their knowledge, and by higher than earthly guidance, award the palm and the honour and the victory to those who, conscious of the immeasurable responsibilities attaching to an hereditary House, have dauntlessly defended, against an arbitrary Minister, the ancient liberties of our race." This is not the sort of speech that the people

17

of Manchester, or of any other place, would have heard from Randolph Churchill's more philosophical and encyclopædic contemporaries, such as Lord Arthur Russell, or Sir Mount-Stuart Grant-Duff. But it is very much the kind of address that, under analogous circumstances, Mr. Disraeli might have delivered ; and as platform rhetoric it reaches a high level of merit, and the furthest point of popular efficiency.

To the eve of the Indian visit, which practically began just as in the Autumn Session the reintroduced Reform Bill, after a good deal of negotiation and amateur diplomacy, conducted by other than statesmen, even by a popular ecclesiastic, acting as intermediary between Mr. Gladstone and Lord Salisbury was read a third time and passed, the extra parliamentary utterances of Randolph Churchill were continued with unabated zeal.

The final speech of the series was that on October 8th, at Carlisle, concluding, as it did, with a description of Liberal politicians as " clouds without water, blown about by the wind ; wandering stars, whose helplessness would compel the English people to turn to

the united and historic party which can alone
re-establish your social and Imperial interests,
and can alone proceed safely, steadily, and
surely along the broad path of social progress
and reform."

CHAPTER XIV.

CHURCHILL AND BIRMINGHAM (1884-5).

A SEPARATE chapter must be allotted to
Randolph Churchill's connection with Birmingham, marking, as the events associated
with it do, the culminating point of interest
and significance in his career as a popular
Tory chief.

During 1883 Mr. John Bright had completed a quarter of a century's parliamentary service as member for the Midland capital. The anniversary was celebrated with popular rejoicings of all kinds, processions and fireworks out of doors; presentations of illuminated addresses, as well as a service of plate and a painting of the veteran tribune within doors. No political position could have seemed more impregnable than that of the great Anglo-Saxon orator in his Birmingham constituency. None, therefore, held out greater inducements to Randolph Churchill for his attack. The Fourth Party's leader had, in fact, during the October following the Bright jubilee, made a visit of electoral reconnaissance to this Radical stronghold, being entertained at a banquet in the Aston Lower Grounds, as well as taking part in a conference of the National Conservative Union at the Masonic Hall, when addresses had been delivered by Lord Cranbrook, Lord Dartmouth, Colonel Burnaby, and himself.

The next year, 1884, the local Tories, in the interests of the Altar and the Throne, determined to reproduce the popular displays

of their opponents a twelvemonth earlier.
Lord Randolph Churchill, as the now undisputed chief of active Conservatism, with Sir
Stafford Northcote, other leading Tories, and
his own personal friend Fred Burnaby, were
invited to take part in the proceedings, the
first item in the programme being a garden
party at Aston.   On this occasion Churchill
gained his earliest experience of a former
and most characteristic phase of Birmingham party warfare.   Mr. Chamberlain's ther
followers had placarded and distributed througn-
out the town circulars protesting against the
Tory invasion, denouncing the Churchill-
Burnaby party in the usual style.   The first
object of this faction was, if possible, to prevent, if not to mar, the Aston Lower Grounds
function.   By way of giving effect to that
purpose, they fabricated and dispersed among
the lowest classes of the inhabitants an immense
number of admission tickets to the afternoon
festivity's scene.   The Conservative stewards,
hearing of the device, closely scrutinised every
proffered admission order, and rejected many
bearers of counterfeit cards.   Upon this he
excluded visitors improvised a meeting of their

own outside the Tory precincts, when the rhetoricians of the local "stump" kindled in their hearers the fire of attack, and, imploring them to abstain from violence, inspired them with an incontrollable impulse to scale the wall which separated them from the garden guests.

The waggon that had served as a platform for the speakers was at once drawn up outside the barrier. In a very few minutes the invaders had poured into the forbidden enclosure, and had even razed to the ground the obstructive brickwork. Meanwhile, ladders, which previously had been smuggled into the gala area, probably by confederates, playing the part of Sinon at the fall of Troy, were placed against the intercepting structure to facilitate the movements of the attacking mob, before whose onset an entirely inadequate police force had rapidly retreated. The "set pieces," triumphs of the pyrotechnic art, were destroyed or ignited by the rioters.

Havoc and confusion followed. The doors of the great hall, in which the speeches were to have been delivered, were battered in with long planks as rams. Immediately, within the covered area sacred to the Conservative orators, a pitched battle ensued. Chairs, small tables, and other missiles which presented themselves, were hurled to and fro. Meanwhile, Lord Randolph and Sir Stafford Northcote were surrounded by a bodyguard of stalwart young Tories, under whose protection they succeeded in reaching the Assembly Room attached to the Holte Hotel. Here a few speeches were delivered, the chief guest and figure of the occasion, Randolph Churchill himself, having received no injury beyond a battered hat, preserving perfectly unruffled composure. He had never shown such command over a mob as in the stinging sentences whose every word went home like a well-aimed pistol-bullet. He began with expressing his "deep and intense pity for the Birmingham Radicals, because of their behaviour to a statesman—Sir Stafford Northcote—by far the wisest that England possesses." "It is," he said, "to Mr. Chamberlain that we owe to-night's scandalous proceedings." This gentleman was said "to look upon the Town Hall of Birmingham as his private property, just as much as he does that great red-brick house which he occupies outside the town."

Notwithstanding the nature of his initial reception by the constituency he aspired to represent, Churchill had, in fact, won a political and personal triumph. The remarkable pluck and temper displayed by a man whose courage came from other causes than his physique created an impression of admiration and confidence in him which nothing afterwards diminished. Two or three weeks later he fulfilled his promise of "drawing the badger"—in other words, of bringing the whole incident before the House of Commons, and re-emphasising to Mr. Chamberlain's face the charges which he had only as yet been able to formulate in his absence. The incriminated statesman repudiated any knowledge of the matter, while on another occasion, dealing with the forged admission tickets, he produced affidavits rebutting the accusation. Ultimately the case was thoroughly sifted at the Birmingham Police Courts, when it was proved that some of the roughs had perjured themselves for a few pounds. The fabricating process had been carried out with remarkable ingenuity, the chief or only discernible difference between the original and the copy being the faint modification of a single letter.

After the Franchise Bill, with its accompanying re-distribution scheme parcelling out the Midland metropolis into seven parliamentary divisions, had become law, Randolph Churchill reaped the preliminary reward of his courage by being definitely chosen to contest Central Birmingham against John Bright.

Conservatism in Birmingham had, indeed, already made strides towards success, which only just before the dawn of the Randolphian era would have seemed impossible. The negotiations for his candidature were conducted mainly through his friend and colleague Colonel Burnaby, Mr. Joseph Rowlands, and Sir James Sawyer. The result showed that against any other opponent than Mr. Bright the latter-day founder of militant Toryism would have had something more than a mere chance of success.

The Conservative tactics in the other six divisions of the city were cleverly contrived. Mr. Chamberlain was occupied by the opposition of Mr. Dumfries. In North Birmingham Mr. Kenrick was engaged by

Mr. Henry Matthews, while Mr. Hawkes, a converted Liberal, was put up against Mr. Powell Williams, and Mr. J. W. Showell, a wealthy brewer, was pitted against Mr. Broadhurst for Bordesley. In East Birmingham Mr. W. Low opposed Mr. Alderman Cook, and in Edgbaston Sir Eardley Wilmot entered the lists as antagonist to Mr. George Dickson. In all the divisions the Liberals were thus fully pre-occupied.

Meanwhile, Randolph Churchill had been elected President of the Midland Conservative Club, and within its precincts was waiting the result of the poll. " I am afraid," he said, alluding to the rather downcast appearance of Mr. E. J. Abbott, who brought in occasional tidings of progress, " our Secretary is a bird of ill-omen. Go and see," he continued, to a friend who was standing near, " if you can bring better news."

To enliven the not too sanguine company, the candidate was called on for a speech. " No," was the reply; " I am now cogitating two orations—one in case of victory, the other in the event of defeat. I will, therefore, pass the torch to my friend Mr. Matthews, and ask him to address you in my stead." Eventually Mr. Bright was declared the victor by a majority of 773, the figures being 4,989 to 4,216.

Certain provincial jokers present up to the very last made small efforts to lighten the interval of suspense. A few moments before the issue was announced a local wag cried out, " Randolph's in!" The shout inspired the more credulous of the company with the customary demonstrations of joy, such as the jumping upon chairs and tables, the throwing up of hats and pockethandkerchiefs. These paroxysms of hilarity having somewhat subsided, the unconscionable jester repeated, " Yes, Randolph's in—in the Club!" after which, wisely enough, he made a rapid exit from the room.

The tidings were received by the person immediately interested with calmness and even cheeriness. " It was what he had expected, but he could not see ultimate defeat in the incident, but only added impetus to further vigour and perseverance. An Englishman who did not know how to take a knockdown blow was not worth a rap."

It was, under the circumstances, no small feat to have come within a few hundreds of the great tribune; and Churchill reaped some reward for his courage in being returned for South Paddington at once.

In the first month of the following year, the elections having given to Mr. Gladstone a parliamentary majority, Mr. Chamberlain put up Mr. Jesse Collings to move the "three acres and a cow" amendment, which had the effect of defeating the Tory ministerialists, of eliciting Lord Salisbury's resignation, and of once more installing Mr. Gladstone in his place. Contrary to the anticipations which had been formed in some quarters, Sir William Harcourt was appointed Chancellor of the Exchequer, while Mr. Chamberlain himself became President of the Local Government Board, and justly recognised Mr. Collings' effective fidelity by nominating him Parliamentary Secretary.

After this there occurred the decisive disruption of Liberalism on the Home Rule question, followed by the formation of the Unionist party, with its Liberal and Conservative wings. Shortly before Mr. Gladstone's appeal to the country in June, an amicable *rapprochement* took place, and communications, close as constant, passed between the erewhile object of the Aston riots and their incorrectly alleged inciter. The National Union Alliance was, in fact, the combined work of Mr. Chamberlain and Lord Randolph Churchill. By the terms of this compact, it was decided that, in consideration of the Conservatives allowing Mr. Jesse Collings, who had been unseated on petition at Ipswich, to be returned without a contest for the Bordesley division, Mr. John Bright being unopposed for Central Birmingham, the Tories should, as of right, occupy the next parliamentary vacancy in the town. This is the precise tenor of that Birmingham compact of which so much has been said.

The circumstances signalising the instrument's genesis were of good Conservative omen; for Mr. Matthews, subsequently Home Secretary, defeated Mr. Alderman Cook by close upon 800 votes—a triumph which was, beyond doubt, largely, if not chiefly, attributable to the admirable management of Sir James Sawyer, then President of the

Birmingham Conservative Association. Mr. John Bright's death, March 27th, 1889, created the vacancy which, by the agreement specified above, the Liberals were pledged to enable their fellow-Unionists on the Conservative side to fill. But when Lord Randolph was invited to present himself, he again adopted a course not unlike that which he had pursued at Sheffield in 1884 ; he was, that is to say, persuaded to place himself in the hands of his friends ; and after conference with Mr. Arthur Balfour, that he might not sever his connection with Paddington, threw over his Birmingham supporters.

The local disappointment was, of course, keen ; and the issue being what it was, there are naturally those who question whether Randolph Churchill's services to the Conservative cause in the Midlands were at all commensurate with those which he rendered in other parts of the country. The greater the distance which separated him from the Tory headquarters in London, the more successful Randolph Churchill's Conservative championship ever was. Notwithstanding the intense citizenship which is a dominant characteristic of Birmingham, its inhabitants do not, after all, differ very much from the average middle-class Londoners ; and however it is to be accounted for, Churchill's temper and rhetoric were alike more congenial to the shrewd aborigines of the County Palatine and to the north, than to the less sympathetic audiences of the more southern shires.

If, on the occasion now referred to, Randolph Churchill had acted in the spirit that so often animated his writings, and, setting at nought the appeals from headquarters, had told those of his admirers at Birmingham, who were ever ready to dare and do all things on his behalf, that he trusted himself to them, and that with them rested the responsibility, the appeal, so far as can be judged, might have resulted in an unprecedented victory alike for the individual, for the Conservative cause, and for its Birmingham adherents.   As it was, the issue proved one thing, and one alone conclusively—that, notwithstanding the existence or non-existence of any contract to the contrary, Mr. Chamberlain's authority throughout the Midlands was so paramount as to induce Conservative and Liberal Unionists alike to act upon the known, though not perhaps expressed, indication of his will. How far this gentleman might, or might not, have been disposed to forward the candidature of Randolph Churchill it is profitless to speculate, because the time has not yet arrived when the documentary evidence that settles the matter can, with due respect to the feelings of those still among us, be published; suffice it to say, as in Mr. Chamberlain's own words I am enabled to do, that the personal friendship between the two politicians was not broken by the Aston Grounds incident, and that long before his friend and rival died all which needed it had been on both sides " forgotten and forgiven." One thing may be submitted with some certainty. If the leader of the Tory "forwards" had, on Mr. Bright's death in 1889, presented himself, he would have found the local Conservatives deeply divided.

For the purpose of this monograph it is interesting to note that the same kind of popularity which, as a boy at school, or an undergraduate at Oxford, he had won among his set, was secured by Churchill during his various visits to Birmingham, where all per-

sons had been touched by the display of
Colonel Fred Burnaby's loyalty to his friend,
as they were impressed · also by Churchill's
grateful reciprocation of the virtue.

Neither felicity nor pathos was wanting in
the allusion made by the survivor to his colleague's death in Egypt in the speech delivered
by Churchill shortly after that event.   " He
was," so ran Churchill's tribute of October
23rd, 1885, "not only one of my closest and
most intimate friends, but one upon whom,
on every occasion, I could confidently rely.
I had looked forward to taking part in this
contest together with him, and had counted
upon being supported by his indomitable
courage, his unfailing and cheering good
humour."   Nor was Randolph Churchill impressed less by the fidelity of his Midland
friends than by that of his Midland parliamentary ally.

Randolph Churchill further marked his
appreciation of Birmingham's kindness by
presenting to the Conservative Club one
hundred and forty volumes of the " Annual
Register," chronicling the period between 1753
to 1893.

On resigning the Chancellorship of the Exchequer, he was, though not unanimously, re-elected President; and his comment on the dissentient voices upon this occasion, " I never thought any member of the Club would have said an unkind word of me," showed the genuineness of his local attachments.

His last visit to Birmingham was paid when the signs of his health's failure were only too visible, and, as he quitted the Club, he left behind him a legacy of melancholy apprehensions too faithfully and too soon to be realised. In these brilliant days, however, now being dealt with, none of the coming shadows had projected themselves.

Never can the metropolis of hardware have beheld a more dazzling and fascinating pair than Randolph Churchill and the graceful and accomplished lady who here, as elsewhere, was ever her husband's most effective vote winner and helper. During the elections of 1885 Lady Randolph Churchill presented at Birmingham a conspicuously picturesque figure, driving about in a dainty tandem securing suffrages wherever she turned her horses' heads.

While Lord and Lady Randolph were the guests of Mr. Joseph Rowlands, a public garden party was given in their honour, and was the occasion of an incident that much appealed to the popular imagination. A poor old woman coming into the grounds made her way up to Lady Randolph, asking a flower from the bouquet she was carrying " to take it back to a good Conservative, her bed-ridden husband at home." The request was smilingly granted, and was immediately pre-ferred by a succession of new applicants who suddenly presented themselves. Without hesi-tation, the nosegay's mistress untied the ribbons holding the blossoms together, and, throwing them into the air, invited the little crowd to scramble for them, while the coveted souvenirs were carried off amid cheers.

The triumphant progress of the Conservative candidate and his wife extended from the environs of Birmingham to a considerable por-tion of the county of Warwick, in which they visited, among other places, Haseley Hall, the seat of Sir James Sawyer, who from the first laboured diligently to promote his guest's can-didature for the constituency of John Bright.

CHAPTER XV.

EDUCATIONAL RESULTS OF INDIAN VISIT
(1885).

Letters from home waiting at Brindisi.—The Cambridge Carlton Club; speech there delivered, showing educational influences of Indian visit; great mental qualities in Randolph Churchill's equipment.—Justice not generally done by the London press to him, except the " Times."—His relations with Mr. Chenery and Mr. Buckle.—Bad results of London journalists' coolness; Randolph Churchill and Aristotle's politics.—A discussion on " la petite" culture at the Orleans Club, between Randolph Churchill and Mr. Shaw Lefevre. —" Reading up" the subject.

WHEN RANDOLPH CHURCHILL, on his home-ward journey from India in the early spring of 1885, reached Brindisi, he found a letter of interest, and, as the result proved, of some fruit-fulness, awaiting him. It was from the committee of the Cambridge University Carlton Club, reminding the Fourth Party leader of a long-standing promise to visit the capital on the Cam as the guest of this particular society, some representatives of whom had, before he started for India, waited upon him in Connaught Place personally to convey the request. The incident has an autobiographical interest, and should therefore be described, as far as possible, in his own words.

There had been during 1884 a time when he happened to be engaged in something partaking of the nature of a struggle, or, at any rate, in a difference of opinion (such are the mildly euphuistic terms in which he spoke of his war to the knife with his own front bench), with men of great position, men of great responsibility, and men of great experience, as to the form which modern Conservative political organisation ought to take. "Well, that difference of opinion at one time became very sharp. I did not know what the result of it might be, and I was getting extremely anxious more for the sake of the Conservative party than for my own. One evening I came home from the House of Commons very anxious and rather discouraged, because there, among the people whom I ought to regard as my friends, I had met nothing but gloomy looks ; and I felt very much inclined to retire from the game, thinking I was doing more harm than good, and rather, to use a slang expression, disposed to cut the whole concern."

On reaching his house, he found the Cambridge deputationists expecting him—three of the most accomplished and able envoys ever sent out on any mission; the only error they committed being, that, instead of going into his house and waiting for him there, with whatever accommodation that dwelling might afford, "they had been waiting for me some time in the street."

In his depressed mood the expressed sympathy and cordial invitation of the academic emissaries refreshed the jaded politician, and filled him with hopes that, after all, he was not going very far wrong, and so encouraged him to persevere.

"Everything," he said cheerily, "settled down, and did come all right, both to the harmony, and I think to the advantage of the Tory party." The invitation had, in fact, been, in his own words, "an encouragement from youth to youth." During his progress from the Italian seaport to the English capital the guest of the evening pondered "what on earth he was going to say at the dinner," because he knew, from experience, a University audience to be more critical than a political audience.

Anticipating, in the June of 1885, just two days before the event actually occurred, the downfall of Mr. Gladstone's Administration, Randolph Churchill summed up his sentiments towards the Government in the words of the judge who has just put on the "black cap" to the condemned criminal. "Unfortunate man! I do not wish by any words of mine to add to the agony of your last moments." After this, the speaker passed on to the topic of political life and thought generally in England. That the man engaged in the first of these has no time for the last was the theme of the address. "The ordinary member of Parliament has perpetually to fly up to the House of Commons, or down to a public meeting, where he is supposed to discuss an illimitable range of British interests with the Government's policy towards them. Having done this, he flies back to the House of Commons, and there takes part, perhaps, either by voting or speaking, in some most complicated question, brimming over with the most serious results to his party or to himself. Besides that, he has, more or less, and generally, I fear, less rather than more, to digest and assimilate an immense quantity of newspaper and periodical literature, and he has to deal with an enormous mass of correspondence, because the great feature of the present day is not only the *cacoëthes loquendi*, but the *cacoëthes scribendi*.

"There are many people nowadays who take a great interest in politics. Everybody doing so thinks it necessary from time to time to write voluminously, generally in very imperfect caligraphy, to his own particular friend in the House of Commons. If these are the duties of an ordinary member of Parliament, what must be those of a Minister, who, in addition to all that, has to think of the business of his department, the condition of his Government, and the prospects of his party? Now, in such a state of things, how can you expect on any subject anything like political thought? How can you expect your Government or your public men to avoid blunders? How can you expect the statesmanship of men like Lord Grey, or like Lord John Russell, or Sir Robert Peel, or Mr. Canning, or, in later years, like Lord Beaconsfield ? I do not believe any of these great statesmen whom I have named, in the whole course of their career, attended half a dozen of those public meetings of the nature which some of us have to attend every week, or every month. Cabinet Councils were very few, the House of Commons rarely sat late, the Sessions were comparatively short; so that these great men had ample time to devote their abilities to the deep consideration of their country's affairs. Yet you had blunders then, and Governments came to grief. If that was the state of things then, what can you expect now ?"

If the lot either of John Stuart Mill, or of his earlier precursor, Adam Smith, had been cast in the latter half of the nineteenth century, these two thinkers' great works would not, as the guest of the Cambridge Carlton believed, have been produced ; "for in this age of action, based rather on instinct, logic, or experience, everything conspired to kill thought. The greatest events of the day, whether the death of General Gordon, the battle of Penjdeh, the vote of credit and Mr. Gladstone's great war speech, were events which caused immeasurable excitement for about twenty-four hours, and were then interred in the political cemetery of utter oblivion.   And yet," argued the speaker, " there never was a time in the history of England when profound political thought and prolonged political study were more essential to the national interests."

The practical guidance offered by the guest of the evening to the Cambridge students was not, indeed, very great.   " To the Russian politician historical study might be useful, because it would tell him the inevitable and speedy end of a grinding and cruel despotism ; so also to a German, because it would tell him that a military oligarchy, acting under the semblance of a constitutional form, is a political system of ephemeral duration ; so again to the Frenchman, because this study will tell him that the transition from a Republic to absolute and irresponsible power in one man is alike easy and regular.   The English politician, however," as Randolph Churchill held, " would derive no such assistance from perusing the chronicles of the past, because the state of things you have to deal with at the present moment is unparalleled in history."

The political problems to be dealt with for the first time since this earth began by the English politician may be given him in the Cambridge visitor's own words : " The duties of the English Government, at the moment of speaking, seemed to him to provide for the security and, as best they can, to minister to the happiness of some three hundred millions of human beings, scattered over every quarter of the world, comprising every imaginable variety of the human race, of custom and religion, of language and dialect. As for the nature of the Government discharging these duties, you have an hereditary monarchy exercising an immense influence indirectly, but hardly any influence directly; precisely the reverse of what was true two hundred years ago. You have an Hereditary Chamber possessing executive and legislative powers, with a Representative Chamber, controlling these two forces, seeking to gather, and gradually gathering, into its own hands almost all legislative power and authority. All these three institutions are of extremely ancient origin, are intensely Conservative in their constitution and procedure, because if the House of Commons were to be elected in November, and were to be composed almost entirely of the Radical party, you may take it for certain the spirit and procedure of that House would be intensely Conservative. By recent legislation the whole of this structure had been placed upon an entirely new foundation—a great seething and swaying mass of some five million electors, who have it in their power, if they should so please, by the mere heave of their shoulders, assuming them to act with moderate unanimity, to sweep away the three ancient institutions just described ; to put anything they like in their place, profoundly to alter, and for a time to ruin, the interests of the three hundred million beings committed to their charge. That is, I say, a state of things without precedent in history. How do you think it will all end? Are we being swept along a turbulent and irresistible torrent, which is bearing us towards some political Niagara, in which every mortal thing we now know will be twisted and smashed beyond all recognition ? Or are we, on the other hand, gliding passively along a quiet river of human progress that will lead us to some undiscovered ocean of almost superhuman development ? "

This doubt emphasised in the speaker's judgment the need of political thought and study ; therefore he invited his hearers to consider how far the five million electors were likely to be controlled or influenced by law or custom, by religion or reason. " I can understand," he said, "that five million people may govern themselves with more or less success. The question is, to what extent will they control and direct the destinies of the three hundred millions whom they have in their power ? This is a problem upon which history throws no light whatever ; and moreover, it is a problem which comes at a time when the persons who are chiefly responsible for the government of our country are precluded by the very circumstances of their life from giving it the deep attention which it absolutely requires."

Here the usefulness of the Cambridge Club seemed to begin. " Its members were not yet drawn into that political machine which kills thought and stifles reflection." Therefore, their President's advice to his hearers was, " to give time, while you have it, to political thought, to the present position of such questions as he had tried to set before them, to discuss and write about them, to endeavour to stimulate political thought on them among the masses of your fellow-countrymen."

More than this even they might accomplish. " By able summaries of statistical information, by precise inquiry into sharply opposing arguments, and by original conclusions put together in an agreeable and literary form, they might do much to restrain politicians from acting heedlessly or hastily at critical moments." Thus, by a different process, in a different, but, for his audience, not less suitable form, Randolph Churchill impressed upon the Cambridge undergraduates the truth which Mr. Disraeli had summed up in his epigram, that a nation may be saved by its youth, while under any circumstances such youth are the trustees of posterity. " Depend upon it," were his actual words, " the mental powers of a man at twenty-one for reaching the truth on any much-contested subject are worth double and treble the mental powers of a man at five-and-thirty or forty, who, harassed and exhausted by ten or fifteen years of active political life and its circumstances, is precluded from giving to the subject the concentrated attention possible for an undergraduate. Do you," he asked, " suppose that a man of forty could go in for the higher mathematics of this University with any chance of success ? He would be mad. Every undergraduate in the schools would beat him hollow ; and yet the extraordinary difficulties of higher mathematics are as nothing compared with the mystery, darkness, and confusion that surround some of our great political questions of the present day."

This appeal to the youth of Granta, on behalf of himself and his brother politicians at St. Stephen's, made by the guest of the evening, was supported by a stimulating expression of his own characteristic optimism. " I am not," he said, " alarmed as to the future. My state of mind," he added, with curious *naïveté*, " when these great problems come across me, which is very rarely, is one of wonder, or perhaps I should rather say of admiration and of hope, because the alternative state of mind would be one of terror and despair. I am guarded from that by a firm belief in the essential goodness of life, and in the evolution, by some process or other, which I do not exactly know or cannot determine, of a higher and nobler humanity. But, above all, my special safeguard against mental annihilation and despair is my firm belief in the ascertained and much-tried common sense which is the peculiarity of the English people. That is the faith which I think ought to animate and protect you in your political future. That is the faith of the Tory democracy in which I shall ever abide; which your Club can, and I hope will, wisely and widely propagate; which, dominating our minds and influencing our actions on all occasions—no matter how dark and gloomy the horizon may appear to be—will contribute to preserve and adapt the institutions of our country, to guarantee and consolidate the widespreading dominions of the Queen."*

In mental grip and literary manner this discourse, delivered directly after his return

* See "Randolph Churchill's Speeches," edited by L. J. Jennings, vol. i., pp. 253-261.

from India, not only shows the educational value of the Eastern experiences he had just acquired, but indicates a real advance upon any of his extra-parliamentary utterances. It is not indeed free from crudities of expression and juvenilities of generalisation. But with more glitter of diction and antithesis of phrase it is very much the kind of deliverance that upon an analogous occasion might have been expected from Mr. Disraeli himself. Nor can any competent and impartial critic doubt that, had such words been uttered by a public man having a reputation for intellectual sagacity or philosophic discourse—*e.g.,* Mr. Goschen or Mr. Balfour—the daily and weekly press would have made them the theme of leading articles or essays, and that the professed critics of such discourses would have lost themselves in admiration of shrewd apprehension of the age's problems, of subtle and penetrating insight into its mental and moral conditions.

Randolph Churchill was, unfortunately for his own career as for his party relationships, without any strong backers in London journalism. The great newspaper to which he might reasonably have looked for encouragement, professing itself shocked by the violence of his tactics towards his own leaders, and the indecency of his onslaught upon Mr. Gladstone —a sentiment in which that great statesman himself magnanimously never shared—except when the journal was obliged to take some notice of him, affected to treat him with contempt or to ignore him altogether. Its editor, not less than Delane, a master in his craft's technique, but less socially accessible than the publicist whose disciple he was, shared in his great exemplar's prejudices against the reckless violators of the traditions or assailants of political respectability's incarnations.

The *Morning Post* was occasionally, through the operation of irresistible agencies in private, less austerely unsympathetic. The *Daily News* on the Liberal side was sometimes appreciative. The *Daily Telegraph* had the perspicacity to see, the candour and the courage in its columns to admit, that Churchill, as a platform personage, might be in a fair way to fill the niche once occupied by the " People's William." The *Times*, under the conduct of Thomas Chenery, who followed Delane at the moment when the Fourth Party first became a phrase, dealt with the Randolphians much as it had formerly comported itself to the Cobdenites. Chenery's abilities were great but not showy. He was, therefore, underrated in that society which he never sought to enter, and where he seldom condescended to shine.

He disliked the affectation of exuberant geniality among publicists at social gatherings ; and though in a country house like Highclere he could be the most agreeable of guests, as in his own little establishment in Serjeant's Inn, which he may be said to have inherited from Delane, he was an accomplished host. The Prime Minister of the Walter dynasty in Printing House Square was alike by temper, attainments, habits, a scholar first, and a journalist afterwards. If, however, he had not been the ablest man available for his post, he would never have filled it. The Walter administration had never been in the habit of mistaking its men ; it did not do so in Chenery's case. So it was that, when the historic letter from the late John Walter to Delane, announcing the arrival of the time when his editorship should reach its close, was placed in the great journalist's hands, the mention of his pension of so-much a year was followed with the statement that his " successor would be the Mr. Chenery whose abilities and wisdom we have all so long admired."

Delane died in 1879, a year before Churchill had become a parliamentary personage. The great editor's successor recognised Churchill's growing popular ascendancy and increasing senatorial influence. Chenery's follower, again, Mr. G. E. Buckle, did not permit himself to be blinded by Pall Mall prejudices, and, upon occasions, accorded to militant Conservatism's protagonist the hospitality of the *Times'* columns. With this exception Churchill had little for which to thank the London press, whose coolness and rather less than personal civility, whether certain of its conductors dealt with him in print or ran across him in private dining-rooms, certainly tended to embitter the object of their criticisms against his official chiefs, and to throw him into the arms of provincial broadsheets.

No politician of the century since the days of Mr. Milner Gibson studied newspapers, whether published in London or the country, with the same catholicity and care as Churchill. Out of Fleet Street he seldom failed to receive usually justice, sometimes appreciation.

I have cited the Cambridge Carlton speech as showing more matured thoughtfulness than is sometimes attributed to this monograph's subject. Another instance of the same kind, or pointing in the same direction, came about this time under my personal notice. He had, it so happened, written and was reading in MS. aloud to me a letter that seemed an unintentional discourse on the famous Aristotelian text describing revolutions as proceeding from small commencements, but having great issues. Hearing, then, from my interlocutor that, as I had expected, he was not acquainted with the familiar passage in the " Politics," I reached the volume from its place on my shelves, and in a few minutes my visitor had mastered the whole chapter. " I had no idea," he said, " these old Greeks knew such a lot." By the time we next met he had provided himself with the Greek text, and with the very legitimate assistance of Dr. Jowett's version had acquired a working comprehension of the general drift of the Stagirite's discourse.

Ignorance itself is not to be imputed as iniquity to any man. The innocence of ignorance ends only where the guilt of Pharisaic pedantry or affected knowledge begins. Judged by these tests, Randolph Churchill's nescience was always upon any topic blameless and inoffensive. Nor during his maturer years, as upon the present occasion, did he ever fail to utilise any chance of filling up gaps in a politically very imperfect education.

Another instance of the same kind recurs to me. In a little company at the Orleans Club, Brighton, of which he, together with Mr. Shaw Lefevre, Mr. Edward Dicey, Mr. Austin Lee, as well as the present writer, was one, a discussion arose on the subject of *la petite* culture between the to-day member for Bradford and the opponent who trusted to displace him. The first day Lefevre had undoubtedly the best of the argument. When, on the morrow, the controversy was resumed, Randolph Churchill had read up in the meantime the whole subject thoroughly, and was at least able to hold his own.

CHAPTER XVI.

ON THE EVE OF OFFICE (1885).

Moving the country; progress towards place during 1885.
*—The Ministry of all the failures.—" Egypt for the
Egyptians."—Castlereagh's legacy to Churchill.—In-
dictment against Mr. Gladstone.—Negotiations with
the Irish.—Randolph Churchill's parliamentary and
platform manners contrasted.—Randolph Churchill
and Mr. Parnell; preparations to defeat the Government on the Budget.—The Opposition victory; scene
in the House.—Mr. Gladstone writing to the Queen
amid the tumult.—Dividing line between two stages of
Randolph Churchill's career.—The free-lance and the
official.*

THROUGHOUT the years 1884-5 Randolph
Churchill devoted his energies to attacking,
upon two distinct lines, the Government of
Mr. Gladstone, which had come into existence
after the Conservative overthrow of 1880.
True to his own methods, as enunciated in
those manifestoes examined in a preceding
chapter, he seized every opportunity of dividing
the House against Ministers ; while on popular

platforms he exerted his now established reputation as an extra-parliamentary speaker
to undermine Mr. Gladstone's influence, and
✓ to emphasise the administrative blunders and
inconsistencies of the Liberal Government.

Among the earliest of these onslaughts was
that delivered in the June of 1884 at Aylesbury,
which, independently of any political importance, is noticeable from a biographical point
of view, as applying to Egypt the same principles of support to petty nationalities that
in the case of the smaller European peoples
Churchill's great - grand - uncle, Castlereagh,
differed from many of his colleagues in advo-
cating after the Vienna Congress of 1815.
On the present occasion the Liberal policy in
Egypt was described as being from beginning
to end " a tale of shame." The Soudan
fighting was distinguished by the speaker from
the Conservative Zulu, Natal, and Afghan wars,
in that while Churchill condemned them all,
the latter " preserved our fellow-countrymen
in Natal from annihilation, or expelled the
Russian envoy from Cabul, so relieving our
Indian possessions from a great danger and
serious menace," although it was at the same

time admitted that "with more wisdom these results might have been attained without bloodshed."

Mr. Gladstone had recently described the native Egyptians as "a people rightly struggling to be free." After his usual habit of castigating his illustrious opponent with a scourge of Gladstonian manufacture, Churchill elaborated the point that "English intervention in the land of the Nile had begun and continued in a manner and with results which Liberalism and humanity alike must condemn. In Egypt misgovernment and oppression had at last produced a great movement for freedom. Mr. Gladstone had it in his power to have discovered the true nature of the movement, to have controlled it and utilised it; instead, he and his colleagues cajoled it, threatened it, and finally, when the fabric of the Egyptian Government was utterly shattered, when every European interest in the East had been imperilled, by an English fleet and army Ministers suppressed the Egyptian national movement at the cost of a great commercial capital on the Eastern highway, of ten thousand lives, and of between five and ten millions of

English money. After Tel-el-Kebir, Egypt was as unresistingly in English hands as clay in the potter's."

Such was, in effect, Churchill's charge : " All the responsibilities of power and opportunity were evaded by the English Cabinet ; the most corrupt and vicious Pachas, against whom the people had revolted, were replaced ; tens and thousands of Arabs, guilty of no other crime than that of struggling to be free, were put to the sword, while swarms of fanatical and savage barbarians, under the Mahdi, let themselves loose upon Lower Egypt."

The belief that the maintenance of our Empire depends upon the sharpness of our swords was scouted by Churchill in words that might have come from Bright. " Such may have been the case with the Empires of Attila or Tamerlane, or with the Asiatic Empire of the Russian Tzar ; but the British Empire depends upon the determination of the British people to pursue a just and righteous policy."

The address was not critical or destructive only : " having begun, England must continue its task. ' Egypt for the Egyptians' must be our aim ; to be secured, paradoxical as it might seem, by prolonged British occupation, under which 'Egypt for the Egyptians' would not be confused with 'Egypt for the French,' or the bondholders, under the name of an international control."

Every phase of the Gladstonian policy during this year was dealt with by Churchill in the same manner. The Government was, in fact, "one of failure and ruin. So in 1882 Mr. Gladstone had to confess, first, that his Coercion Act had quite miscarried, and that he must invite Parliament's sanction to his arrangements with Mr. Parnell in Kilmainham. Next the Prime Minister acknowledged that compact itself to have been a blunder, and his Irish Secretary to have fallen a victim to it." This line of criticism was followed throughout, the result being that "from one cause or another the national expenditure was five millions in excess of what the Tories left it, and that Ministers were diverting popular attention from their blunders by a Reform Bill," which, though he subsequently supported it, Randolph Churchill described as "likely only to misrepresent the people."

The enthusiasm which on this occasion the

Tory democrat found for himself and his friends at Manchester convinced him "that the English people were about to decide in favour of the politicians who, like the Hereditary Chamber at that moment, were dauntlessly defending against an arbitrary Minister the ancient liberties of our race."

These addresses were continued at various points throughout the country during the eventful summer and autumn of 1884-5. Whatever the deficiencies of these harangues in respect of knowledge, whatever their sins against political judgment or literary taste, they were thoroughly adapted for their immediate purpose, and were all delivered in that platform style which was an entire contrast to the speaker's House of Commons manner, but which never failed to tell with provincial galleries. At St. Stephen's Randolph Churchill modelled himself chiefly after Disraeli in his more conversational moods, who himself in these aspects of his eloquence reproduced the oratorical traditions of Palmerston or perhaps Melbourne.

On his favourite spot below the gangway, whence he had successively ejected Mr.

Frederick Lygon and Mr. Cavendish Bentinck
—just as Mr. Parnell appropriated an analogous
position formerly occupied by Mr. Butt—the
member for Woodstock, except in his more
declamatory moments, avoided all approach to
vehement gesture or intense tones. It was the
style of the club committee man who, having
also the *entrée* of the Westminster society,
delivers himself of such sentiments as may be
to the purpose in the well-bred phrases and in
the perfectly self-possessed manner which seem
best suited to the assemblage.

At Manchester, Leeds, or Sheffield, it was
a very different affair. Lord Lytton in *St.
Stephen's* has described in memorable lines
Palmerston's great rival when steam was on,
" and languid Johnny swells to glorious John."
So, too, upon the occasions now spoken of,
the passionless and indolent dandy who at
Westminster thought apparently more about
his moustache than his invective, was solicitous
rather for the fit of his boots than the effect
of his periods, divesting himself of all self-con-
sciousness in the excitements of the moment,
indulged in superabundant gestures and now
and again wildly melodramatic attitudes.

Not content with striking one hand's open palm with the other's clenched fist, he sometimes emotionally raised both together above his head, as if to signify despair at the Republic committed to inveterate blunderers like Mr. Gladstone and his friends.   There were even moments in which in an access of uncontrollable feeling he seemed as if he were literally about to follow Mr. Parnell's example, when that patriot talked of taking his coat off for his country's liberation, and as if Randolph Churchill were seriously struggling to divest his body of its outer garment.   This action, however exaggerated, had often exercised a remarkable influence upon his auditors ; and repeatedly the more excitable among them, as if magnetised by the orator's example, were observed apparently to be emancipating themselves into the *déshabillé* of shirt sleeves.

Sooner than many persons expected, the result for which the Fourth Party's leader, with his followers, had laboured and waited since 1880 was realised.   After the death of General Gordon and the failure of the Khartoum expedition, with the Soudan warfare which followed, and the Afghan boundary difficulties with Russia that developed themselves a few weeks later, the popularity of the Government had disappeared in the country ; their authority was on the wane at Westminster. Night after night Randolph Churchill was occupied in parliamentary manœuvres and negotiations with Mr. Parnell and his lieutenants in the resolute attempt to detach from the Gladstonians the Irish vote.

A less patient and pertinacious manager than Churchill proved himself to be would have been discouraged from pursuing his enterprise by the moral rebuffs he received. It was not indeed Mr. Parnell's way to be actually or gratuitously rude to any one. He was constrained, distant, unconciliatory, with all. He made no distinction between the son of an Irish peasant and the descendant of an English duke. Through all this period he continued apparently to treat Lord Randolph's approaches in the same way that he might have done among his indigenous followers the courtesies of Mr. Tim Healy or the blandishments of Mr. T. P. O'Connor.

But, unpromising as the transaction might often appear, Randolph Churchill did not desist from it. He was rewarded by an agreement with the Irish leader, that on consideration of the Tories pledging themselves not to renew the Crimes Act, and to deal seriously with local government on the other side of St. George's Channel, the Celtic brigade would unite with the British constitution's champions to support Sir Michael Hicks-Beach's resolution dooming the Liberal Budget, or its increase of the Beer, Spirit, and Death Duties.

The 9th of June, 1885, was for many reasons memorable in the career of this monograph's subject. The division which followed the Budget debate, and which by Randolph Churchill's personal agency alone reinforced the Conservatives with 39 Home Rulers, placing the Government in a minority of 12, coincided with the line separating Churchill, the reckless and juvenile free-lance, from that individual in his capacity of sobered and mature official.

While amidst inarticulate noises of all kinds, that would have shattered nerves less firm than those of the octogenarian Premier, announcing, as they did, his fall, Mr. Gladstone concentrated his whole attention upon the letter to Her

Majesty, which he was writing on his knees as upon a desk, apprising her of the debate's issue.   In defiance of all parliamentary order, the noble lord who was the moving cause of the whole incident had leapt upon the bench below the gangway, was waving his hat over his head with one hand, waking the echoes with his shout, while his other was placed trumpet-wise on his mouth that the clamour might the more surely reach the fallen Premier before he left the Treasury bench. But, in truth, Randolph Churchill was proclaiming and bidding adieu to something more than the 1880 Cabinet.   He was, in fact, saying farewell to his own earlier self—that stage of irresponsible aggression to which the Representative Chamber was only a continuance of the Eton schoolroom.

Within a very few hours, or at the most days, the old identity with which we have thus far been conversant in these pages was to disappear for ever.   An interval of more than years separates the personality of the Churchill of the " fourth party " from the Churchill of the reigning Administration to whom the reader is now about to be introduced

CHAPTER XVII.

LORD RANDOLPH ON TURF AND TOWN (1885).

The Marden Park Yearlings' sale on the day after the Conservative triumph.—Lord Randolph as a turfite and Lord Dunraven's partner; skill in stable management; performances of partnership horses. — The Church and Turf as centres of Conservative organisation.—Types of past and present sportsmen compared. —Effects of second French Empire's fall on English society; consequences of London's fashionable popularity.—Parties for the play; the Continental and the Bristol restaurants.—American bucks and beauties in London society.—Randolph Churchill as patron of the play; his theatrical talk with Mr. Henry Irving.

WITHIN a week of Mr. Gladstone's defeat, chronicled in the preceding chapter, Lord Salisbury had formed a Ministry, in which Randolph Churchill's party services were rewarded and his Indian experiences recognised by his appointment to the Secretaryship of State for our Oriental Empire. On the day succeeding the outburst of boyish exultation within the House of Commons at the division's result, the new Minister was engaged with pursuits less of politics than of pleasure.

The turf, at this time, if it was without the presence of pillars so distinguished, not less in the service of the State than at Newmarket, as Lord George Bentinck, the fourteenth Lord Derby, or Mr. Charles Greville, was still pre-eminently the sport of statesmen.

Mr. Disraeli, at Hughenden, took his pleasure, not in the production of yearlings, but in the contemplation of flower beds and the breeding of pea-fowl; yet he showed his appreciation of the racecourse as an institution by socially cultivating its human ornaments, and when, as in the case of Lord Bradford or Cadogan, he had an opportunity of doing so, giving them places in his Cabinets; he became, too, if I mistake not, towards the close of his career, not unknown, whether in the capacity of occasional guest or honorary member, at the Turf Club in Piccadilly, whose domicile was the mansion once occupied by Monmouth's original in "Coningsby," the old Lord Hertford, and quitted by him in disgust, "because it had no reception-rooms."

The Turf Club had sprung from the ashes of

the old Arlington Club, dedicated though the latter especially was to the playing of whist, and frequented as it had been by personages in the world of pleasure not less puissant than Mr. George Payne, or by the diarist of the Privy Council, whose "horrid friends," when he was a guest in Bruton Street of that accomplished diplomatist, Lord Granville's lady used to meet upon the staircase. But Charles Greville had disappeared before this monograph's central figure was known on the town.

From Mr. George Payne, however, Randolph Churchill might have formed a fair idea of those turf patrons, who have left behind them, unfortunately, few successors. Mr. Payne, like Mr. Craven, both of whom Churchill knew well, showed the members of the Turf Club in the last decade of this century a faithful specimen of those men of fashion and culture who thirty years ago reminded their juniors that it was a gentleman's duty to be a scholar first, a turfite, if he wished, afterwards. How Randolph Churchill, on the more studious side of his character, tried to profit by that example we have already seen. How, as a man of society, he conformed to the pattern, it will not be amiss now to show.

During the summer of 1885—immediately, in fact, after Lord Salisbury had been entrusted with his Sovereign's commission—an unusually distinguished company gathered round the sale ring at Marden Park, where Mr. Tattersall was selling Mr. Hume Webster's yearlings. Among the many coaches present was that of the Marquess of Londonderry, with his cousin, Lord Randolph Churchill, by his side.

In view of the Ministerial crisis which had just been reached at Westminster, most spectators would then have looked for the politician, destined by the popular voice to official cares, anywhere rather than in the Surrey park. Not a few, therefore, doubted for a moment as to the identity of the slight youthful figure who, to all appearance, was solely preoccupied with the fillies which, in conjunction with his relative, he was purchasing. On the whole, Randolph Churchill's investments upon this occasion seemed to win the expert's approval.

That the present visitor to the Marden enclosure could buy wisely as well as widely is perhaps proved by the performances of Lord

Dunraven's and Lord Randolph Churchill's partnership horses, for which the reader may be referred to the racing calendar, and of which it seems enough here to say that in 1888 St. Serge won the Fitzwilliam Plate at Newmarket, L'Abbesse de Jouarre the May Plate at Newmarket, as well as the Two Year Old Plate and some stakes at Pontefract; that in 1889 the Abbesse carried off the Oaks; while in 1890 the same mare was victorious in the Prince of Wales' Handicap, at Sandown, in the race for the Manchester Cup; was also second for the Gold Vase at Ascot, and the Liverpool Cup, respectively, actually triumphing in the Portland Plate at Doncaster.

The Abbé Morin, Blue Peter, Inverness, Trapezoid, Sea Urchin, and Larkaway also carried off turf prizes for the Churchill and Dunraven colours between the years 1881-91. Mockery, Apostate, Carlina, Lady Morgan, and Whiteknight were also successful, if not so conspicuously. The Abbesse de Jouarre was bought by Lord Randolph entirely on his own judgment, while the fact that he parted with his own half share in her to his noble and remarkably acute and experienced confederate,

Lord Dunraven, for £2,000, together with the circumstance of his practical disposal of his entire interest in the sporting stable at the end of the '91 season not at a loss, indicates that with added years, and the gravity of accumulated experience, the subject of this monograph might have become an oracle of the Jockey Club. As it was, he did not often appear at its meetings ; and, when there, seemed to be thinking of graver subjects than turf legislation or the classical authorities in that calendar whose hagiography comprises the names of Richmond's dukes, Knowsley's earls, Bentinck's barons ; his turf aptitudes were, however, shown in the great skill with which Randolph Churchill for some time managed Colonel North's large stud.

The new Indian Secretary, like Disraeli himself, had the shrewdness to perceive in the racecourse one of the central points round which Conservatism organises its social forces not less certainly than round the State Church. If a democratic or levelling spirit animated occasionally some of those gentlemen of the ring who had made inauspicious wagers with the late Marquess of Hastings, the Glad-

stonian bookmaker is probably not less
rare than the licensed victualler who has
become converted to the patriotism of the
Local Veto and the equity of "No Compensation."

Even Lord Rosebery's personal favour with
an Epsom multitude and the popularity of his
Ladas victory have not yet detached the givers
and takers of odds from the politics of the
music hall. The most trusted leader whom
the House of Commons, in Lord Althorp, has
ever known, thought it a kind of duty sometimes to look in at a prize fight. The parlia-
menteer now promoted from his seat below the
gangway to the Treasury bench confessed the
Tory democrat's obligation to attest in practical
shape, and by personal presence, his sympathy with the oppressed promoters of the
national sport.

Nor is the turf the only institution around
which Conservatism is impelled naturally to
organise itself. The interests of the body that,
at the West End of London, calls itself pre-
eminently "society," are as dear to the Conservative politician of the popular hue as the
turf itself, with which indeed, more than with

any other of our national pastimes, that polite organisation is socially identified.

If all men are equal upon the greensward and under it, the racing stable is the thing which divides all fashionable sections the least, as well as furnishes the social cement that unites representatives of varied political schools the most. The Turf Club was thus, and for the same reason, politically useful to Randolph Churchill not less than the Carlton.

Sir Robert Peel the second, among the members of that assembly, was indeed already a convert to something more advanced than even Randolph Churchill's democratic Toryism ; but for the rest, Lord Dunraven's partner might hope to instil into the breasts of such unpromising converts as Lord Dorchester the wholesome leaven of his own enlightening principles.

Equally indispensable from another point of view were the politically educating influences of the Newmarket rooms and Heath, where he was brought into contact with exponents of popular thought on national affairs unknown to more sequestered statesmen, and had the opportunity of plumbing the political depths beneath that white hat in whose wearer Palmerston humorously recognised the incarnation of public opinion.

Randolph Churchill was not, indeed, altogether pre-eminently qualified to derive the maximum of gain which such emporia of popular predispositions and talk as the resorts now spoken of may yield to temperaments to which they are instinctively congenial. Those persons who on whatever social levels retailed the good or droll things that " Randolph " had said to them across the walnuts and the wine, or recounted the political programmes he had drawn up for their instruction between the whiffs of his cigarette, were generally exercising their invention rather than displaying their memory. Churchill did not invite, and certainly did not bestow, indiscriminate confidences. As he had much of Disraeli's resourcefulness and courage, so he did not at times lack the spirit of moody isolation which caused that statesman to keep many of his followers at a distance, and was not calculated to improve his fortunes in the division lobby.

In general and mixed society Randolph Churchill was often silent. With years, and the consciousness of weak points in his health, that disposition to reserve increased. In the private dining-room of the Turf Club, as in his own dining-room at Connaught Place, playing the part of host with conversationalists like Lord Justice Barry, Lord Justice Morris, Fitzgibbon, Sir Henry Drummond Wolff, or his own brother the Duke of Marlborough as guests, Randolph Churchill was to be seen and enjoyed at his very best. Intensely modern in many of his ideas as we have seen him to be, there still seemed to linger about him in general society a flavour of old-world courtesy and personal restraint. He possessed, or at least it pleased him constantly at unexpected moments to invest himself with, the distant dignity of a bygone century's *grand seigneur*. He could show by turns an exaggerated and rather artificial courtesy, a friendly geniality, or a freezing remoteness. The unfortunate person who might have been a few minutes before recounting his intimacy with " Randolph " was not likely to elicit from that personage any sign of reciprocally close knowledge when the pair actually met, and had usually reason to regret the *còntretemps*. Living though he habitually did in the most progressive, the most modish and showy latitude in London, his inherent Conservatism asserted itself upon many occasions very strongly, and upon two sets of conjunctures with severity as well as warmth.

From his childhood to youth, and through maturity, his intense reverence for his father and his tireless devotion to his mother were dominant traits of his being. As at school and college, so in later life was he, times without number, held back from some precipitate course or ill-advised action by the remonstrating inquiry, "What those he loved at home might think of his so doing or speaking?"

Had the life of the seventh Duke of Marlborough been prolonged, there may be much reason to think that his son's "fourth party" leadership would have been moderated in many of its aspects, and so have been delivered from many of its results; while as regards the Duchess of Marlborough, the model of a mother for such a son, he retained to the last the same childish devotion to her as when he had played with the Blenheim spaniels by her side. His mother's birthday was to him the most sacred of festivals; he refused systematically all invitations upon that day, and reserved, as a token of his special regard for a very few personal friends, the summons to attend the anniversary banquet held at the Dowager's house in Grosvenor Square.

The second of those social usages redolent of the antique was to be seen in his detestation of that exuberant familiarity in which he saw vulgarity's nadir. His very intimate friend, perhaps during some years his closest, and the one whom he consulted most confidentially, the then Chief Income Tax Commissioner, was in mixed society always given the honour of his baronetcy, and spoken of by him invariably as "Sir Alfred." The Yorkshire baronet, whose farmers supplied his own and the Carlton's larders with bacon and hams, never ceased to be "Sir George." His own devoted henchman, the late Mr. Percy Mitford, drew from his chief a rather sharp reprimand because in a miscellaneous company he had alluded to Sir Henry Drummond Wolff without giving him the titular benefit of his K.C.B.

Yet with all his reverence for time-honoured distinctions, as for good breeding's conventional etiquette, stiffly as he could resent any infractions of that portion of the social decalogue invested by his tastes with inviolable sanction, Randolph Churchill embodied in his own person, illustrated in his own social life from day to day, the tastes, the habitudes, the caprices, the modes, which are the last half-century's leading novelties. His guests were as cosmopolitan in their *personnel* as the Hyde Park loungers in the week between Epsom and Ascot. He divided with Lord Rosebery the distinction of being the best friend whom the American stranger has ever known in society. His own experiences comprised a remarkable change in the social status of the Anglo-Saxon visitor from beyond the Atlantic.

The British exclusiveness of which N. P. Willis complains in his " Hurrygraphs," which was satirised by Hawthorne in his " Old Home Glimpses," ceased to exist, and to some extent through his influence, during Randolph Churchill's lifetime. Within the limits of his career the great Republic's citizen, from being merely tolerated with equanimity or welcomed with hospitality, became, to some extent, the true autocrat of the breakfast table or the arbiter of the luncheon party.

It was during the Churchillian era that the late Mr. Samuel Ward, that venerable and polished cynosure of New York or Washington, was elevated by his British partisans to the position of London society's "uncrowned king." "Uncle Sam" was only one of the types of his time. Mr. Henry Hurlbert, Mr. Marion Crawford, the novelist, Mr. Henry James, the late Mr. Thorndike Rice, editor of the *North American Review*, but indistinguishable from an English gentleman, Mr. Smalley, correspondent of *The Tribune*, were only a few of those who had achieved places as recognised and enviable as were once occupied by Mr. Charles Greville or Mr. Alfred Montgomery.

One characteristic London society possessed, at the time now spoken of, which was absent from it in the bygone dandy's epoch. The man of the world, of the period, had become identified with the social trifler. Charles Greville lived for sport and society as much as most men, but *viveur* though in these respects he was, he hated frivolity. He took, as his posthumous papers show, the most serious interest in politics ; he applied himself to the turf with the gravity due to an exact science.

The diffusion of the associations of the *coulisses*, the dissemination of green-room gossip through groups of fashionable men and women, who, when they were not dining at each other's houses, were making up parties for the play, and dining or supping in battalions at " smart " restaurants, were developments un-dreamed of in Greville's day ; nor, as a matter of fact, were they known among us till the French Empire had fallen, and the British capital, from being the most sombre, exclusive, and inhospitable of cities, was transformed suddenly into the most cosmopolitan of pleasure haunts.

New amusements had to be found for a society thus essentially novel in its composition and its tastes. The attractions of " Lords " or of Hurlingham during the day were supplemented by the theatre as a scene of fashionable display at night. American ladies are at least as prominent and powerful in that society near to the heart of which Churchill lived as American *littérateurs* or dandies.

The highly gifted lady from the other side of the Atlantic whom, shortly before he

entered Parliament, Lord Randolph had led to
the altar at the Paris Embassy, retained her
interest in those theatrical *premières* which are
so great a feature in the polite world of Paris,
and communicated her own enthusiasm to her
husband.   The theatre in London had become
as much the mode for pleasure-seekers, *comme
il faut*, as the Anglo-Parisian restaurants of the
West End.

For the same reason that he made himself a
figure on the turf, the new Secretary of State for
India was an indefatigable patron of the stage
in its most sparkling aspects ; and just as he
seldom missed an important race meeting, so
was he rarely absent from any of those first
representations whither he was summoned by
fashionable wont.   He had, too, an appreciative
eye to and taste for the severer forms of drama
associated with Shakespeare. So shrewd a
judge as Henry Irving was impressed by the
sagacity and penetration of Lord Randolph's
comments on the effects which, as it seemed to
him, the great dramatists desired to produce in
certain more obscure and controversial passages.

The politician aimed, in fact, at the realisa-
tion of that ideal worshipped so generally in

England during the eighteenth, as it had been also during the sixteenth century ; he wished, that is, to be what Lord Herbert of Cherbury, or Sir Walter Raleigh, and Sir Philip Sidney before him, would have called " a complete man."

CHAPTER XVIII.

LORD RANDOLPH AS INDIAN SECRETARY
(1885).

*Surprises of the late Sir Louis Mallet at the India Office.
—A twofold astonishment about Lord G. Hamilton
might have been followed by a third in Randolph
Churchill.—Special attention to Indian topics after
return from Indian travels.—His Birmingham speech
on India; his first Indian Budget in House of Commons; its main points, and how received.—The secret
of Lord Randolph Churchill's parliamentary and
official popularity to be found in House of Commons'
dislike of professional politicians of the French type.
—How Randolph Churchill had studied the House of
Commons and knew how to reflect its temper and hit
its taste.—Journalistic element in his politics.*

SIR LOUIS MALLET, the accomplished and able Permanent Under-Secretary of State for India, had more surprises than one during his official career. The first came when Lord George Hamilton was appointed to the parliamentary headship of the Department ; the second when this ex-Guardsman, whom Sir

Louis knew only by reputation as a brilliant young man about town, proved himself not less industrious in routine than his predecessor, Lord Hartington, nor less vigorous in initiative than his forerunner in another department, Sir Michael Hicks-Beach, the admiration of the permanent Colonial officials.

Had not, to the great loss of the public, Sir Louis retired in 1883, he might have experienced a third surprise in the aptitudes, greater than his most sanguine friends had credited him with, which Lord Randolph Churchill brought to his new portfolio, as well as the unexpected ability and efficiency with which, down to the minutest details, he discharged the duties of the post.

Immediately after his return from his Eastern travels to England, in the spring of 1885, the future Secretary of State in a Primrose League address, at Birmingham, had defined England's duties upon the Ganges, and in a bold figure of rhetoric had sketched the character of our Indian rule. " That rule," he said, " was a sheet of oil spread out over a surface of, and keeping calm, an immense ocean of humanity. Underneath that rule lie hidden all the

memories of fallen dynasties, all the traditions
of vanquished races, all the pride of insulted
creeds ; and it is our most difficult business
to give peace, individual security, and general
prosperity to the two hundred and fifty millions
of people who are affected by those powerful
forces ; to bind them and to weld them by the
influence of our knowledge, our law, and our
higher civilisation, in process of time, into the
great united people ; and to offer to all the
nations of the East the advantages of tranquillity and progress in the West."

As for the loyalty to England of the Indian
princes, while believing it, Churchill reminded
his hearers that " this sentiment is strictly con-
ditional on our will and ability to protect them,
not only from internal conflict, but from foreign
aggression. If," he contended, " in any of
these respects English pledges were not redeemed, then," he asserted, " our Indian rule
would have received a mortal blow ; that the
deadly decrepitude which fell upon the Hindoo
and Mogul Empires would overtake us in our
turn, and that the annihilation of our power
must be but a question of time."

Another of Randolph Churchill's Anglo-

Indian addresses, that on the vote of credit, May 4th, 1885, deserves notice here, because it received the high compliments of Lord Salisbury, who referred to it as " the very clear and vigorous description of Russian proceedings, given by Lord Randolph Churchill in the House of Commons last night," as being "historically unimpeachable, and a warning to the Ministers of the English Crown."

Notwithstanding this high and merited testimonial, the discourse in question was rather a well-contrived recapitulation of details already familiar to students of the subject than an exposition of original views or a narrative of personal experiences. Its delivery, however, was opportune, and justified the new Prime Minister's selection for the office just vacated by a Liberal statesman.

On August 6th, 1885, the House of Commons was crowded to a degree very unusual at that period of the session, especially when the traditionally unpopular theme of Asiatic finance is under discussion, to hear Randolph Churchill, as Indian Secretary, bring forward his first Budget. The speech, which had to face the awkward fact of a £5,000,000 deficit, had not

a little of the old polemical "fourth party " ring,
and contained criticisms unacceptable indeed to
the admirers of Lord Ripon's policy, but based
upon historical facts, and rendering a tribute
that was simply just to the too often and
too ignorantly abused Administration of Lord
Lytton.

The new Indian Secretary took, incidentally,
the opportunity of enunciating those principles
of retrenchment which were henceforward to
be his political watchwords, and his adherence
to which was, within eighteen months, abruptly
to end his Ministerial career.

Randolph Churchill's platform manner differed, as we have already seen, in important
respects from his parliamentary. His first
official speech contained some of the characteristics of both. Usually, when addressing the
House of Commons, the present Secretary of
State dispensed with the exordium, which in
his popular addresses he employed, less to
foreshadow his line of argument than to discover the temper of an unknown audience.
The telling phrases, often fortuitous combinations of simple words taken accidentally from
a newspaper paragraph, were habitually em-

ployed by him as a refrain to fix the anticipations of his audience, or at periodic intervals
more closely to arrest their attention. Thus,
in one of his most effective country harangues,
he played with the phrase identifying Liberalism with humbug; just as, to quote a French
critic's simile, a juggler toys with the daggers
or balls he catches, or the clown in the circus
ring kneads, compresses, and expands that
miraculous felt hat with which such prodigies
are worked.

The normal method in Parliament of
Churchill was almost conversational in its
simplicity and directness; there was little
variety of vocal cadence; there was usually a
juvenile uniformity of inflections; the same
tone being observed from first to last, unbroken even when the interposition of an
incidentally fresh topic called for a parenthetical digression. To-day, however, the
Indian Secretary in the House of Commons
presented specimens of both modes. and the
Minister of State was also the "people's
Randolph."

In 1882-3, at a supreme and obvious crisis,
when frontier railways, roads, preparations of

every sort for a rainy day were needed, Lord Ripon was described as having slept, "lulled by the languor of the land of the lotus." The speech, however, contained also touches which attested its author's desire to raise the topic above the level of party strife. "Although to-day Hindostan's affairs seemed to be either beneath the attention, or above the comprehension of Parliament, that," the House was reminded, "had not always been the case; and in the last century, when our Indian Empire was forming, the greatest men, Mr. Pitt, Mr. Burke, Mr. Fox, did not disdain to apply their minds to the most careful examination and exposition of the complicated questions of India. Therefore, the new Secretary ventured on an appeal, or even almost a command, not only to his hearers, but to those who might be his successors, to shake themselves free from the lassitude, the carelessness, the apathy which have too long characterised the attitude of Parliament towards India, and to watch with the most sedulous attention, to develop with the most anxious care, to guard with a most united and undying resolution the land and the people of Hindostan, that most bright and truly precious gem in the crown of the Queen, the possession of which, more than that of all your colonial dominions, has raised in power, in resource, in wealth, and in authority, this small island home of ours far above the level of the majority of nations and of states; has placed it on an equality with, or perhaps even in a position of superiority over every other Empire, either of ancient or of modern times."

The general preparation received by Lord Randolph Churchill for Cabinet office had been his parliamentary experiences since 1874. His special training for the department whose head he now found himself had been his Eastern travels a year earlier. Among the Anglo-Indians of eminence whom, as Lord Dufferin's guest at Calcutta, or at his entertainers' in other Presidencies, Randolph Churchill had met, were Sir Charles Crosthwaite, Sir Steuart Bayley, General Chesney, Sir Alfred Lyall. With all these, as members of his Council, he was brought into contact again when he became Secretary of State. Few public servants have had a more diversified experience of official colleagues or chiefs than the Indian Viceroy of Randolph Churchill's epoch.   Generally popular throughout his department and his province, as during his tenure of office the young Minister was, he not only proved himself in the words of his most distinguished associate as "the most charming of men to work with, equally quick and sympathetic, not more clear than appreciative," but astonished the oldest of the staff by his extreme rapidity to apprehend the bearing of new ideas, and his thoroughness of application in tracing unfamiliar principles in all the aspects of their practical adaptation. The initial attitude of most parliamentary chiefs towards the suggestions of expert subordinates is complained of by these gentlemen as "instinctively hostile." With Lord Randolph Churchill, the document from which these extracts are given continues, "the reverse of all this was most certainly the case."

His incumbency of this, his first office, was not uneventful. The period of 1885-6, during which the *ci-devant* "fourth party" champion was responsible for Indian administration, comprised the successful conclusion of the difficult negotiations with the Afghan

Ameer, the construction of many new fortifi-
cations and railways, the initiation of military
manœuvres which brought together a larger
British army than India has ever seen, that
was most valuable to the officers engaged,
a theme of admiration to the agents of many
foreign powers invited to witness them;* the
whole military pageant culminating in the
great Delhi parade, at which officers from
all the great European armies were welcome
and impressed spectators. In addition to the
annexation of Burmah, Randolph Churchill's
Indian Secretaryship was signalised by the
construction of two commercially remunerative
railway lines, opening up for the first time
to British industry the great market of Thibet,
hitherto hermetically sealed by Chinese jealousy
against the trade of England. The same reasons
which subsequently in 1886 made Randolph
Churchill's appointment to the Chancellorship
of the Exchequer and leadership of the House
of Commons popular, conspired to commend
to most members of the parliamentary body his

* Lord Randolph Churchill's speech at Manchester after
the fall of Lord Salisbury's first Administration, March 3rd,
1886.

selection for the Indian Secretaryship of State, followed by the performance, painstaking and successful as it was, of his duties in that capacity.

Our own popular chamber has ever been predisposed in favour of those belonging to the class of country gentlemen. On the other side of the English Channel it has witnessed representative bodies, controlled mainly by the professional politicians, the lawyers, advocates, engineers, and financiers, who seem, under popular institutions, the inevitable alternative to men belonging to the same order as a Peel, a Gladstone, a Balfour, a Canning, or an Althorp.

The English House of Commons dreads and dislikes nothing more than the idea of assimilating itself too closely to a directors' board, with Ministers, chosen chiefly for their business-like powers, by way of managers. So long as its traditional prejudices are respected in the social quality of its official members, it does not exact scrupulous propriety of bearing on their part; nor does it expect them upon all occasions too exactly to measure their phrases. Very human itself, it is, in a measure, gratified by the reminder of its controllers' composition out of the same common clay ; by their knowledge of its own temper as of the world ; a vision limited, it may be, but, so far as it goes, clear ; a thorough acquaintance by the person addressing it of his own mind, together with some skill in reflecting that self-knowledge in his words.

The readiness to perceive what the parliamentary mood at any moment is, the skill to adapt his remarks to this passing temper, above all, the tact which will prompt him to bring his speech to a period before the premonitory symptoms of boredom are felt— these are the prime attributes in its favourites demanded by the first representative Assemblage in the world ; and if such conditions are complied with, the parliamentarian in whom the desired qualifications are united may, in process of time, hope to emulate the great Sir Robert Peel, of whom it was written by Disraeli, that " he played upon the House of Commons as if it had been an old fiddle." If Randolph Churchill had not profited as much as he could have wished by the strictly academic opportunities of his education, there was nothing on its social side, acquired whether at Eton, Oxford, or during his subsequent travels, which he had failed to turn to good account.

His remarkable powers of swift acquisition had been, from the first day of his entering into St. Stephen's, employed upon studying the romances of Westminster life, in mastering its humours, in comprehending its genius, in identifying himself with its antipathies or partialities, very much as an industrious student aspiring to honours masters his books for the " schools " ; and if he is an astute undergraduate as well, does not omit to fortify himself personally against the foibles, fortes, or specialities of those particular examiners, themselves the authors of treatises or editors of text-books, who are to have the honour of interviewing him across the table in the Oxford " cockpit."

The same French critic, to whose " profile " of the present sketch's subject reference has been made, happily compares the topic before a deliberative chamber at any moment to a statue upon a revolving pedestal. The figure itself is motionless, but the aspect in which the assembly sees the image is protean in its mutability.

Throughout his Indian Secretaryship, as, indeed, in a more or less degree at every period of his career, Randolph Churchill studied to fix his auditory's attention upon those angles of his theme which the illumination of actual events brought into prominent relief. This was not the oratory of the scholar or of the jurist; just as his politics themselves were not those of Mr. Gladstone, any more than of Sir William Harcourt. Actuality was the keynote alike of his declamation and his *repartee*. He spoke as a reader of newspapers and blue-books to men finding their mental pabulum and interest in these sources of information. If opportunity had not made Randolph Churchill a parliamentarian, time and toil might have transformed him not unsuccessfully into the professional publicist of the daily press.

CHAPTER XIX.

ARRIVAL AT HOUSE OF COMMONS LEADER-SHIP (1885-6).

Birmingham exchanged for Paddington; ladies of the Churchill family as electioneering agents.—Return for South Paddington, first, in 1885; secondly, in 1886; denunciations of Mr. Gladstone the Home Ruler too strong for some of his electoral friends.- Local interest and popularity in Paddington affairs; characteristics of Leadership of the House of Commons; industry and good opinions won; Mr. C. P. Villiers' verdict.—Review of Churchill's career up to this point.—Contrast between his and Lord Salisbury's character.—Congenital dangers of collision between two such temperaments.

THOUGH Randolph Churchill had failed in his attempt at the 1885 appeal to the constituencies to carry the Midland capital for the Tory democracy, the general results of the dissolution, including his own creditable fight at Birmingham, could scarcely fail greatly to strengthen his own party position. As was to be the case again in 1886, the Conservatives, whilst losing seats in the counties and agricultural districts, gained considerably in the boroughs, where the decentralised organisation advocated by the Conservatives below the gangway against their bureaucratic chiefs had taken effect.

Exactly a month before Christmas Day in the year now reached by this monograph, Randolph Churchill left Birmingham as the selected candidate for the southern division of Paddington. His opponents were Alderman William Lawrence and Mr. J. E. Hilary Skinner, who by their placards appealed to their supporters not to allow their borough to become a refuge for a "political traducer," and to poll early for the two Liberal candidates, who did not appear to be too well pleased with each other, since Mr. Lawrence's posters set forth that there were already one hundred and twenty-three gentlemen of the long robe announced as parliamentary candidates, and asking the question, "Will you vote for a lawyer or a lord?" suggested the answer, "Say no! and poll for Lawrence."

Together with his indefatigable agents, his mother, the Duchess, and Lady Randolph, the Tory candidate visited the various polling stations, and showed in many ways the interest he was prepared to take in the borough where he had long been a resident. This promise he fulfilled after his return, generally by his readiness to preside over public meetings of every kind, especially by his interest in the South Paddington Working Men's Club, whose business proceedings and whose smoking concerts he attended, while, following the example of Sir Charles Dilke in the South-Western district, he was constantly an attendant at the " Paddington Parliament."

By this time the Primrose League, indebted for its existence to the ingenious initiative of Sir Henry Drummond Wolff and Sir Algernon Borthwick, acting under Randolph Churchill, had become a power in the land, and had already fulfilled the definition of its purpose given by Lord Randolph by transforming into political energy the affectionate enthusiasm elicited on the successive anniversaries of Lord Beaconsfield's death.

In this department of organisation the efforts of a Churchill were seconded, politically

alone, by the co-operation of the great financial
dynasty or their compatriots. Shortly before
the defeat of Mr. Gladstone's first Home Rule
Bill, the Lionel Cohen habitation of the Primrose League was inaugurated June 1st, 1886,
in Dr. Danford Thomas' grounds, Park Lodge.
There were those who had, on the eve of
the Home Rule propaganda being accepted
by the Liberal leader, anticipated for the
country a quick succession of short-lived
Administrations, little thinking that Lord
Salisbury's second Government would prove
among the most powerful and durable of the
decade.

The address to his Paddington constituents
issued by Lord Randolph after the Liberal
overthrow on Irish government of June 7th,
1886, was not less denunciatory than the
occasion required, and struck the keynote of
innumerable other addresses to their constituents by the Conservatives within the next few
weeks. The Indian Secretary spoke of Mr.
Gladstone as " deserted by all who could confer
upon his policy character or reputation, and
signalising his career's close by a conspiracy
against the honour of Britain and the welfare

of Ireland more startlingly base and nefarious than any of those other designs which during the last quarter of a century have occupied his imagination. It was not only a design for the separation of Ireland from Britain, but an insane recurrence to heptarchical arrangements, a condonation of crime, an exaltation of the disloyal, an abandonment of the loyal ; a monstrous mixture of imbecility, extravagance, and political hysterics, professing to convert a nation of tributary slaves into exuberant lovers of the Britain which they now hate, but with which it is on a footing of perfect political equality."

The chief absurdity that this address for the first time seized upon in the Gladstonian project was that of converting a people like the Irish, longing for protection to create and foster manufacturers, into free traders. " The new financial system proposed was one under which by no possibility can revenue be adequate to expenditure."

On July 2nd, 1886, the polling stations of South Paddington were once more opened. Lord Randolph Churchill was opposed by no weaker candidate than one likely to unite the

suffrages of all Nonconformists, and equipped
with a special letter of recommendation from
Mr. Gladstone himself, Mr. Page Hopps.
In the sequel, the Gladstonian was defeated
by a majority larger than his opponent commanded at the General Election some months
earlier, 2,576 votes to 769 ; and this notwithstanding that more than one Conservative
voter considered the indictments and epithets
of the Tory candidate's address too strong
for him to endorse. " I don't consider these
words gentlemanly, or kind, or true," was the
comment of one elector, who, while he walked
along, read aloud the Randolphian manifesto,
commenting on it in an audible whisper, till
the ballot-box was actually reached, when he
plumped promptly for Mr. Page Hopps.

So far as the Member for Paddington was
concerned, the result of the 1886 election had
been almost, not, as Mr. Gladstone had hoped,
a plebiscite for Home Rule, but a national
vote justifying apparently the most aggressive
tactics and the most vituperative language of
the Indian Secretary.

The repeated choice of a middle-class Metropolitan borough had confirmed the long

registered preferences of innumerable constituencies throughout the country, from Lancashire
to the Land's End.   Lord Randolph Churchill
had the bulk of the electorate behind him.   No
other variety of Conservatism than that which
he had popularised proved successful at the
ballot-boxes, or could unite a working majority
in the House of Commons.

When, therefore, the Government of 1886
was formed, none were surprised, public expectation was only fulfilled, and, on the whole, gratified, by Randolph Churchill's kissing hands on
his appointment as Chancellor of the Exchequer,
carrying with it, as of course the office did, the
Leadership of the House of Commons.   At the
same time, Sir Michael Hicks-Beach making
way for the triumphant *frondeur*, whose rising
star he had long since recognised, returned
to the Irish Office, while Sir Stafford Northcote, having, with the titular rank of First Lord
of the Treasury, already received the style of
the Earl of Iddesleigh, was Foreign Secretary
in the House of Lords, as a preliminary to a
tragically pathetic departure from existence
itself within the precincts of his office.

In less than nine months Randolph Churchill's

electoral anticipations had been verified with noticeable fidelity. Speaking in the previous February, shortly after the revolt of the counties from Conservatism had brought Mr. Gladstone into office, the now Chancellor of the Exchequer, in words having a permanent interest, traced the gradual progress of the Tories to power, from apparently irrecoverable disaster, since 1832.

Upon the admission of the ten-pound house-holders to the Franchise, the Conservatives in the House of Commons were 170 all told, as against 300 Liberals ; by small degrees the hostile balance was in nine years extinguished, and in 1841 there was a majority under Sir Robert Peel of 78. Similarly, in 1868, another great Reform Bill was carried through by a Tory Minister, with the result that the elections first held under it placed his supporters in a minority of 106, which, in its turn, within half-a-dozen years, was converted into a Conservative preponderance of 52.

In 1885 the Liberal advantage was estimated numerically at fourscore. " I should think," said Lord Randolph, " it would not take many months to convert the present Liberal majority

of 80 into a Tory majority of more than 60."
This prediction was, as a matter of fact, verified
in just under nine months, when the Conservatives, obtaining 47 votes more than were won
by the aggregate of Liberal sections, gained 66
seats, as compared with their state in 1885.

The rest of this address, remarkable as
it is for shrewdness of foresight, predicted
Mr. Gladstone's imminent acceptance of Mr.
Parnell's propaganda, which took place almost
before the words had left the speaker's lips.

Mr. Disraeli's leadership of the House of
Commons had shown that statesman as a
pattern of punctuality, courtesy, consideration
for his opponents, not less than his followers—
in a word, of that deference towards the
Chamber in its collective capacity which the
House of Commons never fails to appreciate.

Lord Randolph Churchill had no sooner
taken up his official position, which was itself
only the recognition of his national position
with the new democracy, than he set himself
to work upon the lines of his great master's
example.   He was throughout the autumn
session of 1886 never absent from his place, save
during a short interval for dinner ; his natural

irritability and impulsiveness were not allowed to show themselves in his manner ; his discretion, good taste, and temper were universally admitted, and, as the despatch of business showed beyond mistake, felt upon all sides.

So experienced a parliamentarian as Mr. Charles Villiers spoke of him as " the best Leader he had ever known." Nor is there to-day any member of the House who has not, whatever his politics and personal predispositions, a pleasing recollection of the courtesy and conciliatory tact displayed during this period by Lord Randolph, to whom there may be applied Rosalind's remark about Orlando, that " he overcame more than his enemies."

The result of the session was, that although no phase of obstruction was left untried, while twelve nights, the equivalent of three working weeks, were wasted in aimless speeches on the Address, Government got all its Supply without difficulty, and that a week before pheasant shooting began, by September 25th, Parliament was prorogued.

Lord Randolph Churchill, it must be remembered, had first entered the Cabinet, not only as a popular statesman, but also in his

capacity of Lord Salisbury's enthusiastic follower; nor is there any necessity to believe
that the homage which, in many speeches
throughout the country, from the year 1880
downwards, he rendered to the Prime Minister
was not perfectly sincere. Humanly, therefore, the unhappy ebullition of petulant self-
will which, before the end of 1886, caused him
to sever his connection with the Government,
and at the same time to close his own career,
could not be anticipated.

Before proceeding to the facts themselves,
it seems well to say a few words about the
different idiosyncrasies of the two individuals
prominent in the episode we are now approaching.

Amid many dissimilarities of training and
culture, temper, associations, and taste, there
were still certain qualities perilously alike
possessed in common by the Prime Minister
and the Chancellor of the Exchequer. The
nature of both was traversed by a strong
vein of arbitrariness which their respective
experiences had deepened and confirmed rather
than corrected or modified. Each of them
had experienced the misfortune of subjection

to an infelicitous discipline. Each, at different occasions, with no beneficial consequences to his character, had been indulged unwisely, or unfortunately withstood.

The circumstances under which Lord Robert Cecil's youth and early manhood were passed were not calculated to develop in him the attributes of sweet reasonableness or apostolic charity. When he started in his distinguished career, he brought with him therefore to the business of life not only intellectual gifts of the highest order enhanced by the ripest study, but a bitterness of heart which sometimes caused his speech and pen almost to distil gall.

Essentially by ancestry and personal endowments the reverse of opportunist, Lord Salisbury had been constrained, by the accidents of political circumstance, to accommodate himself to an alliance, that with Lord Beaconsfield, under which, even when the achieved results were the most splendid, he must inwardly have chafed.

The nature of the ordeal submitted to by Randolph Churchill had galled his sensibilities perhaps in nearly the same degree. Conscious of great parts improved by courageous industry and patient application, the central figure of these pages could not forget that his titular chiefs, whatsoever their names, had only given his party services any recognition when his unwelcome personality had been forced upon the Westminster managers by the long-resisted united impulse of provincial crowds. Obligation, therefore, was not a sentiment he could be expected to feel, when the moral success of his Birmingham demonstration against Mr. Bright left Her Majesty's chief adviser no alternative but to offer him the second post in his Administration.

Hitherto Lord Randolph's opponents, whether inside or outside his own party, had constrained him to fight for his own hand; he had, in effect, been defied to do certain things by the Whitehall officials, and had persisted in continuing them not only without loss of his influence with the mob, but to the appreciable increase of his popularity. Now, therefore, that he had made good his position, had arrived at the highest office as well as at a pinnacle of popular influence, it needed slight knowledge of character to perceive the probability that he would use place without much regard to the prejudices or convenience of his colleagues, but with a keen eye to the approval of those partisans from outside who had been instrumental in helping on his promotion as well as for the purpose of furthering his own personal ideas.

Lord Salisbury's peculiarities, independently of his political or social experiences, had been intensified rather than chastened by his favourite studies. Nature had given him that pre-eminently scientific mind which his colleague, the late Lord Derby, possessed, and which presents so striking a contrast to the intellectual character of the statesmen of the preceding pre-scientific age, of which the fourteenth head of the Stanleys was a type; still more distinguished exemplars of which were George Canning and his associate in the *Anti-Jacobin*, as at the Foreign Office, John Hookham Frere. All that there was of the political and, therefore, essentially the opportunist mind in Lord Salisbury, as the statesman, was neutralised by the passionate dogmatism of Lord Salisbury, the man of science.

The condescension to petty expediences, the

accessibility to mutual accommodations and surrenders which are the politician's appanage, and which must be illustrated in action if success in practice is to be obtained, were in perpetual antinomy to the craving for precision and certainty which marked the student of abstractions or the experimentalist in the laboratory.

Had Disraeli's immediate successor in the Conservative leadership been born in a different age, or lived amid other circumstances, he might have won in astronomy or chemistry the same place occupied in statesmanship by his great ancestor Burleigh, many of whose moral or mental features he has reproduced so faithfully. One of the most amiable, kind-hearted, and chivalrous of men, Lord Salisbury has ever found a political charm in the atmosphere of prerogative, in the traditions or the exercise of authority, and has lost no opportunity of showing in practice that intellectual scorn for compromise which Mr. John Morley has reflected so brilliantly in his classical treatise on the subject. When, therefore, the same fortune that made in 1886 Randolph Chancellor of the Exchequer, destined him to hold this office under such a chief as the Marquess of Salisbury, it really seemed as if fate, in a mood of exceptional irony or perversity, had raised up Randolph Churchill to a position from which she had concurrently foreordained his inevitable and irremediable fall.

CHAPTER XX.

THE sensation caused in London and throughout the country by the announcement in the
Times of December 20th, 1886, that the
Chancellor of the Exchequer had resigned,
will not readily be forgotten. Yet, apart from
the general possibilities of such an event dis-
closed by a comparison between Lord Randolph
Churchill's and Lord Salisbury's personality in

the preceding chapter, and the presumptive chances of a collision between the two at no very distant date, there were clear indications contained in Randolph Churchill's long vacation utterances this year, that any overt cause, however slight, might be sufficient to precipitate such a rupture.

His speech at Dartford, in Kent, unless—which of course it was not—it had been delivered after consultation in Cabinet with Lord Salisbury's approval, amounted to a scarcely veiled impeachment of Ministerial expenditure ; and to all who heard or read it constituted a bid for independent support from his countrymen. Much of the phraseology employed was studiedly authoritative and oracular ; the first person, singular or plural, was used with significant reiteration and emphasis, transparently with the set purpose of identifying the speaker with the true wielder of popular power and administrative control.

Notwithstanding, therefore, the popular astonishment expressed at the leading journal's intelligence, more thoughtful observers .had, after the Dartford manifesto, held the view that the alternative to the Chancellor's retirement must have been the Premier's abdication. There is no reason to suppose that the explanation of the step given by Lord Randolph Churchill himself from his place in the House of Commons next year, was not substantially correct and practically exhaustive. The retiring Chancellor had acquired a social intimacy with " business princes " and representatives of *la haute finance*, who, by their consummate knowledge of practical affairs, had become first-class forces in the intercourse of nations.

Just as Churchill lent a ready ear to the permanent officials of the public service, with their traditional predispositions in favour of economy and retrenchment, so it seems reasonable to suppose he was not likely to forget the contemptuous denunciations of that alleged commercial mismanagement in the great spending departments, which, as he had been assured by the great Continental financiers, by successive magnates of the Bourse at various capitals during his trip through Europe in 1886, if perpetrated by private firms, or individuals, would plunge them and their concerns in the abyss of bankruptcy and ruin; nor had he

studied the remarks of Mr. John Morley on
Civil List Reform, in his monograph on Burke,
without deeply taking to heart their moral.
His Birmingham opponent, Mr. John Bright
himself, had more than once declared that in
peace time no Government ought to spend
more in administering the country than seventy
millions a year.

To the same effect, if not in the same words,
Randolph Churchill had declared himself at
Bow, on June 4th, 1885, at Sheffield, in
September of the same year, while his own
unchallenged statement in the House of Commons on the subject of his resignation, 1887,
showed that immediately after the formation of
Lord Salisbury's second Government he had,
in conversation with the Premier, insisted upon
the necessity not only of conducting Imperial
expenditure upon commercial principles, of
seeing that every sixpence spent yielded its
full worth, but of actually fixing the maximum
sum laid out upon the country's business at a
lower figure.

The "Dartford programme," as it is called,
was but the last of a series of utterances
in which he pledged himself to place retrench-

ment and departmental reorganisation in the very front rank of objects aimed at, and to devote whatever strength or energy or influence he might possess to attain some general and considerable reduction in taxation. During the same month of October he had also told distinctly the Prime Minister and Secretary of State for War that unless there was an effort to reduce the expenditure he could not remain at the Exchequer. These words were written on paper, and are beyond dispute, while within a week of the resignation being actually announced, it was, not for the first time, as will be seen, definitely foreshadowed.

Whether Randolph Churchill was prepared to be taken upon this occasion by the Prime Minister at his word must for the present be mere speculation. The chances would seem to be that he was not. He knew that up to this point the negotiations always favoured by himself for a fusion between the Liberal and Conservative wings of the Unionist connection had failed, and that Mr. Goschen had loudly expressed his determination not to serve under Lord Salisbury. Churchill may, therefore, plausibly have assumed the acceptance of his resignation to be impossible without involving the disruption of the Government.

Thus far his official superiors' treatment of Randolph Churchill had done much towards encouraging his belief that, to obtain any concessions he needed, some parade of menace of obstinacy was alone required. Both in the matter of the Franchise Bill in 1884 and of Conservative organisation in 1884-5, he had differed from his chiefs, had refused to surrender any substantial point, and eventually had obtained from Lord Salisbury and Sir Stafford all in effect he wanted and far more than all he had hoped. Nothing calculated to induce in him a conviction of his own indispensability had been omitted in their treatment of him by the Tory chiefs. He had thus every reason to believe that the reduction in the estimates for which he contended would have been assented to, although with an ill grace and reluctantly. That his demands, though denied at the time, were not unreasonable, is proved conclusively by the fact of the concessions urged by Randolph Churchill as Chancellor of the Exchequer in December 1886 being actually yielded to his successor in that office, Mr. Goschen, in January 1887.

Lord Randolph's retirement, therefore, disastrous for himself though it was, deserves no stronger epithets than ill-judged, impolitic, quixotic. He ought to have known the Tory Premier better than to have supposed him to be altogether a willow lath, painted to look like iron ; should have exercised enough knowledge of human nature to have perceived that Lord Salisbury at this crisis of his own career was not likely to write himself down a *roi fainéant* ; and that after the challenge thrown down to him by his lieutenant before a Kentish audience, in view of the impeachment of Tory administration at the bar of public opinion which that defiance carried with it, the head of the historic house of Cecil could have morally no alternative but to advise the Queen to send for Lord Randolph in his place, or to get rid of his rival at any cost.

As a fact, the man whose career we are tracing was not without reason for thinking that the bold, even presumptuous stroke he now played might have been successful.   The

Cabinet was divided on the subject, and there were not a few who believed the high military estimates to betoken a "spirited" policy, likely, as others than Churchill thought, to involve England in foreign embroilments. Churchill's personal following was nearly as numerous as, and possibly to himself seemed in weight more considerable, than that of the Premier. Within a few hours of his secession becoming publicly known, two hundred members of the House of Commons called at his private house in Connaught Place, suppliantly to ascertain how they stood with him in whom they recognised the fresh depository of power and dispenser of patronage.

If there was nothing preposterous in the expectation of the Salisbury Cabinet not surviving the withdrawal of its popular Chancellor, equally little was there anything in his contentions which was not justified abundantly by subsequent events. At Blackpool Churchill had demanded an inquiry into the whole of the Civil Service, to include the amount of work done in each department, the number of hands employed, the salaries received. He further wished that these results should care-

fully be compared under corresponding head-
ings with the arrangements in some of our great
commercial establishments.   Lord Randolph
actually succeeded in getting a Royal Commission appointed for this purpose, which was
sitting as late as the spring of 1889 ;* he
further secured the nomination of select commit-
tees of the House of Commons to investigate
the causes which, notwithstanding an annual
expenditure of thirty millions, make our national
defences so unsatisfactory and inadequate.

If in the press, or from any powerful body
of friends throughout the country, Randolph
Churchill had received the support he fairly
might have hoped for, results would have
made his resignation to be hailed not as a
blunder, but as a master-stroke of patriotic
policy.   The facts were really not in dispute.
That the national expenditure was profuse,
that the taxpayers were not receiving a proper
return for their money—these truths were
known to all well-informed critics no less
than to the Chancellor of the Exchequer.

But in the particular month of December

---

* See footnotes *passim*, in Mr. Jennings' second volume
of Lord Randolph's speeches.

1885 the public opinion necessary for the enforcement of a sweeping policy of retrenchment and reform had not been generated. The taxpayers were content to leave all to Lord Salisbury and the titular First Lord of the Treasury, as the statesman who had been Sir Stafford Northcote then was ; in a word, the moment was not well chosen, and so the defiantly adventurous step miscarried. Nor was there anything in the circumstances of the resignation for which unexceptionable precedent, in the case of statesmen whose political integrity and sobriety were unimpeachable, could not be found, as Lord Salisbury, of all men, had good reason to know.

Twenty years had not passed since the Lord Cranborne of that day, in the hope of wrecking Mr. Disraeli's Government on the rock of Reform, not only resigned himself, but by his personal influence induced Lord Carnarvon and General Peel to follow him. At that crisis Mr. Disraeli acted with a felicitous courage and promptitude which, after an interval of nineteen years, Lord Salisbury not unsuccessfully imitated.

On the same day as the secession of

Mr. Disraeli's three colleagues in 1867 was known, the Prime Minister named their substitutes. Within a week of his throwing up his portfolio in 1886 Lord Randolph Churchill, when seated at lunch, heard with a sensation of dismay, resembling, as he said, a cold-water douche to his back, that the supple and capable politician who so recently and openly had protested his resolve not to sit in a Salisbury Cabinet, had easily been won over, and that the new Chancellor of the Exchequer was to be that Mr. Goschen whom Randolph Churchill had ignored or forgotten.

CHAPTER XXI.

LORD RANDOLPH IN OPPOSITION (1887).

Exact state of parties at Westminster in 1887, subsequently to Churchill's resignation; Mr. W. H. Smith's leadership.—The Unionist party in name and substance Churchill's offspring.—John Bright's death; Birmingham Conservatives thrown over through official pressure on Lord Randolph; sustained parliamentary influence and oratorical vigour, 1887-91.— Channel Tunnel speech; "Who-will-press-the-button" Cabinet.—Parnell Commission debate.—Terrific denunciations of Pigott; breach with Mr. L. J. Jennings. — Jennings' distinguished career, and good influence on Churchill.

THE results of the dissolution to which the country had been committed by Mr. Gladstone on the rejection of his Home Rule Bill in 1886 were, as we have seen, the organisation at Westminster and throughout the country of a dissentient Liberal party, led by Lord Hartington with Mr. Chamberlain as his lieutenant, and the creation by the constituencies of a new House of Commons, composed of 317 Conservatives, 74 Liberal malcontents, 191 Liberals, and 84 Parnellites, who thus held the balance of power. Mr. Gladstone had resigned before Parliament met. Lord Salisbury, having been sent for by the Queen, proposed Lord Hartington as Premier—an overture which that statesman declined, while pledging himself and his friends in every way to support Lord Salisbury's Government.

When the session following Lord Randolph Churchill's resignation at the end of 1886 opened, on the 27th day of the new year, Mr. W. H. Smith, whom in the past the "fourth party" had carefully distinguished from his other front bench associates, was installed as leader of the House of Commons. His *ci-devant* predecessor, according to custom, by permission of the Queen, stated the circumstances of his resignation, which have already been set forth sufficiently in the account given of this incident, and which there seems no reason to assume, as in some quarters has been done, included a private letter to Her Majesty in addition to and apart from the formal notification sent by post to the Premier.

One other remark upon the opening day of Mr. Smith's leadership the late Chancellor made. Notwithstanding that the Unionist party was then in power, and that he had christened it with its name as well as more than any * one advocated and contributed to its existence, he now expressed himself so disparagingly of it as to compare it with a crutch " to be thrown aside when a Conservative Government was strong enough to walk by itself."

Generally, at first, the member for Paddington's attitude towards the colleagues he had quitted promised to be one of benevolent neutrality. Mr. Sclater-Booth, transformed into Lord Basing, was no longer visible in the Representative Assemblage to excite his indignation by a portly presence and a dual patronymic. Mr. Cross had been promoted from a G.C.B. to a peer. The magnate of the Strand was from the first day of his management a success in his new position, and was preparing the way for the more permanent leadership of Mr. Balfour, himself long since

* Manchester, March 3rd, 1886. See Mr. Jennings' edition of speeches, vol. ii., 15, and following pages.

detached from Lord Randolph Churchill, as
also were Sir John Gorst in his capacity of
Under-Secretary of State for India, and
Sir Henry Drummond Wolff, about to take
possession of the Embassy at Madrid, travelling
thither *via* Teheran, where he was now, and
Belgrade, where he was soon afterwards to
be ; while the "fourth party's" leader himself
had actually held the second place in Lord
Salisbury's Cabinet, still seemed that Ministry's
indispensable supporter, and had the satisfaction of witnessing the installation of a
Government formed on the impartial principles
laid down in his Manchester speech, stamped
with a title of his own coinage.

The surprises of politics which intensify
their purely human interest alike to partici-
pators in and spectators of the game were to
be illustrated before the following session, that
of 1888, was many weeks old by Lord Randolph
Churchill's support given to Mr. Bradlaugh in
his measure for abolishing the Oath, as well
as in the carrying of a Bill for this purpose
under a Conservative Government by a
majority of 100.

A subsequent debate towards the end of

April in this year, not only showed Churchill
at his very best as to clearness of language
and cogency of argument in the discussion
on Local Government, but gave him the
opportunity of vindicating the views he had
put forward on popular platforms in favour
of Irish autonomy, by pointedly reminding his
former colleagues in the House of Commons
that when, in 1886, he had advocated the
treatment of local administration in Ireland
with, in relation to the English question,
similarity, equality, and simultaneity, he had
spoken with the full approval of the whole
Cabinet. Some consternation was, as might
be expected, produced on the Treasury bench
by this unwelcome but incontrovertible statement. The new leader's face fell. Mr.
Balfour looked the other way. Mr. Smith's
followers hesitated between a denial or a
hiss. Mr. Gladstone showed intense interest,
and, according to his habit, when Lord
Randolph had risen, leaning forward, placed
both hands to his ears, that he might lose
no syllable of the revelations from that
opponent whom he always complimented with
the closest attention.

24

It is not to be supposed that Randolph Churchill ever seriously contemplated in regard to Ireland a coalition with the Parnellites, whom he never failed to denounce. He probably felt that a Home Rule Administration such as Mr. Gladstone was eager to form would afford a better field for the display of his Opposition powers than the continuance in office of the statesmen from whom he had separated himself. One fact is certain. A tide of popular opinion and political thought set in against the coercion of the Salisburians from the day of this speech to a degree not noticeable before.

During the remainder of the session Randolph Churchill isolated himself more even than usual from members of his own party inside the House itself as in its social observances and in the lobby. He gave no encouragement to men who would have liked to address him, and, as has been said, notwithstanding his occasional geniality and his frequently artificial courtesy, it required no common amount of temerity to force oneself upon him when he evidently preferred the meditations, painful though they very likely were, of himself to the kindly gossip and well-meant banalities of others.

A few weeks later, Ministerial reverses more specifically showed themselves, and the Government's chances in the race they had set themselves to run against Mr. Gladstone's life appeared decidedly less promising. An important section of the Local Government Bill, the session's chief measure, had been withdrawn; Ministers had found themselves twice defeated in House of Commons divisions, had in the country lost the Scotch constituency of Ayr, and had elicited a rebuke for their Irish procedure from the highest of legal tribunals on the other side of St. George's Channel.

Lord Randolph Churchill, however, diminished rather than increased his attendance at parliamentary debates. He paid fresh attention to affairs at Newmarket, but from his corner seat behind the Treasury bench watched, with growing languor, proceedings at St. Stephen's, being in fact as often in the Scotch highlands or in the French capital as in his new place at Westminster.

Yet it was during this session, on June 26th,

1888, that Randolph Churchill made one of the best and brightest speeches, in a manner that would have charmed Mr. Disraeli, which the House of Commons had ever heard from him. The occasion was Sir Edward Watkin's Channel Tunnel Bill. The word-picture drawn by the ex-Minister of a Cabinet, menaced by a French invasion, discussing tremblingly in Downing Street who was to press the button that England might recover her insular defence, was really humorous, and for its brilliance of fancy and lightness of touch was commended by none more warmly than by Sir Edward Watkin's champion, Mr. Gladstone himself.

In the autumn session of this year the parliamentary attendances of the man whose career had now passed its zenith were more frequent, and the action which he. had taken while Chancellor in abolishing the post of official referee, supplied material " in another place " for a discussion of the late Lord Chancellor's patronage while Lord Halsbury sat upon the Woolsack.

The next year was of equal significance to the House of Commons itself and to Lord

Randolph Churchill. At the beginning of April 1889, Westminster lost its greatest orator of this generation, and Birmingham its most historic representative, by the death of Mr. John Bright.

Now occurred the vacancy in the Midland capital which Lord Randolph's enthusiastic workers there had long anticipated, and which they confidently relied on him to fill. But once more the man here being dealt with showed, as at Sheffield four years earlier, that his courage did not suffice to raise him above deference for the party conclaves of Westminster. During some days deputations were visiting him frequently, either in Connaught Place or at the House of Commons. Had Churchill at this juncture embodied in his conduct the full daring of his words, he would have told Lord Salisbury, Lord Hartington, Mr. Chamberlain, that, much as he regretted to interfere with any plans of theirs, his word was pledged to the Midland Conservatives; that this promise left him no free agent in the matter; have then taken the first train to Birmingham, and informed the electors there that he came in redemption of an honourable obligation, personal to himself and them, but against the wish of the party wire-pullers, or even in spite of certain hole-and-corner arrangements which he had conceived it his duty to ignore. The result of such a step is hardly doubtful. Birmingham would have appreciated the compliment, and Churchill would have enjoyed to the close of perhaps prolonged life a constituency that would exactly have realised the ambitions and satisfied the needs of his very peculiar and complex temperament.

But, whether from new-born loyalty to the chief he had so often flouted, or regard for the colleagues whom he had so frequently ridiculed, from failure of nerve, or from less superficial causes, Lord Randolph once more effaced himself, and exposed the spell of his popular ascendancy to the risk of fatal rupture by justifying his opponents' taunt that on an emergency his friends, no matter who they were, could not count upon him.

Even as it was, during the sessions from 1887 to 1891, with which this history now deals, there were some signs, as in the House, so in the country, that Randolph Churchill's

abdication of office had not impaired his parliamentary position or weakened his popular
prestige.   Upon   his   appearances   at   St.
Stephen's, now always irregular, and often
for long intermitted, he spoke with his old
brightness, commanded his former attention.
He invited, indeed, no new parliamentary
acquaintances, and dropped many of long
standing.   Yet, had he cared to do so, he
might, on several occasions, have formed a
new and later edition of the " fourth party."
He did not, however, assert himself to this
extent, but in a different, though not less
independent manner, elected to play the part
of the Government's candid friend ; thus,
during the summer of 1889, after having drawn,
for the terror of Lord George Hamilton,
a gloomy picture of the ordeal in store for
the First Lord of the Admiralty when his
estimates got into committee, Randolph
Churchill went to Norway, and the votes only
occupied two nights.

It was also during this session that, in
another of the apparently interminable Bradlaugh debates, Churchill made what many
competent critics still hold to be the. very best

and most brilliant of his contributions to the
more sparkling eloquence of the House. Somewhat later—in the next year—the member for
South Paddington engaged in an attempt to
deal with the licensing difficulty which well
illustrates not only his position on this question, but his relations to Liberal and Conservative principles respectively ; he neither
believed in the capacity of legislation to effect
moral reforms, nor in the necessity of always
waiting till public opinion in favour of legislative amendments is ripe. Thus, in regard
to State control of public-houses, his contention was, not that men could be made sober
by Act of Parliament, but that some of the
temptations to drunkenness might be taken
away.

There were at least two considerations which,
long before the informer Pigott confessed his
crime, caused Randolph Churchill to regard
with something more perhaps than suspicion
the letters published in the *Times.* The first
was the notorious fact of the Irish leader
avoiding on all possible occasions epistolary
correspondence of any kind. He was rarely
seen to volunteer a letter to any one. He was

seldom induced to answer one till it had become almost a matter of ancient history, cynically justifying this neglect with the remark that " it was surprising how many epistles answered themselves in the course of two or three weeks." The second circumstance favouring Churchill's incredulity was that of Mr. Parnell's caligraphy being so enigmatical, and, of set purpose apparently, so subject to change, as to defy identification except by an expert. No one probably to-day defends the policy of the Parnell Commission. Its mistake was proved sufficiently by the necessity under which the House found itself of inscribing on its journals a substantial apology for having been misled by à forger.

The episode was so far to be regretted on Lord Randolph's account that it led to a break of his friendship for a gentleman who, though not, as was his nature, exuberantly, was still sincerely attached to him ; who has done his memory good service by that edition of his speeches to which reference is made so frequently in these pages, and whose obstructive and critical temperament was calculated to operate as a wholesome check upon the sudden impulses of the politician whom he wished loyally to serve.

Mr. L. J. Jennings was a man of wide and varied experience in both hemispheres. Originally an active member of Mr. Delane's staff, he next served the great newspaper as its chief Indian correspondent,—writing in that capacity an account of the Calcutta hurricane still accounted a masterpiece of graphic des-scription. After this, Mr. Jennings went to the United States, where, as editor of the *New York World*, he displayed equal sagacity and courage in breaking up the notorious Tammany Ring ; to return to England, it is needless to say, with all his Tory prepossessions intensified by his Republican experiences, to give forth the ripe fruits of his genuine culture and incisive style in *Quarterly* or *Blackwood* articles that by their uncompromising championship of political reaction, and gritty, rather than frothy, denunciation of Liberalism in all its aspects, might have satisfied the exacting shades of Lockhart or Wilson themselves.

The speech with which, in March 1890, in the debate on the Commission Report, Randolph Churchill denounced it and the informer, sent a thrill of horror, by language that, in a healthier state, the speaker could scarcely have used, through the House, and drew forth from Mr. Jennings a refusal to " stab his party in the back."

CHAPTER XXII.

SOUTH AFRICAN VISIT—AND AFTERWARDS
(1891-4).

Visit to South Africa decided on : Would not six months in an English farmhouse have done more good ?—Departure for South Africa ; special correspondent at fancy price for " Daily Graphic "; arrival at Cape Town ; travels up the country, and general route.— Return home ; reappearance with beard in Parliament.—Health improved, but still unsatisfactory.— Personal influence undiminished ; sets the fashion in parliamentary costume.—Leave-taking of friends and foes before starting on ill-advised voyage round the world.—General course of Lord Randolph Churchill's disease, and last scene of all.

Long before this date, there were signs in his personal appearance and manner, that Randolph Churchill might at any moment find himself threatened with a failure of power. The parliamentarian who, in these days of all-night sittings, and popular speechifying, would enable even an iron constitution to hold its own, must combine the application of a double first-class man with the regimen of a champion sculler, in training.

Violent delights of any kind must altogether be unknown to him. He must be as much of an ascetic as Sir Wilfrid Lawson, as great a prodigy of sleep commanded at will as Mr. Gladstone,—must, in fact, lose no chance of adding to the reserve fund of energy and strength on which to draw at the hour of need. True type and product of his age in other respects, Churchill reflected its foibles, especially, as we have seen already, in this, that repose and rest were words unknown to his vocabulary, that his only idea of recreation was change of exhausting excitement.

So early as 1880 his sense of *ennui* admonished him of the drain made by his parliamentary attendances on his energies. By way of recruiting himself for the heated warfare of the Bradlaugh discussions, he would hurry through his dinner to play a rubber of chess, a game he had liked at Oxford, with the professional expert, Mr. Steinmetz.

To ensure a holiday, not to be broken in upon by such inroads as these, in the course of 1890, Randolph Churchill, reappearing from

Newmarket, in the House, told his friends that he was, before very long, to start for a protracted tour in South Africa, blending, during his sojourn there, the *rôle* of the sportsman and the journalist.

In the former capacity he was accompanied during part of his travels by his intimate friend, Sir John Willoughby, of the Blues; in the latter he received from the *Daily Telegraph* the offer of £100 per column. Eventually he engaged his services to the *Daily Graphic*, two thousand guineas being paid for twenty letters, consisting of four thousand words each.

At this time, with the exception of Mr. Gladstone himself, no public man possessed the quality of personal interest and attractiveness to the same extent as the member for Paddington. He had long since attained that measure of affectionate popularity which calls its possessors by diminutives of their Christian names. The " Randolph " of the middle classes was the " Randy " or sometimes the " Randy Pandy " of provincial assembly rooms, or of metropolitan cabmen. As he never spoke without hitting his audience, whatever and wherever it was, by satire, ridicule, metaphors, just fitted to their intelligence, "between the wind and water," so newspaper conductors might feel sure that whatever the writing he might produce, it would send up the sale of their broadsheets.

Early in the spring of 1891, Randolph Churchill left England, reaching, at the end of April, Cape Town, *en route* for Mashona-land, Johannesburg, Pretoria, Salisbury, which last place he arrived at towards the close of July.

During his shooting expedition, on the Umfuli River from Salisbury, his companion was Sir John Willoughby; afterwards, in August of the same year, the route was to the Hartley Hills, fifty miles west of Salisbury, whence the caravan returned through Bechuana-land, visiting on his way Mafeking, Kimberley, the diamond mines, reaching England again, December 1891.

When he next took his seat in the House of Commons, his health had visibly improved, though in person he was very unlike the slim, smooth-faced Eton buck who led the " fourth party." The freshness of youth had left his face for ever, and his moustache was now

accompanied with a short beard ; but the mag-
netic influence that he had always asserted
upon those about him remained.

He was the first member of Parliament who
trod the floor of St. Stephen's in tan boots.
Within a few days, this example was copied
on every side, and foot-coverings of the novel
hue and manufacture were discovered by Conservatives and Liberals alike to be " the only
wear."

Although he spoke not infrequently nor in-
effectually, his constitution had but too evidently
received an organic shock, while he was already
at times a victim to a painful form of nervous
ailment.   If, at this moment, some friendly
coercion, such as physicians and relatives can
occasionally apply, had been laid upon him to
deny his thirst for variety and to seek repose
amid some environment the most intolerably
tedious but therefore the most physically beneficial, one cannot help cherishing a hope, almost
a belief, that the indomitable courage which made
his strength " as the strength of ten " might
have enabled him to shake off the infirmity that
had already assaulted his system.   But it was
not to be.   At least eight years before this,

Churchill had been painfully conscious of vulnerable points about him, and in a call upon the late Cardinal Manning, perhaps upon Irish politics, would seem to have spoken despondently as to his physical resources ; for between 1880-5, Manning's words to a friend were : " I have to-day had a long talk with Lord Randolph Churchill, and am grieved to think he will never live long enough to make the mark he might have done on his country."

The struggle during the years from 1891 to 1894 was as plucky as it was pathetic. The season during which his final speech was delivered was the same as that which, fourteen years earlier, had witnessed his first triumph.

During the Uganda debate of June 1894, he showed some of the educational results of his South African travels, and answered Sir Charles Dilke, interrupting Mr. Storey, who had spoken of St. Paul and St. Peter as missionaries, by exclaiming, in a voice of reprimand, " Paul, and Peter ; the apostle Paul ! " He alarmed friends and foes by his painful appearance, his ghastly pallor, his sunken eyes, as well as by his extreme nervousness, and it was the physical distress under which the

25

sentences were delivered, more than the argument's weakness, that impressed so deeply those who in a few minutes gathered round him as he passed out of the lobby which he was never again to enter. The three final words, therefore, which fell from him in the House were, "The apostle Paul!" being a part of his correction of Mr. Storey for mentioning "the missionaries Paul and Peter."

Commenting on this occasion, that accomplished historian of parliamentary life, Mr. H. W. Lucy,* remarks that "Lord Randolph Churchill was another parliamentary debater of the first rank who went back to the use of manuscript; that notwithstanding the extent to which it suffered in delivery, his parting effort of rhetoric was, in Mr. Bryce's opinion, who from his place on the Treasury bench immediately opposite heard every word of it, cogent in argument, admirably phrased, and illumined by happy illustration."

It will be less painful, and perhaps at the same time more conducive to a clear apprehension of the facts, if a few general words are

---

* See the *Strand Magazine*, March 1895, "From behind the Speaker's Chair," page 267.

said concerning the malady from which Lord
Randolph Churchill was now suffering, and
which remains an opprobrium of medicine,
being a morbid condition that therapeutic
science characteristically boasts of its power
to " diagnose," but is, as a matter of fact, impotent to cure or prevent. Progressive general
paralysis, most frequently occurring between
the ages of thirty-five and forty-two, is practically limited to the first half of adult life,
and to the period preceding the fullest brain
development. Heredity ranks as a predis-
posing cause in about one-third of the cases,
while so subtle and insidious are its advances
that many bodily or mental irregularities, sometimes loosely spoken of as causes of malady,
strictly ought to be regarded rather as the
effects and the evidences of the ailment being
already established. Men who lead an am
bitious and stormy life, in which exhausting
brain-work is added to emotional strain and
consciousness of responsibility, are, I am told,
pronounced by the most competent authorities
to be the likeliest victims of this appalling
affliction.

Ten years before the disease seems actually

to have declared itself in Lord Randolph Churchill, there is good ground for believing he himself must have had clear suspicions as to the imminence of a visitation that would try him to the utmost.

In 1884, when to the world the brilliance of his star was undimmed, he thus foretold his future to a friend: " I shall lead the Opposition for five years; I shall then be Prime Minister for the same period; and then I shall die."

Frequent consultations with the general practitioner whom he habitually employed, and with the experienced specialist, sometimes called in, had familiarised the incipient invalid with the terminology of the profession. In a speech during 1885, the Union is referred to as the " new centre of the Queen's dominions ; if you sever It, the Empire is dead ; if you injure it, the Empire is paralysed." Read by the tragic light of the accomplished sequel, these expressions seem almost an echo of words that may have first lodged in his mind after an interview with one or other of the physicians with whom he was constantly conversant. Well indeed would it have been for the professors of the healing art, as for

their patient and for his friends, if so early as
1891 they had told him that what his constitution required was not the sporting excitements
of the African jungle, but rather the uneventful
repose of an English farmhouse, and that
any disregard of such a warning would assuredly
bring him within the category of those who are
said by the Roman poet to sacrifice life itself
for the sake of living. When the great Apostle
of the Gentiles, whose name Randolph Churchill
had so strangely emphasised ere he left the
scene of his triumphs for ever, bade the elders
adieu on the sands of Miletus, that which chiefly
moved his friends to tears was their knowledge
that they would see his face no more. A like
presentiment was diffused throughout the parliamentary precincts on that June day of which
we are now speaking.

Lord Randolph and his friends, on their
voyage after health, left England in the summer of 1894. In September, the travelling
party reached Japan. One of the invalid's
arms was now disabled. At Yokohama,
further weakness and semi-coma became frequent, culminating, as they did, in the attack
of unconsciousness from which the sick man

had not recovered when Marseilles was gained. After the memorable Christmas eve when Lord Randolph Churchill was driven from Charing Cross station to Grosvenor Square, and placed in bed, there were the customary periods of rise and fall in the symptoms' urgency, but there was no real improvement ; the tendency to coma increased, the heart's action became weaker, till, on the early morning of January 24th, at 6.15, in the presence of those he loved best upon the whole earth, there passed away the fiery and chivalrous spirit who for more than a decade had divided with Mr. Gladstone his countrymen's chief attention, and who in much recalled Lord Lytton's phrase, summing up the fourteenth Earl of Derby :

"The brilliant chief, irregularly great."

Deprecating the tendency to judge practical politicians by an ideal standard, Sir Henry Bulwer, during his estimate of Canning, quotes Cicero's remark as to the necessity of remembering that we are not in the Republic of Plato, but in the mud of Romulus ; and goes on to observe that if, by however questionable

means, Canning had not made himself Prime
Minister when he did, his patrician censor,
Lord Grey, would never have been able to
create his reform Administration three years
later. With analogous cogency may it be
asserted that, however just the criticisms,
passed by Lord Salisbury and those about
him, on the "fourth party" tactics from 1880
to 1884, Conservative reaction would never,
but for Randolph Churchill, have called the
present Tory leader to office, first in 1885,
and again for a longer period after the Home
Rule defeat, in 1886; while both before and
since that date, the Conservative statesman
and his friends have repeatedly seen, and
practically confessed, that in these days of
virtually manhood suffrage, it behoves the
Constitution's champions to follow Churchill's
example, and as against their enemies to do,
not perhaps all that they might wish, but
whatever they can.

Opportunity may here be taken, by one who
is in a position to know, to say that the reports arising out of Lord Randolph Churchill's
repeated contributions to newspaper columns,
and crediting other pens than his with the

authorship of compositions identified with his
name, are mere inventions.   As a youth, the
crudities and deficiencies of his first electoral
addresses called indeed for editorial revision
and completion, before they appeared in a
permanent shape.   Thus far Sir Herbert
Maxwell's narrative of the Woodstock incident, as related in the *National Review* for
April 1895, is correct.   " But," as Sir Edward
Clarke obligingly writes to me, " to attribute
Lord Randolph's first electoral success to me,
is not exactly to represent the facts, because
the report which I prepared for the press only
appeared in the *Globe*, and was probably unknown at Woodstock."

           *   *   *   *   *

Too short for his friends, as for the
established maturity of his political reputation,
the life of him whom in these pages we have
followed from the cradle to the grave, was not
so brief as to prevent his leaving a permanent
mark in English politics, or to debar the observers of his career from an estimate of his
abiding contributions to the volume of Conservative statesmanship.   Like all prominent
members of the historic connection into which

he was born, and for which, according to his lights, he spent himself; like, that is to say, the younger Pitt, Canning, Peel; like Disraeli himself, Randolph Churchill was not only the product, but to some extent considerably in advance of his age. Randolph Churchill's illustrious opponent at Birmingham, John Bright, lived to see those of his doctrines that once were chiefly scouted as subversive of our civil, religious, social, and commercial polity, passively accepted as first principles of the Constitution, as truisms of political progress or domestic well-being.

Randolph Churchill had not ceased to take an active part in public affairs before he had made something like the experience of his great adversary his own. That confidence in the moderation, common-sense, as well as patriotism of Englishmen, must be the keystone in Conservative statesmanship, and that for this condition's fulfilment Conservative leader must show themselves possessed with a love of popular liberty in its broadest sense, at least as deep as their attachment to political prerogative in any meaning of the term—these were the two principles for which from his beginning to his close, alike in his "fourth party" days, during his tenure of office, and in his subsequently less responsible declarations, Randolph Churchill ever contended.

Long before he died, the different articles in his Sheffield propaganda of 1884 had been accepted as essential doctrines in the creed of official Conservatism. A little later he had the shrewdness to perceive the popular weariness of worn-out shibboleths and effete divisions of political partisanship, as well as the courage to declare that if the tide of destruction was to be stayed, it could only be by the combination of moderate politicians of all parties, irrespectively of the schools into which they had been titularly split up. The entire accuracy of this forecast was verified by the transactions which, in 1886, checked the progress of the Home Rule movement in England, and which up to this day render its consummation impossible. Whenever the party, at this moment of writing, in Opposition is called upon to construct a Government, it will be because its chief members listened in due time to Randolph Churchill's appeal.

The Unionist party not only derives its

name from the man who more than any other stimulated it into existence, but has embodied from its commencement in its policy the principles he laid down, and will in the future stand or fall accordingly as it does or does not, regulate its course by the chart which Randolph Churchill mapped out.

The 24th of January is, in common gratitude, entitled to the same sanctity of Conservative observance as the 19th of April; and "Unionist Day" ought henceforth to be celebrated throughout the United Kingdom with a pomp not less general, and more affectionate, than "Primrose Day" itself.

INDEX.

Adullamites, The, 96, 110.

Americans, prominent, in London society, 320; their amusements, 321.

Anglo-Indian press as an exponent of public opinion, 238; its favourable attitude towards Lord Randolph, 239-40.

Ashmead-Bartlett, Mr., his antagonism to the "fourth party," 201-2.

Aylesbury, Lord Randolph's Egyptian speech at, 297-9.

Balfour, Mr. A. J., returned for Hertford, 78; an occasional member of the "fourth party," 141.

Balliol College, Oxford, special features, 41-2.

Barnet, Mr. Henry, contests Woodstock, 75.

Beaconsfield, Lord, when indispensable as a statesman, 5; his historic letter to Lord Randolph's father, 6; situation of the Tory party after his death, 9; his modish imperialism, 96; underrates the gravity of the Irish question, 100; fails to divine the potentialities of Lord Randolph, *ib.*, 129; his inexplicable neglect to aid Sir Stafford Northcote, 128-30; anticipates the result of the dissolution of 1880, 172; his death removes the last check to Lord Randolph's revolt, 183; his estimate of Lord Randolph, 184-5; his apothegm on the normal course of ministries, 208-9; his advice to his party at the Bridgewater House Meeting of 1880, 210.

Biggar, Mr. Joseph G., his personal appearance, 145; his attractiveness to Lord Randolph, *ib.*; his power of talking against time, 146.

Birmingham, party warfare at, 262-4; conservative tactics at, 266-7; Lord Randolph's defeat at, 268; his popularity there, 274.

Blandford, Marquis of (*see* Marlborough, eighth Duke of).

Blenheim Palace, birth of Lord Randolph at, 13; reception at,

Printed by Hazell, Watson, & Viney, Ld., London and Aylesbury.

NEW WORKS PUBLISHED BY

Messrs. HUTCHINSON & CO.

BY COUNT PHILIPPE DE SÉGUR.

AN AIDE-DE-CAMP TO NAPOLEON I. Translated by H. A. PATCHETT-MARTIN. In demy 8vo, cloth gilt, 12s. With Photogravure Portrait of Napoleon after Delacroix.

The *Daily Chronicle* says:—"We thank the publishers for this translation of the most absorbing portion of a most interesting work. There is no part of the book more profoundly interesting than that relating to the famous countermarch across Europe from Boulogne, when the victory of Trafalgar had dissipated the dream of an invasion of England."

NEW VOLUME OF THE POETS AND THE POETRY OF THE CENTURY.

RELIGIOUS AND DIDACTIC. Edited by ALFRED H. MILES. Selections from the Poetry of John Keble, J. H. Newman, Stopford Brooke, E. H. Plumptre, S. Baring-Gould, S. J. Stone, W. W. How, Richard Wilton, Dr. Alexander, and others. In cloth, gilt top, 4s.; buckram, gilt top, 6s.

This Volume, which completes the work in Ten Volumes, will contain biographical and critical notices by leading critics.

BY W. G. THORPE, F.S.A.

MIDDLE TEMPLE TABLE TALK. With some talk about the table itself. In demy 8vo, cloth gilt, with Photogravure Portrait, 6s.　　　　　*[Cheap Edition.*

A Fine=Paper Edition of Zola's Masterpiece,

With about 100 fine Wood Engravings from Original Drawings by
F. THEVENOT.

A LOVE EPISODE.

A NOVEL.

By ÉMILE ZOLA.

With a Preface by the Translator, Mr. ERNEST A. VIZETELLY.
In large crown 8vo, richly gilt, cloth, 6s.

Extract from Translator's Preface.

" ' I will make all Paris weep,' said M. Zola to a friend, when he had schemed out the plot of ' Une Page d'Amour,' here presented to the English reader under the title of ' A Love Episode' ; and certainly, though one explore the entire domain of fiction, it is difficult to find a more pathetic story than that of Hélène Grandchamp's struggle with passion, her fall and bitter punishment. Hélène, as Mr. Andrew Lang has rightly pointed out, is a good and pure woman upon whom the fate of her family falls, with the result that she loves a kind of Dr. Brand Firmin, like the father of Philip in Thackeray's story. Critics have frequently contended that M. Zola's realism is confined to outward and visible things ; but 'A Love Episode' embraces psychology of no mean order, and repeatedly shows us that the author can, when he chooses, probe the human soul to its utmost depths."

Alphonse Daudet's Masterpiece.

FROMONT JUNIOR & RISLER SENIOR.

Translated by EDWARD VIZETELLY.

In large crown 8vo, artistic binding, with 88 Wood Engravings from original drawings by GEORGE ROUX.

*** An *Edition de Luxe*, limited to 100 copies for England and America, with 88 Illustrations by GEORGE ROUX, and 20 full-page Etchings by FERNAND DESMOULIN. In royal 8vo, price £1 1s. net. Only a few copies of this edition remain unsold.

The *Observer* says :—" The most popular of Alphonse Daudet's novels. The characters have the human interest and fantasy of those of Charles Dickens, and there is no more charming or pathetic creation in fiction than that of ' Désirée,' the little lame milliner.' "

3

HUTCHINSON'S
SELECT NOVELS.

In Crown 8vo, handsome cloth gilt, 3s. 6d. each.

A HOUSE IN BLOOMSBURY.

By MRS. OLIPHANT.   [*Fourth Edition.*

THE STORY OF AN AFRICAN FARM.

By OLIVE SCHREINER.
[*Seventy-eighth Thousand.*

THE CUCKOO IN THE NEST.

By MRS. OLIPHANT.   [*Sixth Edition.*

THE TRAGEDY OF IDA NOBLE.

By W. CLARK RUSSELL, with 40 Illustrations by EDWARD HOPKINS.

A MARRIAGE CEREMONY.

By ADA CAMBRIDGE.   [*Fourth Edition.*

THE HERITAGE OF LANGDALE.

By MRS. ALEXANDER.   [*Third Edition.*

LONDON: HUTCHINSON & CO., 34, PATERNOSTER ROW.

www.ingramcontent.com/pod-product-compliance
Lightning Source LLC
Chambersburg PA
CBHW021327110726
47900CB00005B/1381